THE
BURGERS
BROTHERS'
Family Funeral Home

by Clayton Tune

a novel

THE BURGERS BROTHERS FAMILY FUNERAL HOME

This is a work of fiction. Murray, KY, and all surrounding towns and parks mentioned are real places. Those familiar with Murray and Land Between the Lakes may recognize historical landmarks, certain structures, or geographical layouts mentioned. However, the characters, businesses, and incidents are a product of the author's imagination and are used fictitiously. Any resemblance to actual persons, living or dead, events, or locales is entirely coincidental.

www.claytontune.com

For Gina.
For encouraging me to write this story,
And complaining to me that you weren't in it.

Until now.
moves hand over the page to highlight the dedication

THE
BURGERS
BROTHERS'
Family Funeral Home

I think the family is the place where the most ridiculous and least respectable things in the world go on.

—Ugo Betti

There is a little boy inside the man who is my brother . . .
Oh, how I hated that little boy.
And how I love him too.

—Anna Quindlen

Murray, Kentucky

Summer 2017

1

Donnie Burgers stared at the black trash bag of human remains on his closet floor.

He lifted his leg and tapped the bottom with his toe. Something shifted inside causing the bag to stretch open and reveal a skull resting on top, staring back at him. "What is that?" He turned back toward the door of his room and yelled for his brother, Frank.

"Yeah?"

"Can you come up here?"

He heard his younger brother begin to walk up

the steps, then watched as Frank entered the room holding a bowl of cereal. Donnie stood away from the closet to gauge his reaction. "You notice anything?"

"No." Frank took in a mouthful of cereal and chewed as he scanned the room. "Oh, you got new sheets. Nice." He paused and sniffed the air. "Did you fart in here?"

"Frank, look in my closet."

Frank's gaze shifted down, and he released an audible "mmm" while nodding. He swallowed his cereal. "My bad. I forgot to tell you that was in here. That's Sarah Piddleton."

Sarah Piddleton, Donnie thought. The name rang a bell.

"She died a while back; fell out of the hot air balloon," Frank said. "Sorry, I'm sure that totally caught you off guard."

"Not at all. Perfectly normal for there to be an entire skeleton stuffed into a trash bag on my closet floor." The sarcasm was lost on his brother. "Damnit, Frank, why the hell is there a corpse in my room?"

"Keep your voice down." Frank closed the door behind him. "The bag was bulkier than I thought, and your closet had hardly anything in it. She wouldn't fit anywhere else. Cliff and I dug her up last night and figured this would be a safe place to hide her. I was hoping you wouldn't notice."

Donnie now noted the two pair of slacks unfolded and laying across the top of the bag as if to hide it.

"You dug up a bo—" Donnie stopped. He rubbed his forehead with his palms before forcefully dragging them down his face. "I can't believe I actually have to ask this question, but why did you dig up Sarah Piddleton?"

"First off, we didn't mean to dig her up. The thing is—and don't get mad—when you came back, you told me that if we didn't start making more money, we may have to sell." Donnie groaned, leaning back against the wall. "Look, I understand. We're not making much, and with the economy how it is, people can't afford elaborate funerals anymore." Donnie began scooting down the wall as Frank continued: "I got it all figured out. You know how sometimes people get buried with these expensive items? Well, I found a couple of people who will pay to have those items dug back up. And, they pay well. So, I was thinking, we do a few of these odd jobs, use that money to update the home, and actually have a chance to compete!" He took another bite of cereal. "The thing with Sarah is that I met this guy who wanted a necklace and he was willing to pay ab—"

"Shhhhh," Donnie cut him off. "Just, be quiet a second." Donnie sat with his eyes closed and took in a deep breath. "If you were looking for a necklace, why the hell is that in my bedroom?"

"That's a funny story. We intended to get the necklace but . . ." Frank sat down next to his brother and looked back at the corpse. "To make a long story short, some stuff went down, and I had to bag her up so we could look for the necklace in a better spot. And," Frank let out a cough as he said the next part, "we dug up the wrong person."

"You dug up the wrong person," Donnie repeated.

"It's a minor hiccup."

"A minor hiccup? Frank, are you crazy?"

"Hey, don't worry, we'll get it straightened out." Frank slapped his brother's knee and then used it to push himself up. "Get dressed and come downstairs. I'll show you what Cliff and I are putting together. Oh, and get this," he brought his voice down to a whisper, "Apparently, there's this whole online market for body parts—like off a corpse. I've got some guy right now offering us money for some limbs. That's insane, right?" He spooned more puffs into his mouth. "Some people are crazy."

Donnie was speechless. He sat by his closet for several minutes after Frank left. "Selling body parts?" he whispered. For a moment he thought the incident was a dream. He closed his eyes, telling himself that the bag wouldn't be there when he opened them.

He was wrong. It was still there: a trash bag full of human remains, sitting underneath khaki dress pants on his closet floor.

2

Donnie left the bag in his closet and walked downstairs, still partially in a daze. He figured that calling the police would be the responsible decision, but there would be no way to make sense of Frank's logic, and he would be implicated by default.

Donnie walked into the kitchen. Cliff Samson was there over the stove, cooking eggs and sausage. He raised up a spatula and slapped him on the butt as he walked by. Cliff was a former intern at the funeral home while getting his degree in kinesiology and physical fitness from Murray State until his graduation in 2014. He then convinced the brothers to let him open a small gym out of their detached garage, which he now owned and operated.

"You want some breakfast?" Cliff asked.

"Yeah that'd be great, thanks." Donnie filled a mug with coffee and sat across from Frank hoping his brother would elaborate on the corpse. Frank, instead, poured himself another bowl of cereal and continued reading the Sports section. Donnie gave his brother a frustrated stare for several seconds before finally saying his name.

"Yeah?"

"Are you really going to act like there's not a prob—"

"Good morning, everybody," Dave Burgers said as he walked into the room. Donnie and Frank greeted their dad in unison. Cliff offered a fist to bump.

"Morning Mr. B. You want some breakfast?"

"No thanks, I gotta meeting out in Mayfield in thirty minutes and I'm running late. Can one of you boys do me a favor?"

"What's up?" Frank looked up from the paper.

"Your mom has an appointment this morning with the specialist and I forgot all about it. Can one of you run her up there? Or let her use your car?"

"To Paducah?" Donnie asked.

"No, they're meeting her at the doctor's office here in town."

"I've got an appointment soon, but she can use my truck," Frank said.

"You know your mother is not going to drive that truck," Dave said. "Donnie, you mind if she takes your car?"

"I'll take her up there. I don't have anything going on."

"I owe you one," Dave said, pulling a mug from the cabinet.

"Hey, question. I need your consulting advice," Frank said to his father.

"You realize I make other funeral homes pay to have me on retainer, right?"

"But we're your kids. And, we're letting you have an office in our funeral home."

"Oh, you mean my and your mother's bedroom? Yes, that's most kind. Thank you." Dave patted Frank and Donnie's shoulders as he walked toward the door.

"I have a girl coming this morning whose dad died. Her mom died a few years back and was handled by you know who. It's not inappropriate to ask why she's coming here instead of there, is it?"

"As long as you don't bad-mouth them if she gives a negative review of their work. See you all later."

"Probably shouldn't ask then." Frank's gaze shifted back down to the paper as Dave walked out into the foyer.

"Who's your meeting with?" Donnie wondered if maybe this had something to do with the sack of bones in his closet. *Is someone really going to buy those bones?*

"Mimi Markham. Her dad died yesterday—Mitch Markham, I think. Those whores over at Life Memorial took care of his wife and I'd really like to know if they screwed something up."

"I don't know why you dislike those guys so much," Donnie said.

Frank finished drinking the blue milk in his bowl and walked over to the sink. "Because they're a couple of poon slingers."

"I don't know what that means." Donnie sighed and sipped his coffee. "You need me to do anything before I take Mom?"

"Nah, I got it. Do you recognize that name? Markham?"

"Nope."

"She looks our age and her Facebook says she grew up here."

Cliff brought Donnie over a plate of eggs with hash browns and sausage links, and set down a protein shake.

"Thanks." Donnie ate and skimmed through the Sports section. Frank went to refill his coffee and walked toward the foyer with the Living section tucked under his arm. "Hey!" Donnie yelled.

"Yo!"

"What are you doin'?"

"Goin' to poop."

"Frank! What are you doing with that bag in my closet!"

"Oh, sorry. Can it wait until after my nine-thirty? Or

actually—Cliff, can you run Donnie through what we're doing with Sarah?"

"I can't. I've got a nine-thirty."

Frank promised his brother they would chat once the Markham girl was gone. He left and the bathroom door closed at the other end of the house. Donnie could faintly hear his brother singing, "I've got the magic in me."

He turned to Cliff who was putting the remaining dishes into the dishwasher. Cliff looked down at his shirt and flexed his arms together, jolting his pecs up and down. Up against the wall was a large curio cabinet which housed several nice sets of china and offered a reflection in the glass. Cliff gave a quick front flexed pose, then shifted to check his side as he lengthened his arm to see his triceps. When his phone dinged, Cliff checked the notification and moved toward the back door, grabbing his gym bag off the chair, and fist bumping Donnie on the way out.

Donnie shook his head as the door closed and let out a sigh. "Ridiculous."

3

A blue '99 Honda Accord sped past Sergeant Monty Suthers' cruiser. Monty sat in plain view on the side of Highway 121 to eat his breakfast and act as a warning for drivers who used the rural highway as a faster means of getting through town. It was a convenient time to enjoy his coffee *and* keep drivers safe. Blue Accord, however, wasn't paying attention and missed the warning.

Monty cursed and pulled out from under the tree's shade. He followed close behind him at nearly fifteen over the limit hoping to avoid having to issue a ticket. Other officers joked that Monty was more upset at giving tickets than the offender was at receiving them. He tried to will Blue Accord to notice him and slow down. Monty could avoid having to talk, and Blue could avoid a ticket. Monty finally flashed his lights. He could see the driver eye him through the rearview mirror and jerk his head forward.

Don't yell at me. I've been behind you for two miles.

Monty could already feel himself starting to sweat from the morning humidity when he opened the door. He put on his sunglasses and hat and walked toward the car. Blue had his window down by the time Monty approached and was texting on his phone. "P-P-Please put your phone down, sir, and p-p-pass me your license and r-registration."

"Was I speeding?" Blue asked, tossing his phone onto the passenger seat.

"You don't know why I p-p-pulled you over?" Monty replied.

"I was goin' pretty fast, huh?"

Then why did you ask me, jackass? "I f-foll-followed you for more than two miles at nearly fifteen over. That's reckless driving. Wh-w-where are you going?"

Blue handed over his license and began rifling through the glove box. "I'm sorry sir, I'm running late for a gym appointment." He passed over a sheet of paper.

"This is insurance. Should be a w-w-white paper, about this big," he said, sizing it with his fingers. "You-You're going to a gym?"

"Yes, sir. I've been trying to get an appointment with this guy for a couple of weeks, but he's booked all the time. I got out the door late and just wasn't thinking while I was driving."

Monty studied the license. "You up at Murray State?"

"I am."

"W-What are you studying?"

"Theatre. The guy who runs this gym said he could help me get in shape for a role. I got six weeks."

Monty handed the license back. "This wouldn't be the guy who r-r-runs a gym out of a funeral home, would it?"

"I think so, yeah. Cliff Samson. Over on Poplar Street."

"That's him," Monty said. He eyed the boy for a second and then, "Look, I'm gonna let you go with some tips. F-F-First off, never tell a police officer that you weren't thinking while you were driving. Second, ch-check your mirrors while you drive. Had you just slowed down, I wouldn't have p-pulled you over."

"Yes, sir."

"Very good. *Now*, I'm g-going to do you a favor. I'll f-follow you over to this gym and let this guy know that you were pulled over. That way he doesn't j-j-jip you out of a session because you were late. That sound okay?"

"Really? Thank you."

"No problem. Pay attention next time?"

"I will, sir."

"See you there."

Monty had finished his breakfast by the time they arrived at Cliff's Edge gym. He sat waiting in his cruiser while Blue went to check in. The building wasn't fully visible from the road. Monty had driven down Poplar numerous times but had never stopped to look at the actual facility, hidden from view by the Burgers Funeral Home.

The owner kept the original garage design but there had been some signs of expansion to the back and sides. Two garage doors were opened allowing Monty to see the inside where a few people were using the available equipment. Wooden logs of varying sizes were stacked against the outside wall. Blue was talking to a large, muscular Filipino man who looked like he was the inspiration for the demi-god Maui. He was standing with his arms out over a bench, speaking loudly to a young woman bench pressing a log. When the set finished, Blue pointed out to Monty's cruiser. They both waved.

Monty gulped the remainder of his coffee and got out of the cruiser. He walked past the kitchen window of the Burgers home just as Donnie glanced up from washing the protein residue out of his glass.

4

"Mom, we gotta go!" Donnie was standing at the kitchen sink when he looked up and through the window to see a cop walking up the driveway. *Oh shit.* "Oh, shit."

The cop walked toward Cliff's gym. *Shit. Someone saw Frank. Or he left something behind.* Cliff noticed the cop and made his way over to shake his hand.

Ginny Burgers strolled into the kitchen and asked if Donnie was ready to go, but he didn't answer her. "What are you staring at?"

"Nothing," he lied. "Watching Cliff."

"Are you ready?" his mom asked again.

"Yeah. Let me get my wallet."

Donnie peeked his head into Frank's office to see if the Markham girl had arrived. He saw Frank alone, sitting in his desk chair and typing on his phone. He rapped his fingers on the door to get his brother's attention. "Hey, there's a cop outside ta—" Suddenly a young, redheaded woman stepped into view from behind the door holding a phone to her ear.

"Hang on, hang on," she said, lowering the phone and putting her hand to the speaker. "The police are here?" She turned to Frank, "Should I go?"

"Sorry," Donnie whispered. "No, no. He's a friend of ours. Sorry, I didn't realize you were in a meeting."

"It's okay," she replied, lifting the phone back to her ear.

Donnie looked toward Frank who was smiling and mouthing *Hot!*

"Come here!" Donnie whispered.

"For what?"

"There's.A.Cop.Outside."

"What?"

Donnie clutched his fists and started to mouth "come here" but was cut off again by the woman behind the door.

"Okay, I will. You too. Bye-bye." She reappeared and looked from Donnie over to Frank. "I'm sorry I had to take that. We have family coming in and it's . . . ugh. Too much right now. And sorry I startled you."

"No problem," Donnie replied. "You mind if I speak with my brother for a moment out here? In private."

"Not at all, please."

Frank apologized to her and closed the door behind him. "What's up?"

"There's a cop outside."

"I know, you said that. So what?"

"Frank! You put a dug up corpse in my closet, what do you mean *so what*? What do you want me to do?"

"What does he want?"

"I don't know."

"He's just standing outside?" Frank asked.

"No, he went into Cliff's."

"Maybe he's working out," Frank said.

Donnie heard Ginny walk into the foyer and stress that they were going to be late.

"Look," Frank said, opening his office door, "you have to go.

Get in your car and if he stops you, say you have to take your mom to her vagina doctor."

"Franklin!" Ginny yelled.

"Sorry. Her vagina specialist. I promise, he's here checking out the gym."

Donnie, frustrated, was at a loss. *What if he wants to search around the house?*

"Go!" Frank said. "We'll talk when you get back."

Donnie sighed. He went to open the front door but when he released the knob the whole thing fell off and clanked onto the ground. Donnie turned to his brother, who was staring at the pieces on the floor. "You haven't fixed this yet?"

"I thought I did. I'll set it back in place and get to it later this afternoon. Go."

Donnie looked at this mom in frustration: "This thing's been broken since I got back."

"Why is that policeman here?" Ginny asked.

"Apparently, he's checking out Cliff's gym."

"Should we go say hi?"

"No, we're already running late."

Donnie turned on the ignition and pumped the AC to full blast. Paranoia was setting in: *Don't move too fast! Don't be awkward. Make eye contact. Wave.*

As he backed out of the driveway, he couldn't shake the feeling something was wrong. Ginny attempted to make conversation, but Donnie couldn't muster more than one or two-word answers. He drove the entire way thinking through logical excuses to explain a trash bag full of bones in his closet that was hidden underneath two pair of slacks.

5

A woman with a lightweight leather jacket and strawberry blond hair had stepped into Frank's office. Her smell was entrancing: honeysuckle and bubblegum—*and burnt . . . asphalt?* Frank noticed the helmet tucked under her arm as the woman smiled and extended her hand. "I'm Mimi."

"Hey, Mimi. Frank. Nice to put a face to a name." He shook her hand. "I'm sorry about your father. You can set your stuff down anywhere you like and have a seat in one of the chairs." She crossed the room and he noticed the helmet held against her side.

"Motorcycle," he said.

"Yup," Mimi replied. "You ride?"

"No. I wish." Frank took a seat opposite her at his desk. He had already done enough preliminary research to know who her father was, but he asked her to describe him and their relationship. She was only a few sentences in before her cell phone rang. She ignored it and continued talking. It rang again. She sighed, and excused herself just moments before Donnie peeked his head in.

Donnie's overreacting. No one could have seen us, and I know I checked the area before we left. What could we have left behind?

"Sorry about that," he said to the woman as he stepped back into the office. They continued to speak about her father and the burial arrangements. Frank listened and occasionally jotted down notes on his yellow pad. "Can I ask you a personal question? You don't have to answer it but, why us? Your mom was taken care of by the Koch brothers at Life Memorial. Normally, people keep the same arrangements unless . . ." Frank stopped and looked at her to finish the sentence.

"I wasn't in charge of that one. That was my brother, Peter."

"Oh." Frank flipped back a couple of pages on his legal pad. "Did I read right that you have two brothers?" Frank asked.

"I did. The oldest one passed away years ago."

"Oh my gosh, I'm sorry."

"We aren't sure exactly what happened. He ran away in high school. As far as we know he could still be alive, but I'm not holding my breath. My parents *talked* like he was still out there but, I kind of think—inside—they gave up hope a long time ago." She sat quiet for a moment, staring at the surface of Frank's desk. "Sorry. Anyway, my *other* brother made the arrangements with the other home and he wanted to go back to them again, but they were a disaster."

"What happened?"

Mimi paused. "She didn't look like Mom. The makeup job was shit. It's funny you mention them. Someone from over there called me yesterday afternoon after I got off the phone with you."

"Really?"

"Yeah. Said they had heard about my father's passing and wanted to know if they could help with the arrangements. I lied and said that you and I were friends so I would have you all take care of my father. Should have just said they did a shit job. Sorry, again. Shouldn't say that."

"No apology needed. I know their artist—Antoine. It's not

normal for me to bad-mouth our competition. Having said that, Antoine has about as much artistic talent as a flaccid penis with a paintbrush tied to it."

A laugh snorted out of her mouth and nose before she could lift her hand to cover it.

Frank smiled. "Probably shouldn't say that."

"Leaving this morning, of all the things racing through my mind, I did not ever imagine the words *flaccid penis* to be a part of our conversation. I needed that," Mimi replied.

Frank reassured her of their artist, without saying it was himself or Donnie—in case they botched the job. Botched jobs would be blamed on Dusty, an imaginary intern who would immediately be fired. "Now, you said you wanted the funeral . . . tomorrow? Is that right?"

"Yes. Is that still okay? I know it's last minute."

"It won't give family much time to get here."

"There won't be many coming in. And we won't need a visitation."

"Oh. Then, we should be able to swing that. As long as it can be later in the afternoon. Maybe two p.m.?"

"That's perfect. Thank you so much. I really expected my brother to help with all this but . . ." She raised her eyebrows and threw up her hands, letting out a sigh. Frank could see new tears forming. The loss of the father was not as heartbreaking to her as the apathy of her family. She gently wiped the edges of her eyes.

"Were you close with your dad?" Frank asked.

"Not really. He left my mom just after I turned five. We talked, saw each other on Christmas, and I would come up for his birthday—July fourth. Unfortunately, he never liked to talk about any of this." She motioned around her. "He didn't have a will." When she mentioned the will, her eyes met Frank's and held his gaze for a second before moving away.

Frank knew where this was going.

"He didn't leave us anything and I'm kind of having to do this alone, you know?"

The Kochs didn't botch the makeup. You just couldn't pay them. "It can be a little pricey, yeah. Your brother isn't going to help?" Frank asked.

"Let's just say I'll be surprised if he comes. He tends to use the demand of his job as an excuse to not participate in family stuff. Oh wait!" She straightened up and reached inside of her purse. "I wanted to ask you—I found this online, but I wasn't sure if it was real. It was on your website." She pulled out a piece of paper.

Frank smiled when she held it up; it was a coupon.

A year earlier, Frank implemented a different method for funeral costs by designing a package system. He believed funerals were so emotionally difficult that people had a hard time thinking rationally. There were too many choices. People

were so consumed with finding an outfit for their loved one and selecting songs that they gave little thought to the officiant, the coffin model, or the type of service. Since most clients had little to no experience with funerals Frank wanted to make their experience easier.

When Cliff brought Frank his idea about a tier level system for the gym—different levels of membership—Frank got the idea to do something similar. He designed a tiered menu of funeral service packages. There were seven to choose from, beginning with the most basic service package—low-grade coffin model, three typical funeral songs played over the sound system, and a prayer with a eulogy by Frank. Each package added more to the service. The most expensive—the "Day of the Dead" package—included a well-known minister, an a cappella quartet, a PowerPoint presentation done by Frank, a professional storyteller to deliver the eulogy, and a reception to follow with a catered meal.

For those who were experienced funeral planners, Frank offered an a la carte menu. He also commissioned Cliff to create an online coupon and embed it in the small picture of Frank and Donnie in the left corner.

"Clicked on the picture, huh?" Frank asked.

"It's real?"

"Sure is. I forgot all about these."

"I've never seen a funeral home offer a coupon. Then again, I've never seen a funeral home with a basketball court either. Was that picture on the site real?"

"Yep. It's out back. We try to stand out."

She smiled. "So, with twenty-five percent off, how much do you think—I mean, with everything I need and all the arrangements, do you . . ." and then she trailed off. Her gaze shifted to the floor. "I'm sorry. I don't have much money, and I don't even know where to start. The one person I want to call for help is gone. I should have had my brother come take care of this; he knows what he's do—"

Frank moved around his desk to sit beside her. "Hey. Hey, it's okay. Listen, I'm going to help you put this together, okay? You'll give your dad an amazing memorial, and we'll take it as slow as you like. I promise, this memory of your father will be something you can be satisfied with." He looked at the paper.

The coupon was created to apply only to the top package, but Frank kept forgetting to add that wording to the picture. Applying twenty-five percent off to the bottom packages would barely get them over breaking even. He took a breath and gave the coupon back to her. "Let's go over some of our less expensive packages. I'll show you some coffin models online, and then we'll talk price."

6

"Hey, I'm Cliff," the young, muscular Filipino said, stretching his hand toward Monty.

Monty extended his hand and offered a James Bond-like introduction—last name followed by his first and then last name again—to avoid the stutter. "Nice place you got here."

"Thanks. It's cool of you to come down here to vouch for him being late."

"N-No problem," Monty replied. He looked around the funeral home driveway, then pointed at the few parking spaces next to the gym. "Let me ask you something; w-w-where are p-people supposed to park? Seems like you'd have an issue there."

"Not really. The Burgers let me use their spaces when there's no service, and with the street there's more spaces than members. Because it's a smaller gym I have to do business a little differently. I can only have a certain number of members at one time. When they sign the contract, they agree to coming here at least three times a week. Their membership's revoked if they go ten days without showing up. Someone doesn't show up for a week, they get a warning, happens again, they have to reapply and wait for an open spot. It's working well, surprisingly. Plus, it makes us more exclusive. Where do you work out?"

It took Monty a moment to register the question. "Nowhere right now."

"Oh. I figured with you on the force . . ." Cliff paused, and motioned toward his arms, "and those cannons."

"Oh." Monty laughed. "No, the d-d-department has a small gym. The only lifting I do is over there on the weekends."

"Any interest in working on stamina or cutting those arms up more?" Cliff smiled.

"W-W-Well, I don't know. Never really thought about it. Both, I guess."

"How 'bout this," Cliff said, "you give me one hour to assess you and see what you can do. After that, if you still want to work with me, we'll discuss price."

Monty hesitated. This conversation had taken a quick turn. He had no intention of getting a gym membership. *This kid's fast.* "That might work. What's your schedule like this weekend?"

"Can I give you a call after I'm done with your perp? Maybe in about an hour or so?"

"Sure. Call me on this number." Monty passed Cliff a card and offered his hand to shake before making his way back to the cruiser.

Out of the corner of his eye he caught a young woman in blue jeans and a bright pink t-shirt walking down the steps of the adjacent home. She exchanged words with a young man in the doorway wearing khaki slacks and a blue polo. The man reached out for a handshake, but the woman moved in for a quick hug—surprising the man—before getting on her motorcycle.

After she drove off, the young man in the blue polo walked confidently down the steps and toward the cruiser. Monty reached his hand out from the driver's seat window. "Morning."

"Hey. How are ya? Frank Burgers." Frank shook his hand.

"Great. Interesting s-se-set up you have here with the gym and funeral home."

"Oh, it's a separate thing. He needed a space, we needed our garage cleaned." Frank laughed. "You thinking about joining?"

"We talked about it."

Frank reached into his pocket and pulled out a card. "Well, hey, if you're a gym member, we offer a fifteen percent discount on funerals for family members—even yours."

Monty took the card. "You have discounts for funerals?"

"Yeah, a few of the business owners in town are trying to do some inter-business promotions. Like when we do a funeral for a family member you get a coupon for a dozen donuts over at Virginia Jan's, or a free draft at Vitello's; small stuff like that."

Monty wasn't sure if this was a joke. "I'll be honest, that's one of the weirdest things I've ever heard."

"Don't knock it too much. If you can prove we've provided funeral services for you in the past, you get a discount at the gym. It's a community."

Monty smiled. "No kiddin.'" He examined the card before placing it in his pocket. "I'll do some d-d-digging and see if I have any connections.

"Let me know. It was a pleasure to meet you, sir."

"It was a p-p-pl—" Monty stopped and cleared his throat. "It was nice to meet you too."

Cliff dropped a large duffel bag at the theatre major's feet and gave some directions to him before walking over to Frank. The actor lifted the bag off the ground, hoisted it on his shoulder, held it over his head, and then dropped it. "Do that fifteen times," Cliff said. "What was that about?" he asked Frank, watching Monty drive down the road.

"Just being polite. You think he suspected anything or was he curious about the gym?"

"He seemed interested. But he only came to vouch for my guy being late." Cliff yelled, "Ten more, come on!" Back to Frank, "Did you recognize him?"

"No, why? You know him?"

"Yeah. He used to teach at Murray High. Mr. Suthers."

"That's Mr. Suthers?" Frank asked.

"Crazy, huh?"

"He would sub for us sometimes. Except we called him something else."

"Stutters?" Cliff asked.

"Yeah." Frank laughed. "Mr. Stutters. Man, I haven't thought about that guy in years. He's put on weight."

"He's still got that stutter, too."

"I guess we should get that bag out of Donnie's closet sooner than later," Frank said.

7

The voices crackling through Monty's scanner were no match for the internal conversations going on in his head. He reminded himself of Marion Crane from *Psycho* as he drove back into town, imagining conversations between others behind his back. He had done his best to hide the stutter—changing words around, taking a breath before saying something, stopping midsentence and taking each word's syllable slowly—but it didn't always work and *always* felt awkward. No doubt others noticed the abrupt pause, the occasional face stretch, or the awkward word he sometimes substituted. The gym owner asked his name, and he led with his last name, then followed it up with the first and last name again. Saying *Montgomery*, or *Monty*—most M words—had always given him a tough time. But *Suthers* was easy, and *Montgomery* followed just fine after it.

"Unit three-four-two come in," the scanner sounded.

He snapped out of it. "Three-four-two, go ahead," Monty replied.

"Got a call on a cemetery disturbance at the Frazier cemetery, over on Poplar. Are you out that way?"

"What's the disturbance?"

"Unsure. Sounds like vandals. Groundskeeper suspects robbery. Can you take it?"

"I'll check it out."

Frank was in his office editing a eulogy when a white mail truck pulled up on the side of the street at 11:15. He saved the document, closed his office door, and promptly removed his dress pants and shirt, leaving on his wife beater and tall red socks with tacos in the shape of a stegosaurus. He slipped on a pair of running shorts and misted himself with cologne before swiping a bottle of water from his mini fridge and going outside.

The woman in view was still one house over. Frank did a quick set of twenty-five jumping jacks and counted out fifteen pushups. He splashed water on his shirt and face, jogged in place, and took off on a slow jog around the house and down the driveway. He made it to the mailbox as the young woman reached out to place mail inside of it. "Hey Ally!" Frank said.

"Hey Frank, how are you?"

"Great. Finishing up a workout. What are you up to?"

"You know, delivering your mail."

"Good timing." He looked at his watch. "It's almost eleven-thirty. I figured you would have already come by."

"No, going slow today. I've got a new audiobook so I keep getting distracted."

"What are you listening to?"

"Usual. Cowboys, vampires, high school drama."

"Erotica, huh?"

"Why do you think I keep getting distracted?" She smiled and held out a small stack of envelopes. "I heard Donnie was home. How long is he here?"

"For good, I hope."

"Wait. He opened a restaurant like five months ago. Is he still running that?"

"No. He quit. The owner got involved in some pretty shady stuff. I think he's looking at opening something in Nashville though. He's scouting out places. Don't tell him I told you that though."

"I'll have to drop by later and see him. Invite us over for dinner one night and tell him to cook."

"I will if you leave Gary at home." Frank smiled. "And if we can go out instead of eat here. And if Donnie can't be there."

"I can probably make that work," Ally said. "Here you go. That top one is Donnie's. I know that name." She pointed to the return address.

"What is it?"

"I see him on the Food Network. He's got some restaurants in Florida."

"Sweet. So, we doing dinner Saturday night?"

"You'll have to ask my husband."

"You think there's a good chance he'll say yes?"

"If you show up with your dress socks and shorts combo, you've got a good shot." She laughed, pointing down to Frank's legs.

"Yeah, this was Cliff's idea. Says it works your calves more."

"Goodbye, Frank." Ally put her earbuds back in and continued her route.

"Tell your husband I said hey."

"Tell him yourself when you come pick me up."

Donnie was sitting at the kitchen table on his phone when Frank came back in. "How's Mom?" Frank asked.

"She's good." He looked up from his phone and noticed his brother's running shorts and tall socks. "Really?"

"What?" Frank asked.

"Dude."

"It's working."

Donnie shook his head and looked back down at his phone. "At least change the socks before you talk to her."

Frank turned and went to his office.

"Mom's fine," Donnie yelled out into the hall. "Doctor said she looks good."

"Where is she?" Frank reentered, tucking in his shirt.

"Downstairs, looking for something to thaw out for tonight. Hey, listen, we don't have to do it now, but you mentioned earlier this week something about the Kochs giving you an offer for this place a while back. Did they say how much they were willing to p—"

"You know those cracker jacks called that girl I met with today? I think they're watching the obits and contacting family members."

"How'd that go—with the girl?"

"Good," Frank replied. He rifled through the mail again and began to open the top envelope. "Super cute too."

"You schedule her in?" Donnie asked.

"Yeah. Rush order—wants it tomorrow. She's strapped for cash, but she and I will figure something out."

"What does that mean?"

"It means we'll figure something out."

Donnie sighed. "Why are we the ones figuring something out?"

"Because money's tight for her right now and her brother isn—"

"So, we're doing charity cases now?"

"What do you want me to do, tell her no?" Frank asked.

"Yes! That's exactly what I want you to do! This is a business. Do you want me to tell her?"

"We can't refuse service to someone because they're low on funds."

"We're not an ER. You can absolutely refuse service."

"I'm not doing that. She has some money, and we need all we can get."

"But not if it means we're footing the bill for the majority of it!"

Frank held up an opened envelope and letter in his hand. "What is this?"

"What do you mean?"

"You're trying to start a restaurant in Florida?"

"Are you serious?" Donnie sprang out of his chair and advanced toward his brother. "Why are going through my stuff?"

"That's not important. I thought you said you were trying to—"

"It *is* important. It's not your mail. Gimme that!" Donnie attempted to swipe the letter out of Frank's hand, but Frank quickly moved his hand out of reach and stiff-armed his brother.

"Florida! When were you going to tell me?"

Donnie took hold of Frank's wrist and instantly pulled him closer into a headlock. Frank threw the folded letter across the room onto the table and tried to wiggle out of the position without success. "I cannot believe you were going through my mail! What the hell is wrong with you?"

"In my defense, I thought it was mine," Frank replied as Cliff walked in from outside through the kitchen door.

"Hey guys, just getting a drink." Cliff opened the refrigerator while Frank let out a couple of threats to Donnie to let him go, but Donnie only tightened his grip.

"You thought a letter addressed to Donnie Burgers meant Fra—" He didn't get to finish the sentence because Frank jammed his extended fingers, with great force, into the crack of Donnie's butt and began to forcibly tickle his brother's rear. Donnie cursed and eased up long enough for Frank to get his head out of Donnie's arm and interlock his own arms around Donnie's sternum.

"Those guys from Florida liked your proposal? That's awesome man, congrats!" Cliff said from the table. He was sitting with a bottle of fermented tea and reading Donnie's letter.

Donnie shoved his brother off him, knocking him to the floor. "What is wrong with you two?" He yelled. "Are you serious? Can neither one of you mind your own shit?"

"Sorry man, it was just laying here."

"So what! It says Donnie on it!"

"Wait, he knew?" Frank asked.

Donnie shook his head and took the letter from Cliff.

"Cliff, you knew about this?" Frank asked.

"Yeah. You didn't?"

Donnie sighed. "No. He didn't. Look, Frank . . ." Donnie took another breath. "I'm considering going to Florida. Cliff knows because he was in the room when I got a call last week. I was going to tell you, but I just, I don't know. I wasn't sure what they'd say or if they'd even entertain my proposal."

"You told me you wanted to stay here," Frank said.

"I never said I wanted to stay here. I said I would look around—"

"You at least said you were gonna help me out for a little while. Chill here and scout out some places. That's what you've been telling me."

"I know. I know! I spoke with this guy a few months ago and I thought—"

"You really have no desire to keep this place going, do you?" Frank asked.

"Honestly? No. I don't want to work here. I want a restaurant. It's part of the reason I came home. I meant to tell you about the Florida thing sooner, but I just—"

Frank rolled his eyes and walked out of the kitchen and back into his office. Donnie still finished his sentence. It was only to himself. And Cliff.

". . . never found the right moment." Donnie stood silent for a moment, before cursing under his breath and moving to pick up the other pieces of mail on the floor.

"He still thinks you quit, doesn't he?" Cliff asked.

Donnie instantly turned and put his finger over his lips. "Hey!"

"Come on, man. You gotta tell him."

"I'm going to. Just let me worry about it, okay?"

"Okay. I'm just sayin, if he knew you got fired he wouldn't—"

"Cliff!"

"Okay. Your deal. But I wouldn't wait too much longer."

8

Monty noticed the disturbance right away. He asked the groundskeeper if he'd touched anything after he found it; he hadn't. The surrounding plots had been mowed and cleaned not more than twenty-four hours prior to the discovery, and the fresh landscaping only accentuated Sarah Piddleton's disturbed plot: two piles of dirt rested on either side of a half filled in grave.

"You get in contact with the husband?"

"I'm sure he knew before I did. He's laying right beside you." The groundskeeper chuckled.

Monty looked down to see the tombstone of Franklin "Fred" Piddleton. He had passed away only one year after his wife. The vandals left his plot untouched.

"You see any dirt tracks? Tire marks? F-Foo-Footprints?" Monty asked.

"Nothing."

"You call anyone else besides the police? Any family?"

"Put in a call to next of kin. Haven't heard anything back.

With two piles of dirt, Monty assumed two diggers. There were no footprints on the dirt inside the grave which indicated that they made it all the way down and then refilled the hole. *Why was it left incomplete?* "You happen to know anything about Mrs. P—P . . ." Monty stopped and took a breath. "About Sarah? Was she wealthy? Did she have children?"

"Don't recall. I remember when she died—hot air balloon accident maybe ten years ago. She taught over at one of the schools. I was at her funeral and even helped dig this grave. But I don't reckon I can recall her being buried with anything of great worth."

"She have any kids?" Monty asked.

"Hell if I know."

"You think they got all the way down there? How long would that take?"

"Depends on the digger," the groundskeeper said. "Or diggers. No telling. Two hours? Less or more depending on help and stamina. You want me to call some guys to have them check the body?"

"Don't you need family approval to exhume?"

"There's not even a foot of dirt over that casket. I'm happy to just say it was left uncovered and we took a peek inside, if that'd be alright with you?"

Monty accepted the offer and made his way around the cemetery looking for anything that might pass for a clue while two older men came and started moving dirt off the coffin. He found a cigarette butt and a torn, brown napkin advertising one of the town's most popular restaurants. He placed both the items in a plastic bag and tucked them into his glove box.

Monty surveyed the surrounding area. No other grave was touched: no footprints, no tire marks, no extra dirt where it shouldn't be. He figured it was more than likely a prank or perhaps some form of fraternity hazing.

Monty stood by the entrance of the cemetery and looked out down the road. Several houses lined both sides of the street, including the funeral home he just came from. He made a mental note to check into which home handled the woman's funeral.

Then a voice called behind him. He turned to see the groundskeeper walking toward him, shaking his head.

"You're not going to believe this."

"D-Di-Did they dig all the way down?"

"Yes, sir. Took everything. And tore the coffin to pieces doin' it, too."

Monty wasn't sure how to interpret that statement. "How c-can you tell what they took?

"'Cause they took everything." The groundskeeper forced a slight laugh and ran a hand through the thin patch of stringy hair remaining on his head. "They took the whole body."

9

Donnie was sitting on the porch swing when Frank came outside with a mug of coffee. He stood by the door in silence, staring out in the direction of the gym where Cliff was working with two girls in their backyard. One girl was running up and down the yard with the other girl client on her back. Music played through a pair of speakers sitting right outside the gym entrance. Cliff stood watching, frequently looking down at his phone.

"Cliff!" Frank yelled.

"Yo!"

"What are they doin'?"

"Leg day."

Frank gave a thumbs up and placed his coffee on a nearby table. He spun the basketball onto his foot, kicked it up into his hands and walked over to the area adjacent to the house that had been remodeled into a basketball court. He dribbled through his legs and took shots around the paint while Donnie watched. Frank made every shot he took.

"You think anyone ever farts while they're working out with him?" Donnie asked. Frank's ball sliced through the net. "I mean, all that bouncing up and down, breathing in and out. I'm sure they have to fart." Frank ignored him. Donnie leaned forward and rested his elbows on his knees. He exhaled.

"Look. I'm sorry I didn't tell you." He heard Frank make

another basket. "It wasn't a sure thing, and I didn't see the point in getting you upset if it fell through." Donnie leaned back on the porch swing and extended his arms over the back.

Frank didn't say anything.

"So, you're just not going to talk?" Donnie asked.

"Nothing to say," Frank replied.

"Fine. Be a drama queen."

"Okay." Frank made one more basket and set the ball in front of the hoop. He grabbed his mug off the table and strolled onto the grass toward the gym.

Donnie stood up and called after him, but Frank disregarded his attempts. He called out again and moved to go after him until Frank waved him off. Finally, Donnie grabbed him by the arm and slapped the mug of coffee out of Frank's hand. "Would you stop?!"

"Are you kidding me? That's my midnight blend!" Frank yelled.

"What is your deal? You read my mail, and you're the one mad at me?"

"That was French-pressed, you asshole."

"What do you want me to say, Frank? I'm sorry I don't tell you about every facet of my life? I'm sorry that I don't want to be thirty-three years old and still living in my parents' house? I'm sorry that I'd rather be running a restaurant than an old funeral home with no advertising potential."

"Screw you, man. I do plenty of advertising."

"You created funeral coupons! What funeral home has coupons?!"

"People use them don't they?"

"That's not a good thing!" Donnie cursed. "You are

unbelievable. Look at this place! You're really upset that I don't want to be here? There's no future for it! The Kochs won! Their place, their staff, their customer service; it's ten times what ours is. We can't even compete because we have zero money. And to make matters worse, you're too naïve to understand that! I've not been here two weeks and I can already see why Dad thought we should sell."

"I can promise you that Dad doesn't actually want us to sell."

"He left, didn't he?"

"No, he gave it to us."

"Frank. Come on, man. Wake up. Dad got out because he couldn't beat the competition."

"Well, *we* could beat the competition if you'd actually take some ownership. I'm trying to plug up holes and you're just sitting in the nest looking for land."

"In a sinking scenario, it would probably be wise to look for land."

"Not if you want to save the ship. I don't want it to go down," Frank said. "I'm not selling."

"Frank—"

"Stop. I'm not doin' it. If you want to stay and help, I'd love to have my brother here. But if you think you're going to convince me to sell to those butt fluffers, you're wasting your time. I have every intention of making this place some money. Cliff and I are trying—"

"Oh, I forgot. Your brilliant idea! Well, forgive me if I feel a little hesitant about this company's future hinging on my little brother's brilliant ideas. I should have known this place was financially screwed when I came home to you putting a pool table in our living room. Who the hell's going to use that thing?"

"Everybody uses that thing!"

"Are you this naïve with everyone who gives you business advice, or just me? I'm not trying to be a dick, but you complain to me about money yet look at what you spend it on. You really think a pool table is going to attract clients?"

"You said you liked it!" Frank exclaimed.

"What am I supposed to say! You don't see why I'm so frustrated? You're coming up with idiotic ideas to make back the money you spent on the previous idiotic idea. No funeral home needs this stuff."

Frank tried to counter, but Donnie kept going: "And now, you're telling me that our winning ticket to financial freedom is digging up some old guy's corpse and selling off his body parts?"

"What? No. There're two separate jobs. Selling parts is more Cliff's thing. He found this guy in his online Chess ring that was—"

"Dude! Stop talking! I don't want to know." Donnie stepped toward his brother, raising his voice.

"At least have some respect for the corpse." Frank pushed his brother back. "It wasn't an old guy. It was an old lady and her name is Sarah."

Donnie's eyes widened and his nostrils flared: "Respect the corpse? You're the one who stuffed a corpse into my closet and then talked to me over a bowl of cereal as if it was a bag of Christmas decorations!"

"Yeah, and if you would quit yelling about it, I could explain what it's doing in there."

"You can't explain that! There is no logical way to explain something like that."

"It's not just about digging up body—" Frank began.

"You've got to be kidding! Just—ugh! Quit talking!" Donnie threw his hands up and began walking back toward the house.

Frank watched his brother walk up to the house and kick a long dandelion out of the grass into an explosion of white seeds into the air. He heard Donnie yell something to himself and watched him sit back in the swing. Frank picked up his coffee mug off the ground and drained the last of it onto the grass, sighing to himself. "That was a waste."

Frank avoided eye contact with Donnie as he walked back up to the patio and wiped the grass off his dress shoes before sitting down on the swing next to him. "Look. You wanna keep your life a secret from me, that's your deal, but don't come up in here demanding I sell what I've worked—" Frank was cut off by his father stepping out onto the porch.

"One of you boys have a client?"

"I don't," Donnie replied.

"No. Why?"

"Then I guess one of you is in trouble." Dave smiled. "A police cruiser just pulled into our driveway."

10

Monty noticed the gym owner out in the yard working with two girls when he pulled up. He made his way up the path and rang the doorbell twice before an older woman answered the door, catching him off guard. "Good morning, ma'am. Are y-you Virginia Burgers?"

"Yes, I am. You can call me Ginny. Can I help you officer?"

"Suthers. Monty Suthers. I s-s-spoke with one of your sons this morning—Frank?"

"Oh. I believe I saw you as I was on my way out."

"Is Frank here?"

"He sure is. Would you like to come in?

"Thank you." Monty stepped inside. "And w-w-while I'm at it, I've been going to your re-re-restaurant for years. It's nice to finally m-meet you. You m-m-make the best donuts in Kentucky."

Ginny laughed. "As much as I'd like to claim it, all the credit goes to my mother. A good daughter I am. I'm just making money off her recipes."

"Then my th-thanks to your mother. You have two sons, correct? Are they b-both here?" Monty asked.

"They're coming inside right now," Dave said, walking into the foyer. "Hello, officer, Dave Burgers. What brings you out here?"

"N-N-Nothing too concerning. I met Frank this morning

and w-wanted to get this opinion on something. Is Frank the owner?"

"Half owner," Ginny replied.

"They took over for me when I retired," Dave offered.

Monty stepped farther into the main hall and glanced around. "I do apologize for disturbing you all. I'm coming b-b-by unannounced." Dave assured him it was no bother. The foyer of the home was inviting, although a little disconnected. The entrance rug and light wood floor surrounding it were noticeably worn down, but the crisp, bright color of the walls showed an obvious attempt to update the room. An office on either side of him: one looked to be freshly remodeled with new paint and flooring, while the other looked like it matched more with the floor and rug he was standing on. Several pictures lined the wall ahead: the same individual—Frank Burgers—standing with large crowds of people. A placard tagged each photo: **Burgers Brothers' Family Funeral Home "Dodge Cancer" Dodgeball Tournament 2016; Burgers Brothers' Family Funeral Home "Fight ALS" Fish Fry 2015; Burgers Brothers' Family Funeral Home Mardi Gras "Ball-Cancer" 2017.** "You guys d-do a lot of events here, huh?"

"At least one a year. My son Frank has been heading those up, as you can tell from the title." Dave pointed at the Mardi Gras photo. "He keeps us on our toes."

"I bet. H-H-How is re-re-retirement?" Monty asked Dave.

He chuckled. "What retirement? Who can afford to do that now'a days?" Monty smiled. "I took up consulting work almost immediately after I let the boys take—" Dave was cut off by someone yelling "Mom" from the kitchen.

"In here, Franklin," Ginny called out.

Frank rounded the corner into the lobby.

"Hello, Franklin," Monty said.

"Officer. Call me Frank."

"Call me M-M-Monty."

"Would you like some coffee, Monty?" Ginny asked, moving toward the kitchen.

"I better not. Heart starts beating in Morse code if I have too much caffeine."

"It's decaf."

"Oh. Then, I g-guess I have no excuse. Thank you."

"Coming right up," Ginny smiled.

Frank moved toward his office door. "What can we do for you? Everything okay?"

"Well, not really. I'd like to ask you and your b-b-brother some questions about the cemetery down the road, if you don't mind."

"Sure. Go ahead and have a seat in my office and I'll grab Donnie."

"What's wrong?" Donnie asked.

"Not sure. Cop wants to talk to us."

Donnie sighed and tightened his lips.

"Something about the cemetery down the road," Frank said.

"Which one?"

"Probably Frazier's," Frank replied.

"What's happened at Frazier's?"

"I don't know. That's why the cop is here." Frank stepped back inside and closed the door. Not five seconds later he reopened it and poked his head out. "But if you're going to force me to guess, it may be because one of the plots was vandalized and half full of dirt this morning. Come on."

"Wait a second. Close the door. You took that body from Frazier's cemetery?"

"Yeah," Frank replied as if it should be common sense.

"The Frazier's cemetery that's half a mile from the house?"

"Yeah."

"You robbed a grave from a graveyard that's in walking distance from our house, and—correct me if I'm wrong—you left the grave open?"

"Yes to the first part. We left her grave *half* open because we had to get out of there."

Donnie leaned his head onto the swing's back and took a deep breath. There was a small moment of silence before he whispered out, "You've gotta be kidding me."

"Look, in my defense, Willy never checks in over there. I'm surprised he saw it. And, if you're going to rob a grave, everybody knows that you should rob from a grave close to where you live," Frank responded.

"No, Frank, everyone knows you just don't rob graves!" He yelled in a whisper. "How could you be that stupid?"

"Common sense would say that you're safest when you rob from the place no one expects. If we picked some random spot out of town, we'd likely be the first suspects. But who in their right minds would rob a grave next to their own house?"

Donnie could feel his heart pounding. "I can't. I can't do this right now." He got up off the swing.

"You're just gonna leave?"

"You deal with it."

"If you don't come in here, then I may as well show him the body in your closet. We'll have—"

Donnie immediately turned around and waved his arms. "Would you keep your voice down!"

"Then come inside," Frank said.

Donnie put his hands on his hips and turned around, at a loss for words. He could see Cliff standing with his arms folded watching an older man walk around the yard with weights.

"Fine. I'll go in there. We'll get this taken care of, but I want that body out of here by tonight."

"You got it."

"I'm not kidding. This plan of yours is over. I want it gone." Donnie turned to face him. "Do you hear me?"

"I got it."

Ginny opened the door to the kitchen: "What in the world are you boys doing?" She chastised them for being rude and keeping Officer Suthers waiting.

"We're coming," Donnie said, from the other end of the patio.

"No, *now*," she said. "There's a cup of coffee on the counter; one of you bring it to him before it gets cold." She turned and closed the door.

Donnie moved toward his brother: "We're not done with this conversation. I wanna talk about that deal, but once he leaves, get that damn thing out of my room."

Monty was standing in the doorway of Frank's office looking in when Donnie saw him. "Officer?" He recognized Monty immediately—*Mr. Stutters*.

"Yes, sir. Are you Donald Burgers?"

"Yes, Donnie. I believe you met my brother this morning—Frank. Here's a coffee. Come in and have a seat."

"Listen, I w-w-won't take up much time. I just had some qu . . . qu . . ." Monty paused and swallowed. "Some things I'd like to ask ya."

"Sure. What's up?"

Frank made his way into the room and shook Monty's hand.

"Either of you boys drive past the Frazier Cemetery today?"

"No, sir," Donnie replied.

"Yessir," Frank offered energetically. "I did. I mean, I didn't drive past it. I was there. This morning. Something wrong?"

Donnie's heart jumped. He could feel his underarms beading with sweat, and tried not to look at Frank, or even cough to break the now awkward silence.

Monty asked after a moment of pause. "Can I ask why you were there?"

"Of course. I take a walk early in the morning every day before I start work, and that cemetery is part of my route." Frank said. "I guess you could say it gets the juices flowin'. Pun intended." Frank could see Donnie shaking his head. "Anyway, yeah. It's on my walking route, that's all."

"You notice anything strange when you were there this morning?" Monty asked.

"No sir. Like what?" Frank asked.

"Just, anything out of the ordinary: someone who shouldn't be there, tire tracks, vandalism. Anything."

"Actually, there was something. I saw a hole being dug up on the upper east side, near that black mausoleum. I didn't think much of it but now that you're here, it seems a little strange."

"Why did that get your attention? M-m-may I ask?" Monty inquired.

"Because that part of the cemetery is full. It's been full since, what would you say Don, twenty-fourteen? Thirteen?"

Donnie worked to keep his eyes from bugging. *What is he doing?* "I don't know Frank. Twenty-thirteen?"

"No, it was twenty-fourteen. Doesn't matter. Anyways, that part of the cemetery is full. Nobody else should be buried anywhere near that mausoleum. But, again, I wasn't paying too much attention."

"Why are you asking, officer?" Donnie said.

"It looks like there was a v-v-vandalism there last night or the night before."

"What happened?" Frank asked.

"Well, I can't say too m-m-much right now. Probably told you more than I should. I'll learn more when w-we contact the family. I just wanted to see if you noticed anything unusual and ask that you kee-kee-keep an eye out over there. Check in with Willie if you can. He's having a hard time getting around. I think he just had a knee replaced." Monty handed Donnie his card.

"Both knees, actually," Frank said. "This was the second one."

"Jeez," Donnie let out. "Is his wife still alive?"

"Yes. But she's been legally blind for a couple years now."

"He got any cameras out there?" Frank asked.

"Used to have a couple," Monty replied. "P-Put'em up sometime back—maybe five years ago? They had a p-problem with college kids hitting golf balls and cracking some of the head-stones. It did the trick, but after a few years he s-said he got tired of paying the security bill and turned them off—doesn't know where they are now; thinks they fell off years ago." Monty took a sip of his coffee. "Anyways, it was nice to m-m-meet all of you. If you don't mind I m-m-may drop back by in a couple of days or so to follow up."

Frank shook his hand for a third time and opened the front door. The dense humidity drew sounds of disgust from each of them.

"B-By the way, completely out of left field, but do either one of you smoke clove cigarettes?" Monty asked.

"No sir," Donnie answered.

"You know anyone who does?" Monty asked.

"Do they even still sell clove cigarettes here?" Frank asked.

"Oh yeah, people here are still smokin' 'em." Monty replied, wiping sweat from his forehead.

"Why clove cigarettes?" Donnie said. "You want us to be on the lookout?"

"Nah, just wonderin'," Monty answered. "Alright, I'm gonna get out of here but please tell your mother thank you for the coffee."

Monty left Frank and Donnie standing on the porch.

"Were you smoking?" Donnie asked.

"Nope, but I may have left a smoked cigarette behind."

Donnie sighed. "Please don't tell me one of the Kochs smokes cloves."

"Hunh, didn't think of that." Frank grinned. He turned to go back inside, but Donnie forced a hand onto the doorknob and closed it.

"First off, I want you to get Cliff and I want you to move that bag. Now." He paused. "Okay?"

"Look. I'm gonna get it out ASAP, but I think you should at least hear what—"

"If this isn't about getting that corpse out of my room, I'm not interested." Donnie turned the knob to go in, but Frank grabbed his arm.

"Just hold up, will ya," Frank said, closing the door. "Hear me out. About three years ago, I was up at Vitello's bar with a buddy of mine. He was back in town for his dad's funeral. We went to school with him—Otto Roberts."

"Frank, I don't care."

"Cool. Anyway, while we were out, he started talking to me about a necklace that his dad had. It wasn't anything fancy, a gold chain with a pendant of a cross attached to a boat anchor. Otto said the necklace belonged to his grandfather, and that before he died he gave it to his son—Otto's dad, who promised to give it to Otto. Well, the dad forgot to give it to the son, and got buried with it. You know what he said? He said, 'I'd pay anything to get that necklace back.'"

Donnie's expression changed. "Don't worry," Frank continued, "I didn't take him up on it, but I wish I would have. I've had that moment in the back of my mind ever since. I asked how much. Guess what he told me: he said he would drain his savings—like three grand. Just for a necklace."

"The guy's a moron then," Donnie said. "You can buy that for probably two hundred bucks."

"But you can't though. He doesn't want a necklace; he wants *that* necklace. It's a memory to him. And then it hit me: sentiment can add one hell of a monetary value to the right person—people get stupid with that stuff. What kept eating at him was that the thing he wanted so badly was so close to him and yet he couldn't get it back. A piece of his family history was right beneath him, relatively easy to get, but gone forever." Frank paused. Donnie had stepped away from the door and given him his full attention. "Six thousand dollars."

"What?" Donnie replied.

"Six. Thousand. Dollars."

"I heard you, what does that mean?"

"That's how much that bag of bones underneath your dress pants is worth. Six Gs." Frank leaned against the door and crossed his arms. "You're right. This place is falling apart. And, you're right; I don't want to admit it."

Donnie didn't say anything.

"We've buried most of our biggest supporters in this town, we're doing one funeral a week—if we're lucky—and they're minimal events at most: cheap coffins, no catering, no special add-ons. Just a small service and a quick burial. It's not because people don't want a nice service—or can't afford it—those clowns down the road just look better than we do. We're so out of date that people don't even know we exist sometimes, and we're so poor we can't rebrand to get those people to notice us. I've tried. Hence the basketball court and pool table, both of which I get compliments on by the way."

"So, you stole a six-thousand-dollar skeleton?" Donnie asked.

"The skeleton isn't six grand. Some moron—as you would say—feels that what that skeleton *was wearing* was worth six grand."

11

"Blue Moon," Frank said to the bartender. He and Cliff were sitting in Vitello's, one of only a handful of bars in town, watching the Cardinals game. It was close to campus and usually overrun by college students during the weekend, but Monday through Thursday were ruled by the thirty-and-older crowd. Evan Vitello, the bar's owner and bartender, poured a Blue Moon from the tap and held up a bottle of Hennessy to Cliff who gave a thumbs up.

Three innings into the game, Frank signaled for a second round. "How's your brother?" Evan asked.

"Good," Frank said.

"How's his restaurant?"

"Donnie says he's quitting."

"What?"

"Yeah, some pretty messed up stuff went down a while back."

"Like what?" Evan asked.

"He hasn't talked much on details yet. There's a possibility that the owner is running an underage sex ring."

"No way!"

"I'm serious."

"Jeez," Evan said. "He needs to get out of there."

"Tell me about it," Frank agreed. "I'm hoping he'll open someplace closer—Nashville or Louisville would be great."

"Tell him to open one here."

"I wish. Nashville is as close as he'll get. I'm trying to get him to come home for his birthday, maybe we can convince him then."

"Y'all want food? Kitchen's closing," Evan asked.

"It's nine-thirty," Cliff said.

"It's also Tuesday. Most everyone in here goes to bed at ten. Food, or no?" He backed away, moving his hands up and down as if balancing weights.

"Yeah, I'll take a fried ravioli."

"Order of chicken wings," Frank said.

"You got any breadsticks left?" Cliff said.

"Yeah, I'll throw some in."

The sound was barely audible, but Frank heard someone speaking in his ear behind him. He turned to see an elderly man leaning on his cane.

"Excuse me?" Frank asked.

"This seat." The man pointed at the stool. "Is it taken?"

"Oh, nah. Go ahead." The man slowly maneuvered his body onto the barstool with considerable effort.

"I'm Frank. Frank Burgers."

"Hi, Frank. I'm Tom."

"You here to watch the game?"

"No, just needed a drink." His eyes met Frank's and held his gaze briefly before turning his head back toward the bar. He tucked his hands into his lap as if he was cold and started to look over the chalkboard menu of draft choices on the wall. Frank asked Cliff if he knew him; he didn't. Tom attempted to wave for the bartender's attention and tried calling "excuse me" with no response from Evan.

"The bartender here sucks," Frank said.

"Beg your pardon?"

"The bartender," Frank said, pointing toward Evan, who was leaning with his back turned to them, talking to another patron. "He sucks." Frank picked up a jellybean out of a bowl and threw it at Evan, signaling for him to come over for Tom.

While Evan was getting Tom's order, Cliff asked, "You really think Donnie will move back here? Or open a spot close by?"

"I want him to, but I doubt he'll actually quit and leave. He's been working with the same guy for years and their place just opened. The guy's record isn't clean, but he's got a following—and money—and Donnie wants him to be a backer for his next project. I'm not getting my hopes up that he'll actually come home."

Evan dropped off Tom's drink and chatted with the elderly man. Frank tried to eavesdrop, but the jabber behind them and music playing was too loud. It wasn't long before Tom drained the rest of his beer and slid off the barstool. Frank watched him walk toward the door. "That was fast," Frank said.

"What's up?" Cliff asked.

"That guy," Frank replied. He threw another jellybean at Evan.

"Another round?" Evan asked.

"Did you know that guy?" Frank asked. "He got out of here fast."

"Never seen him before. You recognize him?"

"No. Did he pay?"

"Nah he seemed like he was having a bad day. It was on me."

"What was he saying?"

"It was hard to understand him. I caught bits and pieces."

"Come on, man," Frank made a strangling motion with his hands.

"Why, did you need something from him?"

"No, but he's old, and he looked sad. Somebody probably died. And if somebody died, then he likely needs someone to do a funeral."

"Or a grandson's in the hospital, or a daughter doesn't want to see her dad, or he caught his wife twerking on some teenager. There are a lot of other reasons an old man could be depressed."

"Nah. I'm excellent at reading people. Those were death eyes. Someone died." Frank turned to get down off the stool.

"You might be half right," Evan said. "It sounded like there was a death, but it was a while ago. Something about burying his wife?"

"His wife died?" Frank asked.

"It sounded like he said she died a while ago. He was saying something about his daughter too . . . maybe she died. And there was a necklace, or maybe he called something reckless."

"I'll be back." Frank hurriedly moved through the standing crowd along the bar toward the exit.

12

"He offered you six thousand dollars?" Donnie asked. "For a necklace?" The brothers had moved inside to the kitchen and were sitting at the table. "What kind of necklace costs six grand?"

"That's what I tried to explain earlier: value is relative. To him, the necklace is worth six thousand because it's one of a kind. It was his grandmother's, and then his mom's. Then he made the mistake of giving it to his wife."

"Why did he pick you to get it—how did something like that even come up?"

Frank hesitated. "It was my idea."

"Grave robbing was your idea!" Donnie got up from the table.

"Technically, it's not really grave robbing if the guy who married her approves the job."

"Yes, it is *technically* grave robbing!" Donnie screamed, catching himself before he got too loud. "Plus, they divorced so your idiotic argument still doesn't hold up."

The two brothers sat in silence for a moment before Donnie asked, "Why didn't he ask the daughter to have her exhumed? The city can do that."

"The daughter is dead."

"Then how does he know this necklace is buried with his ex-wife?"

"Because his son-in-law told him about it. The ex-wife refused to give it back to Tom, and when she died, the daughter didn't understand that it was an heirloom. She knew how much her mom liked it and didn't want Tom giving her mom's favorite necklace to some, and I quote, 'street whore.' His words not mine. Tom wanted the necklace back, but knew the city wouldn't grant him an exhumation since he's not married to her, and he definitely couldn't dig it himself so . . . here we are."

"Where's the necklace now?"

"Well, that's the bugger," Frank paused. He got up and walked over to the counter. "We didn't find it."

"So, naturally, you brought the whole corpse back?" Donnie said sarcastically.

"Eh, yes and no."

"There's no *no* in there. She's in my closet!"

"No, I mean, it's not that simple. First off, the coffin was all torn to pieces."

"What does that mean?" Donnie asked.

"Exactly what I said. It was like the thing had rotted. Pieces were coming off and stripping from it the more we dug around. Plus, there was still some water pooling down there from the storm a few nights back—the whole thing was a mess. The box was so weak that when I stuck my shovel into the ground toward the bottom, it went right through the coffin."

"Hang on. When did she die?" Donnie asked.

"Early two thousands—maybe fifteen years ago."

"And she already looks like *that*?" Donnie pointed upstairs to his bedroom. "There's no way it was fifteen years ago. She should still look . . . relatively normal."

"She may not have been embalmed. Lots of people don't get

embalmed. Plus, if there was a leak in the coffin and all that water just sat there, who knows? But, like I was saying, the necklace wasn't on her. After we dug her up we checked around the neck, and then in all the pockets. Nothing. So, we started moving parts of the body thinking it had fallen off or perhaps they just laid it on her person somewhere. Nothing. At that point we figured the necklace had fallen down into the lining, so we started searching around in there."

"You didn't have flashlights?"

"No. That would have been stupid," Frank said. "Someone might have seen us."

Donnie tightened his lips and held back his comment.

Frank continued, "That's when things went south. Cliff thought he saw a flashlight coming up one path, so I hurried out of the hole to hide. We sat for a bit until we were sure everything was clear, and I got back down in there. About that time, Cliff called down that a car was driving up. He said it was sitting idle, and then when he saw people getting out he told me to climb back up and bail. So, rather than dig and dash, I did what I thought was best: I called for a trash bag, threw as much of Sarah as I could into it, and climbed out. Of course, I tripped running to the car and spilled some of her out on the ground, but got everything back in while Cliff tried to push some dirt back on top. The voices were getting closer so I hurried back over to help, thankfully, because that's when I found some of Sarah's clothes that had fallen out of the bag—what was left of some pants and a torn up, pink cardigan with buttons on it. I threw them back into the hole, and that's when I saw her headstone. Well, not hers, but the one next to hers."

Donnie's eyes narrowed. "You dug up the wrong person."

"Yeah. The Sarah we needed was one over."

"So, that's not this guy's wife in my closet?"

"Nope. That's Sarah *Piddleton*. We needed Sarah Middleton. Easy mistake."

"Why didn't you just throw the bag back into the hole?"

"Because we were out of time. In the heat of the moment I figured I'd take the bag and rebury it later. To your point though, I now see the stupidity of that decision."

Donnie shook his head and walked out of the kitchen into the main hall. "Damnit, Frank." He said that a few more times from the hall as he walked back and forth. Finally, he appeared in the doorway and asked, "How do you dig up the wrong body?"

"Dude, in my defense, it was dark. And, who puts two people with very similar sounding last names right next to each other?"

"Who digs up a body?!"

Frank leaned against the counter, not saying a word. He watched Donnie pace back and forth down the hall, through the kitchen doorway. He finally asked if he was going to keep pacing or come back in the kitchen. Donnie walked by the doorway again holding up his middle finger. "Okay," Frank said. "Six thousand dollars. For a necklace. Not a bad night's work."

"You put a body. In. My. Closet." Donnie was back in the doorway. "It wouldn't be a bad night's work if you did the job right."

"So, if I would have walked in here with an envelope containing six grand with nobody in your closet, you'd be okay with all of this?"

Donnie glared at Frank. "You don't have the six grand. For

all you know the guy was a drunk. How are you sure he'll pay up?"

Frank reached into his pocket and pulled out a roll of bills. "Because of this. Right here. This money." He waved the wad around to Donnie. "He paid me half up front. I get the other half when I bring him the necklace."

Donnie stepped back into the kitchen and took hold of the money. "This is three thousand dollars?"

"Yup."

Donnie sat back down at the table. "This doesn't change that you stole a body and hid it in my room. You're dragging me into this."

Frank put the money back into his pocket. "Don't worry about it, we're heading over to Frazier's—"

"Stop! Stop telling me details. I don't need to hear it!"

"Look, if these jobs work out, our money issue—"

"Wait, wait. *Jobs*? There's more than one?"

"Yeah, I told you. Someone is paying us for body parts—bones, actually. I got almost five thousand dollars last week from two bodies."

Donnie's eyes were bugged out of his head. "Those people we buried last week had . . . wait . . . you sold limbs off those clients?"

"Yeah. Five grand," Frank replied.

Donnie sat motionless, mouth still open. It was several seconds of silence before words finally—and slowly—came out: "How did you ever think this was a good idea? I mean, most of your ideas are worthless, but this!" Donnie paused. "Damnit. I cannot believe dad gave—" He stopped himself. He met his brother's eyes and let out a breath instead of words.

"What?" Frank asked.

"Nothing." Donnie paused again. "Doesn't matter."

"Just say it."

"I hate that Dad handed the controlling interest of his business to you."

"You would rather him have given it to you? You had no intention of stay—"

"I'm not saying that. But he should have given the place to someone who was actually serious about running it. At least I tried to get out and do something with myself. What are you doing? You're thirty-two years old, Mom's still doing your laundry and cooking your meals. You've been hitting on the same married woman for two years. You talk all this game about these ideas you have for your future, and for the home and for Cliff, and all these goals you want to achieve, but . . . you're just lazy. We asked you to work on promotions, and business ads, and instead you upload some hyperlinks for funeral coupons. You put a slightly offensive logo on your truck. You bought furniture we didn't need."

"What are you talking about? Those old couches were crap!"

"You bought a basketball court for god's sake. We're bringing in next to no profit, and your solution is selling bones? Cutting off arms?" Finally, "I think we should take the deal from the Kochs."

Frank's eyes lifted to meet his brother's. "Wow."

"I at least want to talk about it."

"Are you just pissed that your restaurant didn't work out and so no—"

"What? No. That restaurant has nothing to do with this. Your irresponsibility is why I want out."

Frank stared down at the floor for a few moments considering how to respond without losing his temper: "You know, despite the fact you think I'm totally incapable of running this business—or any other for that matter—this place isn't doing *that* bad. Could we be doing better? Absolutely. That's what I'm trying to do. And screw you for calling me lazy! I've got ambition coming out of my ass, you prick. There's a reason I bought all that stuff; an actual plan for what I want this place to be, and it's something the anus brothers across town could never offer. But you wouldn't understand any of that, because you've never asked me. You realize the only time you've talked about the home since you got here is to tell me that we should sell it?" Donnie started to interject, but Frank continued: "Even when you call, it's just to talk about you—*your* restaurant, or some new movie *you* saw, or whatever new activity *you're* doing, but you never ask anything about us. You don't ask how things are going, the finances, where we need help, my vision for the place—"

"Your vision includes purchasing a commercial espresso machine and five hundred dollars' worth of old tabletop games?"

"Yeah. Yeah, it does. Because at least twice a month, there's a handful of kids sitting in the parlor bored out of their minds, playing on their phones. Most times, families just sit off by themselves and those games give people something to do. Most important, they get them interacting and enjoying themselves."

"Enjoying themselves? It's a funeral. I don't want people to be miserable, but it's not a birthday party."

"Like I said, you wouldn't understand. You left—and it's fine. But *I've* been running this place for six years. You're acting like dad gave me the company—he gave it to both of us. You backed out. So, because you backed out, you want me to do the same so you can feel like less of a dick."

"Yeah," Donnie said. "Yeah, that's completely accurate." Donnie put his head down on the table, letting out a breath. The two of them were quiet for a moment before Frank spoke again.

"You don't believe me, but I am trying to keep this place together. It'd be a lot easier if I had your help while you're home," Frank said.

"You talk about me helping you with this as if we're doing a simple house remodel. This is illegal. If you're caught, we're all going to jail. Even Cliff!"

"But we won't get caught if you help us!"

"If you don't put that woman's corpse back tonight, I'm going to go to the police. I'm serious. I'm not ruining my name over this."

Frank laughed. Not at anything funny; he was frustrated. He was the one running the funeral home. He was the one making the decisions. He was the one who stayed behind when Donnie left, not because he had to but because he loved the home—he loved the service he provided people. He was proud of his ideas and he was proud of this one. It would get them the money they needed to compete and update. He spent hours thinking and planning: how he would advertise the odd service, how he would execute the jobs, what kind of jobs could be done, and most important, how he wouldn't be caught. He knew it was insane, but there was no other choice—the Kochs had an insane amount of money and Frank couldn't compete without a financial boost. His crazy ideas had given the home some success in recent years—especially in Donnie's absence—and it frustrated him that his older brother couldn't at least offer a hint of trust.

Frank folded his arms and stared at his brother. "Look, I'll get the corpse out of your room, but I'm not selling the place—I have nowhere else to go. You said it yourself, I'm a thirty-two-year-old college dropout. This is really all I know. You and me have been planning funerals since we were kids, and I still love it. This place is all I have and getting caught would mean I can no longer do the one thing I do well. Family funeral homes are dying out and you're right, we can't compete so I'm trying to reboot the place. I've tried to think of ways to stay alive—pun intended—but I've got nothing."

Frank continued: "I know you don't get it, but this *is* the quickest solution for staying in the game. If we can get to a reasonable spot where we can compete again, I'm taking it. In the words of Dr. Dre, you only get one shot, don't miss your chance to blow. Opportunity comes once in a lifetime."

Donnie raised his head. "That's not Dre. And I'm pretty sure that lyric doesn't apply to this situation."

"Agree to disagree," Frank said.

Donnie looked around the room. "I'd be lying if I said I'm not nervous to let this place go. But you're going to have to find a different way to save it. I can't risk getting caught up in something like this—especially if I'm opening a restaurant. So, what if you and I sit down and discuss going forward. Not just about selling, but about if we can actually keep the place open."

"That's fine. Let me and Cliff take care of this first. We'll get the payment, and then we can talk."

"Okay, but once you get that guy's money, no more. Okay?"

"You got it," Frank replied.

"I'm serious. This place is not worth me going to jail."

Frank nodded his head.

"Okay?" Donnie asked.

"Okay."

"And don't tell me about Sarah, or whatever her name is," Donnie said.

"Deal." Frank looked at his brother. "We cool?"

Donnie sighed. "Not until you get that corpse out of my room."

Frank moved toward the hallway while Donnie made his way out the back door. "You know," Frank called out, "if you'd hop on this project with me, we could have enough for you to open a restaurant right here. What do you think? Build it next door?"

"No one will eat at a restaurant next to a funeral home."

"They would if *you* opened it. Just imagine how well we could promote this place if we had a restaurant next door. Hashtag *family funeral home!*"

13

Frank and Cliff loaded the bag of bones into the truck bed just after ten p.m.

The plan in Frank's mind was to return Sarah to her grave at the Frazier cemetery, cover the hole, and dig up the correct Sarah in the adjacent plot—all in one evening.

Willie Frazier was sitting on his porch sipping a can of Pepsi when Frank walked up the front porch steps and extended his hand. He noticed Willie attempt to scoot the empty mini bottles of Crown into the trashcan as he took a seat in the chipped, white Cracker Barrel rocker. They chatted, looking out over the large property, the bright yellow caution tape in the distance dancing in the wind around Sarah's grave.

"You want me to come out and take a walk through later tonight? See if I see anything?" Frank asked.

"I never saw a need to keep tabs on what goes on at night in here," Willie took a sip of his Pepsi-Crown. "Security cameras and cemetery watch volunteers—that's a bunch of hooey. Way I see it, the spirits are watchin' over each other. Diggin' up a body isn't an easy task. Mentally, I mean—it's tough. You're messin' with the dead, and that ain't something you wanna be foolin' around with. I'm sure whoever it was won't be coming back." He went quiet for a second and then reached behind his rocker. "But if they do, I got this here shotgun. Just fire a warning shot—usually does the trick."

"You ever actually hear anyone out there?"

"What?" Willie asked, cupping his hand behind the ear.

"You eve—never mind." They continued talking until Lynette called Willie in for dinner. Frank assured him he would keep an eye out. The two shook hands and Frank made his way back toward home, but not before getting a quick assessment of the Middleton/Piddleton plots.

He didn't have to get too close to see that the Piddleton grave was filled back in. "Oh man," he whispered. He would have to dig Sarah Piddleton's grave all over again, then do Sarah Middleton's grave, putting them in an already sensitive situation for twice as long. It was too risky. Plan B: Sarah Piddleton would have to be reburied somewhere else.

Kentucky Highway 80 leads out of Murray and directly to the US 68 bridge. It is one of only a few access points to the recreational peninsula, Land Between the Lakes—what locals referred to as LBL. The peninsula, now spanning almost two hundred thousand acres, is operated as a recreation area for hiking, camping, and historical exploration. The drive from Murray to the old bridge normally took Frank fifteen minutes, but the time on the dashboard indicated it had already been twenty-five. Sarah's bones encouraged a careful drive.

"I can't stand that thing," Cliff muttered when the dim red lights atop the narrow, two-lane bridge over Lake Barkley came into view. The structure hung over the black water in the dark with an ominous presence, as if warning them not to cross over. "I always feel like it's going to collapse when I'm on it—or there's going to be a hole in it."

"Same," Frank said, rolling down his window and unknowingly slowing down to almost ten miles per hour.

"Plus, I usually think like I'm going to swipe the oncoming car," Cliff nervously gripped the bar above the door, and slid down into his seat. Frank ignored him and continued humming along to the radio. Both exhaled when the truck made it to the other side.

"What is it with this place having no lights?" Cliff said. "No streetlights, flashing signs—nothing. I can't see a thing."

"I mean, that's a good thing for us, right?" Frank replied.

"It's crazy that people used to actually live out here. I don't even like driving through it."

"No, what's crazy is that they kicked everyone out of here and never thought to replace those old bridges," Frank said.

"When did people stop living here?"

"The seventies, I think. There were even a couple of big towns."

"What happened?"

"I'm not too clear on all the details but there was a nasty problem with flooding because of how it was situated between the Tennessee and Cumberland rivers. Tennessee Valley Authority built a dam on the Tennessee River to help, which it did, but then they built a second dam on the Cumberland River and that's when they decided it would be better used as a national recreation area and that anyone living here should go somewhere else."

"They just kicked everyone out?"

"Pretty much. After they built the dams and created the lakes, they started calling it—"

"Land Between the Lakes," Cliff interrupted. "Makes sense. What happened to the people?"

"They moved to different towns nearby. Mayfield, Murray, Clarksville, Paducah."

"So, all the cemeteries are from when people lived out here before?"

"Mostly, yeah."

"Do people still use the cemeteries?" Cliff asked.

"Some. A lot of them you can't get to anymore because of overgrowth or washed-out trails. I'm surprised you've never been up here."

"I've been here numerous times, I just didn't realize until recently that people used to live out here."

"If you know where to look you can still find some of the historic stuff: house foundations, railroad tracks, an old church, a furnace—cemeteries."

Frank turned up the volume when the Stone Temple Pilots came on the radio and began singing along, but Cliff started talking over the volume.

"How many cemeteries are there?"

"Couple hundred," Frank replied.

"Which one did you pick?"

"Otter Pond." Frank leaned over and pointed on the map.

"Is it easy to get to?"

"Yeah. I did a couple of burials out here a few years back."

"No one will see us?"

"Not likely. The place only has like fifteen graves, and it's in the middle of nowhere," Frank replied, turning up the volume a little more for the song's chorus.

Cliff reached over and turned it down again to ask another question, and Frank groaned. "Why are we coming out here to do this?" Cliff asked. "Does it need to be a cemetery? Why not bury them somewhere in Murray?"

"It's not uncommon for older graves to be refilled with dirt. Sometimes the holes sink in or need to be re-treated with grass. Someone walking by an old headstone with fresh dirt wouldn't think twice, but someone walking in a field or out in the woods that catches a glimpse of freshly turned dirt might be suspicious."

"Seems legit," Cliff replied.

"Plus, no one comes out here. A lot of these cemeteries are so old, overgrown and secluded, the chance of someone being in them—let alone seeing us dig there—is really slim."

"How old are we talking?" Cliff asked.

"I've seen graves as old as the seventeen hundreds," Frank replied. "A lot of them you can't even get to anymore; there's no path."

"My dad used to tell me stories about this one cemetery up here, Bethel. You ever hear about that?"

"The one with the witch?" Frank asked.

"Yeah."

"I'm sure that's a myth." Frank smiled.

"Nah man, he's got pictures."

"Yeah . . . probably a picture of another cemetery, and he's calling it Bethel."

"Maybe."

"Was there more than one grave in the picture?" Frank asked.

"No. Maybe like ten or so."

"There ya go," Frank said. "Bethel has one grave. Plus, even if that place is real, it's probably inaccessible and impossible to find."

"You know where you're going, right?"

"It's up here." Frank had been on a back road *of a back road* for almost two minutes. The paved path turned to dirt and finally become a trail of tire tracks through grass and weeds. "Look for a sign."

"I can't even see the road, it's so dark. What kind of sign?"

"That one. Got it!" Frank yelled, driving past the entrance.

"How did you even see that?" Cliff asked.

Frank turned onto another dirt road and the cemetery came into view within seconds. His depiction had been accurate: easy to get to, about fifteen graves, and devoid of any human contact.

Cliff sighed. "I got no service on my phone."

"Would suck to get stranded—"

"Hey. Don't even say it. I ain't tryin to play that," Cliff said.

"Dude, we're in the middle of nowhere and no one else is out here. Plus you're three times the size of anyone I know. I'm sure we're fine."

"People aren't what I'm worried about," Cliff replied.

Frank turned off the car and headlights, throwing them both into total darkness. "Yeah I could have gone without you saying that." He snatched two flashlights from the glove box and clicked them on.

The sun's absence didn't bring much relief from the heat. Cliff stepped out of the air-conditioned truck and cursed at the thick, humid air. A mosquito wasted no time in landing on his arm as he shut the door. Cliff swatted at the sting, leaving a tiny smear of blood across his forearm. "You got bug spray?"

Frank grabbed a can from under the seat and sprayed his exposed skin, before throwing it to Cliff, who afterward looked like he'd taken a shower. "Did you use the whole can?" Frank asked.

"It's possible," Cliff replied. He made his way over to examine some of the graves while he attempted to rub the repellant into his skin. Even in the dark, the flowers on the graves were vibrant in color as if they'd just been planted. A closer look revealed just the opposite: vacant spider webs stretched across the plastic leaves and pedals, and dead bugs littered the bottom of the headstones. "Ew," he whispered. "That's depressing." He turned back to Frank. "I take it no one ever changes out these flowers."

Frank removed two shovels out of the back of his truck and threw the bag of Sarah's bones over his shoulder. The two of them made their way toward the rear of the cemetery with shovels in hand.

It didn't take much time before Cliff began to feel like he was sweating off the bug spray. Sweat poured off his brow and down his legs. He constantly mistook the trickle of sweat for the movement of a bug and instinctively swatted at the disturbance. A light breeze only brought mild relief from the humidity, but after ninety minutes, two pee breaks, two rests, and a cup of iced coffee, the two had dug a hole almost five feet down. Cliff climbed up the step ladder and pulled Frank out. "Finally," Frank panted. He grabbed the bag of bones and held it over the grave. "You wanna say anything?"

"Like what?" Cliff asked.

"I don't know." They both stood there silent until Frank pulled out his phone and started scrolling through his music. "Perfect," he said, placing it back in his pocket. "Sarah Smile" by Hall and Oates played over the night calm.

"I was thinkin you might offer a prayer, but that works," Cliff said. Frank dropped the bag into the hole as he sang the chorus in his falsetto voice, and the two of them began shoveling dirt back in.

By one o'clock they were back in the truck. "Do you know how to get home?" Frank asked.

"Dude, I don't even know how you got here. Turn your GPS on."

"Can't. No service. I think I got it. Check the map and tell me how far up the highway is," Frank said, clicking on the overhead light and pointing to their current location.

Frank cut the ignition to his truck and slapped Cliff's arm to wake him, causing Cliff to jolt back into consciousness. Cliff looked confused and Frank reminded him that they were back at the home. "You good?" Cliff gave a thumbs up and yawned.

The two decided to walk to Frazier's by way of the path through the woods behind the house. Using the truck would not be ideal given the sensitive circumstances.

"I've got an energy drink in my fridge," Cliff said. "Go get it and I'll grab the shovels from the shed."

"Don't need 'em," Frank said. "There are shovels in Willie's shed; he never locks it."

"How do you know that?"

"I used to work there in the summer helping to dig and landscape. He didn't like shed locks because he always lost the key.

"You still wanna grab me that energy drink?"

The two of them dug in silence, taking only a couple of breaks to get water or pee on the tree nearby. Frank was certain that neither Willie nor Lynette could or would hear anything this late at night, but to be safe he and Cliff kept an eye on the Frazier house as they dug. Each watched behind the other, peeking out over the grave's top when it got low enough.

Exhaustion eventually set in and the dig took much longer than anticipated. After nearly two and a half hours, they hit wood. They cleared off what dirt they could before Frank unlatched the coffin and Cliff pulled it open. Sarah Middleton's corpse wasn't nearly as decomposed as her namesake neighbor in the next plot.

"Yup. I'm gonna have nightmares tonight," Cliff whispered, turning his head away. "Can't un-see that."

"Boom!" Frank exclaimed in a whisper. He swatted Cliff's sweaty leg and pointed down at the necklace resting around her neck. Frank reached down and maneuvered behind the corpse's head and neck to unlatch the chain. Cliff made a gag sound behind him. The necklace came off cleanly, and Frank placed it in a plastic bag, which he put in his pocket.

"We good?" Cliff asked, exhaling.

"We're good. Let's get out of here."

As they mustered their remaining energy to quickly shovel

the dirt back into the hole, something cut through the cemetery's silence: voices. Cliff stopped. "What is that?"

"Shhh," Frank replied. Frank peeked out over the hole. People were coming toward them—with flashlights.

"Again?" Cliff said. "What is it with this place? It's almost five."

"Hide!" Frank scrambled out of the hole and hid behind one of the nearby headstones. Cliff followed and squatted behind one adjacent.

Frank peered from behind the stone. There looked—and sounded—to be two girls and three guys. Someone was smoking and they were all being way too loud. Frank's heart jumped when one of the girls suddenly called the others to come and look at something near where Frank was crouching down. She'd noticed the open grave and a collective sound of curses were let out when they all approached it.

One of the boys laughed. "I dare you to jump in."

"Hellllllll nah," a girl yelled.

Shut up! Frank thought.

"There must be a funeral tomorrow," the other guy said. "Here. Get a picture of me down there." Frank heard one of the guys protest, and one of the girls agree. Then a light flashed on from the Frazier's house. "Hey, that house light came on," one of them said.

"So what? This is public property. We're not doing anything ille—"

Then the gunshot rang out.

"Shit," Frank whispered. He heard the kids sprint off, yelling 'go, go' along with several expletives. One of them must have tripped because someone let out a shriek of pain. Frank didn't wait long before he scooted back toward the hole.

"We're not finishing, are we?" Cliff said.

"No. Just making sure we didn't drop anything." Frank picked up the shovels and started to walk.

"Leave it," Cliff said. "It's his stuff anyway. Let's go."

With the college kids acting as a needed distraction, Frank and Cliff ran back toward the wooded trail they used to get in. They kept quiet as they went past neighboring yards, careful not to draw attention if anyone should happen to be outside. When they returned to the back lot of the funeral home, Cliff took a seat on the porch swing and Frank bent over, resting his hands on his knees. "Not at all how I expected the night to go," Frank whispered, catching his breath.

"You at least got the necklace, right?"

"Yeah. I just can't believe we left another grave open."

"Well," Cliff panted, "even if we filled it in, someone would have noticed the loose dirt. What's the point of filling them in?"

"To be nice?" Frank replied.

"Not worth it. No more filling in holes."

"No more Frazier cemetery. Or any big cemetery."

"Good idea," Cliff said. "I'm pretty sure I need to change my pants now, so, I'm going home."

"Thanks again for helping. I'll get you the money when he pays."

When Cliff came out of his office and locked the gym door, the sun was starting to come up and Frank was waiting for him. He offered for Cliff to stay in the guest room, but Cliff declined. "Drive safe. I've got a couple of items to bury still—two bones.

That guy your friend set us up with ended up buying only two of the four."

"Why didn't you bring them tonight? We could have buried them with one of the bodies," Cliff said.

"Didn't think about it. I'll probably head back up to LBL tomorrow, see if I can find a place that's more secluded. Don't wanna use the same place twice."

"I'm gonna be honest; I don't know how much more secluded I can go. I don't like messing around in LBL at night."

"Oh, I'm definitely not going back up there at night," Frank said. "But we'll need to get more isolated if we're going up there in the daytime."

SATURDAY

14

Virginia Jan's Café was nestled in the downtown historic square. The location was troublesome for most businesses due to its distance from the college and limited parking, but the early morning rush for donuts was weekly pandemonium. Open only six days a week from five a.m. to one p.m., the draw of the freshly baked donuts and cinnamon rolls was enough to squash any excuse of poor parking. They were available beginning at 5:00 a.m. and offered until they ran out, which was generally no later than 11:00 a.m. 10:00 a.m. on Fridays and Saturdays. A police officer stood outside during the rush directing the Uber and Taxi drivers in and out of the square.

Donnie took his mother's parking spot when he arrived. With a line extending out the door, people sitting along the sidewalk curb, and nearby benches, and '80s rock playing through the speakers, it was hard to believe that it wasn't yet seven in the morning.

The smell of fried dough and cinnamon hit him within seconds of getting in line. He inched inside with everyone else, looking up from his phone whenever someone called out his name or tapped him on the shoulder. His mother had not done much to change the interior in years: a basic layout of tables and chairs for the select few who wanted typical entrée items. Two lines led to the main counter where an order was placed and received, which fed into another line if customers wanted milk for coffee or napkins. There was a counter against the wall with stools, but it was being overrun with standing patrons talking and eating.

"Mr. Burgers?" Donnie heard a voice say as he was about to reach the counter. The voice was deep and authoritative. He turned around to see a tall, nerdy-looking man with slicked over hair and glasses wearing a short-sleeve button-down shirt and khakis. He had a body that Donnie was sure Cliff could snap into two. "Yes, sir?"

"I was hoping I could speak with you in private."

Oh no. Police.

"I was on my way to your home and noticed your car in the parking lot. I figured I'd try and catch you here—and grab a bite to eat."

What? "I'm sorry, but, do I know you? And how do you know my car? Have we met?"

"No. Not officially—just over the phone. My name is Bill Cobb. I'm a friend of someone you did work for recently. He told me you drove a red truck with a . . . rather crude logo painted on the side."

Donnie turned back to look at the decal on the side of Frank's truck: a casket stretched all the way along the side. Sitting up in the casket was the same skeleton from the coupon, giving a thumbs up. The side of the casket read "Look Alive @ Burgers Brothers' Funeral Home."

"You think I'm Frank?" Donnie asked.

The man went quiet for a second, and then turned to look back at the truck as if he thought he had the wrong one. "You're not Frank Burgers?"

Donnie breathed out a slight laugh. "No. I'm his brother, Donnie. I took his truck this morning because he was blocking mine in."

"Oh." The man paused. "I'm sorry for the mix up."

"No apology necessary." Donnie pointed at the truck. "I told my brother to have our logo and name printed on the truck as a form of advertising. That's what he came back with. I guess the positive is that people always know where we are."

"Is Frank with you?"

"Donnie Burgers." He heard another voice say.

Donnie turned back to see a young woman standing in front of him with jet-black hair and light skin staring at him. He didn't recognize her. "Yes?"

"Oh my gosh! How are you?" She went in for a hug that Donnie didn't refuse.

He smiled and nodded his head as if he knew her. She had a Pepperdine logo on her shirt. *Who do I know at Pepperdine?*

The lady at the counter called for next in line—the girl moved to the counter and addressed the woman standing behind it: "Hey, Mrs. Dale."

"Well, my word! Lexie, what are you doin' here?"

Lexie? Lexie. Who do I know named Lexie?

"Oh, just visiting. Can I get four chocolate glazed, one cinnamon twist, and a strawberry? And, a coffee, please?"

"Sure can. You here to see your dad? I talk with him quite a bit these days. Seems like he's doing well." Mrs. Dale moved down the counter and began picking out the selections.

Lexie smiled. "How've you been? How's your mom?"

"I'm stayin' busy, but oh Lord don't get me started on that woman. She's losing her mind! She had a date last night and never came home. I came this morning to open up the café and come to find out she's been here since 3 a.m. prepping dough—with her date! They were both still dressed up."

Lexie laughed. "Seriously?"

"She turned ninety this year. I can't get her to slow down." Judy Dale handed Lexie the bag. "Three-fifty, darlin'."

"Hey, if she's dating at ninety, she's doing something right." Lexie passed her a five-dollar bill. "It was good seeing you. Take care."

She turned back to Donnie, who was still standing next to Bill. "Gosh, it's crazy seeing you here. It's been what? Since seventh grade? Sixth grade? You look great."

"Yeah, I know. It's been a while." He noticed himself awkwardly nodding his head. "And you look . . . great too." He could feel his face betraying him, turning into a nervous grin.

She took a sip of her coffee. "You don't remember me, do you?"

Donnie shook his head. "I'm sorry. I'm trying to piece this together. Lexie, right? Are you sure you have the right person?"

"Not a lot of guys in Murray with the last name Burgers. You don't remember me from middle school?"

He let out a nervous laugh. "I don't remember a lot from middle school."

"Wow. Ouch." Lexie's smile faded. "Don't know how to respond that one." Lexie pulled her sunglasses down over her eyes and patted his shoulder with her hand. "I'll see ya around, buddy."

Donnie tightened his lips. "Is there a last name?"

"Oh, there is," Lexie replied. "I just thought you'd remember it." She turned back once more and smiled at him: "Tell your mom she still has the best donuts in the country!"

Donnie watched her walk out.

"Mr. Burgers?" Bill said.

"Next in line!" Mrs. Dale called.

"Sorry, can I order first— wait, are you wanting Frank to help with a funeral?" He stepped toward the counter. "Because, I'm happy to help out if th—

The man cut him off. "No. No. That's ok. This wasn't about a funeral. Frank . . ." The man rubbed his thumb and forefinger around his mouth, seeming as if he wasn't sure how to proceed. "You mind if we talk somewhere in private?" He didn't wait for a reply. He walked over to an empty table near the back, away from the crowd at the counter, and took a seat. Donnie dropped his head back and sighed before looking at Mrs. Dale. "Sorry, I'll be back." He followed him and sat down.

"Frank did some work for a friend of mine recently, and I'd actually hired him to do some similar work for me."

"This have anything to do with a Sarah Piddleton?" Donnie asked.

The man cocked his head. "Piddleton?"

"Sorry. Middleton."

"You know about Sarah?" Bill asked.

"That depends. You're not a family member of Sarah's are you?"

"No."

"Then, unfortunately, yes. I know about Sarah." Donnie sighed. "How do you know her?"

"I didn't. I know her husband, Tom."

"My brother isn't doing those projects anymore, so if that's what you want . . ."

"That's what I wanted to talk with Frank about. I wanted to up my offer."

"Like I said, Frank isn't doing any more projects. I'm happy to tell him you and I spoke, but I don't think he's going to have an interest in seeing you," Donnie replied flatly.

Bill leaned back against his chair and sat quietly for a moment. "I'd like to try and persuade him otherwise. I understand that he doesn't want to take the job anymore, but if he's truly set on that, then I'm going to need seventy-five hundred back."

Ten seconds elapsed before Bill started waving his hand in front of Donnie's face. "You alright?"

"Did you say seventy-five hundred? Dollars?"

"Yes. I offered your brother fifteen thousand dollars to do a job for me. In good faith, I gave him half the money up front. That was about a week ago. I told him I would deliver the rest once he delivered my wife."

Donnie was having trouble processing Bill's words. "And I heard you right—you're wanting to pay him more?"

"Yessir. I'm willing to pay twenty thousand if he'll reconsider. He called me last night and he said he couldn't do what I wanted and that he would be returning my payment this morning. Unfortunately, I've spent too long thinking about this and I'm not interested in abandoning the project."

"You're going to pay my brother twenty thousand dollars?" Donnie whispered.

"If he'll reconsider backing out and bring my wife to me, yes."

Donnie's eyes narrowed. "He called you and just said that he changed his mind?"

"Sure did. Didn't give me much reason other than that. Tell you what: you pass along my message, and have him get in touch with me by the end of the weekend. If I don't hear from either of you by Sunday night, I'll consider the deal off. Sound good?" Bill stood up and offered Donnie his hand.

"He has your number?" Donnie asked, shaking Bill's hand.

"Yes. Let him know my request and the new offer." He didn't wait for Donnie to walk with him up to the counter. Perhaps he thought it best to separate after such a conversation.

Donnie stayed sitting at the table trying to take in everything Bill had said, and weigh whether he could be on board with such a scheme. *Is it worth twenty grand?*

He got up and walked back toward the line's end when Mrs. Dale called him to come up front. The interruption alerted several more people to Donnie's presence in the café. His kindergarten teacher left a coveted spot near the wall counter and gave him a hug at the creamer stand. The owner of the restaurant where Donnie first worked in high school scooted out of line to come shake his hand. Even his former high school principal, Eugene Atlas, came over to say hello. Normally he was happy to speak with so many familiar faces, but all he could think about was the twenty grand. And a light-skinned, dark-haired girl named Lexie he supposedly knew.

15

Ginny and Dave were at the kitchen table staring at pieces of the *Murray Ledger* when Donnie returned home. Ginny held a folded section in front of her face and was mumbling numbers to herself. She ignored his "good morning" and began counting the fingers of her other hand. Donnie poured a cup of coffee and set the donuts on the table peering over her shoulder to gauge her progress on the morning's Sudoku. "What about a six in that top left quad—" he began before she waved her hand for him to hush.

He picked up a warm glazed donut from the box and sat down, still not able to shake the encounter from earlier.

"Everything alright?" Dave asked. He sipped his coffee and opened the box of donuts.

"Yeah, I'm good. Sorry. Spaced out." He took a bite of his donut.

"See any familiar faces?"

"Oh man," Donnie laughed. "So many people. That's what took so long. I saw Mrs. Combs, who still looks the exact same. My boss from The Bull Pen was there. Even saw Principal Atlas. He says hi."

"He's there just about every morning," Ginny said from behind her paper. "Did he remember you?"

"Oh yeah. I saw him come in and thought he wouldn't recognize me, but he walked right over and shook my hand."

"How was he feeling?" she asked.

"Fine, I guess. He's looking older. You can see it in his eyes and neck," Donnie replied. "Plus, he was using a cane."

"He's been having some hip issues recently—or back issues."

"He still has that fiery personality, though," Donnie said.

"Was Wanda working?"

"No, her daughter was there. I overheard her say that Wanda was there at three a.m. prepping, though."

"I don't know why she does that." Ginny sighed. "That woman is ninety years old, she doesn't need to be driving that early."

"I'm pretty certain her date was driving."

Ginny looked up from her puzzle and Donnie took another bite, catching the glaze chips with his hand. "I overheard Judy say that she showed up this morning at three with her date from last night and they were still in their dress clothes."

"No."

"Oh yeah," Donnie said. "Looks like one of your employees has been putting some extra love into those donuts."

"I need to talk to her."

"I don't know why," Dave muttered. "Unless you're going to ask her for some tips." Ginny sighed through her nose and shot her husband a sharp glance.

"Plus, there was this girl there that I supposedly knew, but couldn't place in my mind to save me embarrassment."

"Oh," Ginny grinned. "Did you get her name?"

"Not a full one. Just that we went to middle school together."

"Your yearbooks are in a box in the attic. You should get them out and go through them," Dave said. "Maybe even take some of the boxes with you when you go next time and get them out of my attic." He winked at Donnie and then turned at the sound of Frank sauntering into the kitchen in his pajamas. "The master stirs."

"Mornin' everybody." Frank yawned. He kissed his mother on the head and went immediately to the coffee pot. At almost the same time Cliff knocked on the back-patio door and entered.

"Yo yo yo!"

"Hello Clifford," Ginny said, turning around to greet him.

"Good morning Mrs. B." Cliff walked over and gave Ginny a hug from behind. He fist bumped Dave. "Mr. B."

"Help yourself Cliff," Dave said.

"Any strawberry?" Cliff asked.

Frank, who was already at the box, picked one out and gave it to Cliff. "Nope. Just the boring ole glazed and chocolate."

"Excuse you," Ginny sneered.

"Feel free to wake up next time and go yourself," Donnie called back. The five of them sat at the table over coffee and donuts as they did most every Saturday morning.

"Tell us more about this girl," Ginny asked. "Get me her name; I'll make some calls. I'd be happy to set something up."

Donnie laughed. "I'm good."

"I set Clifford up on a date last week, didn't I?"

"You did. Katie," Cliff replied. Then to Donnie: "She was hot, man. Your mom's got good taste."

"I'm gonna act like you didn't say that," Donnie scooted the glaze shavings on the table into his hand.

"Who's Katie?" Frank asked. "How does Mom know more about your dating life than me?"

"First off, I told you I had a date. You just don't listen.

Second, she's the one who set it up. You work with her mom, right?" he asked Ginny.

"I work with both of them. Katie's sense of humor reminded me of Clifford's. Plus when she said she liked to play chess I knew that was a sign of good compatibility."

"She told me she would murder me in a match. Her confidence was cute." Cliff chuckled. "Yeah, the date went fine. We had a little scuffle in the bar which I think made her feel awkward, but it worked out."

"The two of you had a scuffle?" Ginny asked.

"Not us. Somebody else—nothing big. This guy at the bar was being rude about his drink order and went off on the bartender for like two or three minutes. I yelled over 'excuse me' and asked if I could put my order in. The guy got all butt-hurt and started mouthing off. So, I said I was sorry, and then tried to put my order in again. He kept runnin' his mouth and getting closer to me, and finally I turned toward him and was like, 'Dude, could you please calm down?' And then boom, the guy shoved me."

Frank laughed. "I thought you were gonna say the guy hit you in the head."

"I'd've dropped him if he'd done that. Nah, he just shoved me." Cliff used his hands to demonstrate the shove. "The guy was totally hammered, and he was about a quarter of my size. Fortunately, I was standing in a way that stabilized me so when he pushed, instead of me moving, he just sort of . . . fell into me. He caught himself, then stumbled back and stared at me with this puzzled look and said, 'Damn dude, you strong.'"

Ginny laughed.

"I think at that point he sobered up a little. He was totally cool toward me after that, but I think the whole thing made her feel awkward. Said she wanted to hang out again though, so that's good."

"When you gonna set me up with a date, Mom?" Frank asked, getting up from the table.

Ginny looked at him and replied dryly: "When you start doing your own laundry, like a grown up."

"Ouch," Donnie said as Frank put his dishes on the counter.

"She loves doing my laundry," Frank said softly. "So, who's the mystery girl?"

Donnie cut off the water and shook his hands in the sink. "Do you know anybody named Lexie from sixth or seventh grade?"

"Guy or girl?"

Donnie paused. "Wait, you know *guys* named Lexie?"

"Touché," Frank said. "What does she look like?"

"Pale skin. Dark hair."

"Nah."

"She bumped into me this morning while I was getting donuts. Knew my name, knew Mom ran the place. Says we knew each other back in middle school."

"The only Lexie I know is the girl you had a crush on back in the day. Was that her?"

Donnie paused. "No. That was Leslie Porter."

"Hold up. *Leslie* Porter? You thought her name was Leslie?"

"Yeah," Donnie replied.

"Lexie, dude. Alexis Porter. *Lexie.* She was two years above us, always had colored hair—neon bracelets."

"Wow," Donnie whispered. "That *was* her. Lexie? I thought her name was Leslie."

"You told her you didn't recognize her?" Frank asked.

"Pretty much. She introduced herself and I stared at her with this blank look on my face like an idiot."

Frank laughed. "Oh man."

"Yeah, right? It wasn't like she and I ever hung out. I thought she was hot, but I never really talked to her."

"You guys made out in Brian's parents' bedroom," Frank said.

"Nice!" Cliff said, tipping his mug of coffee toward Donnie.

"I didn't ask her name when we made out; I thought I knew it."

"Why were Donald and this girl making out in a parents' bedroom?" Ginny asked, setting down her Sudoku.

"It was nothing. We were at some random house for a birthday party—"

"What is with your memory? It was Brian Pennington's house. You guys were b-f-fs all through middle school," Frank said.

"Oh yeah. I forgot about him."

"How do you forget your bff?" Cliff asked.

"Because it was twenty years ago! I don't keep up with anyone. Plus, he fell of the face of the earth after freshman year. We all thought he ran away, that his parents sent him away for drugs. They were in town a few years after that, but I don't think he ever came back. I should look him up and see where he is now," Donnie replied.

"Anyways," Frank continued, "we had a birthday party at Pennington's house and there were tons of people."

Donnie noticed his mom's look of concern. "This was a middle school party, Mom. Nothing to worry about."

Frank cupped a hand to the side of his mouth and whispered

to Cliff, "*Shit was wild*. As I was saying, birthday bash. The guys were in one room and the girls were in another, but the main bathroom was being renovated or something and so we had to use the parents'. We were standing around and someone wanted to play truth or dare. Donnie wanted a dare. So, I dared him to go and make out with the next girl who walked into the bathroom. And that girl just happened to be the super-hot eighth grader . . ." Frank looked at Donnie for confirmation.

"Leslie Porter," Donnie muttered.

"*Lexie*. You never did really tell us what happened with you two."

"That's because nothing happened." Donnie smiled raising his eyebrows as he took a sip of coffee.

"You told us you guys made out."

"No, I said, 'No one act weird when she comes out of the bathroom, and I'll tell you about it later.'"

"What did you guys do then?" Cliff asked.

"It's awkward saying it now. I went back into the parents' room and waited for her to get out. Being the creeper that I was, I thought closing the bedroom door would help my chances. Instead, when she came out and saw me standing by the closed door, she laughed and asked what I was doing. I played the honest card and told her that I'd been dared to come back and kiss her. She chuckled again and said she had a boyfriend. So, I naturally asked if I could at least say we made out. She said 'no' to that too." Donnie took another sip of coffee. "But, she did say that if I promised to not say we kissed, she would make up for it when she came out."

"What'd she do?" Cliff asked.

"She waited a few moments after I came out, walked by our

group, winked at me, and gave the slightest air kiss." Another sip. "I think that was the last time I talked to her. But I held up my end of the bargain; never told anyone."

"I can't believe you asked to kiss her," Frank said.

"Whatever. We were twelve years old." Donnie rinsed out his cup and put it in the dishwasher. "Besides, all that mattered at the time was that you all *thought* I kissed her. I'm certain that if she said yes, I would have fainted. So hot."

"How's she look now?" Frank asked.

"Hotter."

"Hotter than eighth grade Lexie? Because I still fantasize about that one."

Silence went over the room. Donnie and Cliff turned their heads toward Frank.

"Come on, man . . ." Cliff said, shaking his head.

"Not sure how to respond to that," Donnie added.

"Where's she staying?" Frank asked.

"I didn't get that far," Donnie said. "She left before I could ask any more questions."

Ginny stood and rinsed her cup out and then announced that she was going in to work.

"You want me to drive you?" Frank asked.

"No. Your dad is gonna drive me in so he can go to the store. I'm meeting with a plumber and an electrician and I don't know how long that'll take."

Dave scooted away from the table. "I'm gonna run to the restroom and then I'm ready. See you boys afterwhile."

"Will you be done before one? We have that funeral at two," Frank asked.

"I should be," Ginny replied. "All the food is ready to go. It just needs to be heated up. Do you need me to do that?"

"No, it's okay. I have to run an errand, but I'll take care of it when I get back. Do I need to do anything else besides throw them in the oven to heat?" Frank asked.

"Just put out the plates and silverware. I asked Cliff to set up the tables."

When Ginny left the room Frank pulled out his phone.

"Hey, did you get a chance to finish the woman's makeup?" Donnie called over to Frank.

"Yup, all taken care of."

"You sure I don't need to look at it?" Donnie smiled.

Frank ignored his question, staring at his phone. "So, she's not on Facebook or Instagram. How are you going to call her?"

"I'm not," Donnie said, walking toward the hallway.

"This is your middle school crush! You're going to let her get away?"

"This hardly constitutes her 'getting away.'" Donnie flashed air quotes. "I haven't seen her in twenty years. I think I'll manage. Plus, that would seem a little desperate to try and find her now."

"Why does it have to be desperate? I'll ask around and see if anyone knows her, get her number, and then you can call her. Easy."

"You're an idiot." Donnie walked out of the kitchen into the hallway.

Frank turned to Cliff. "Donnie pulled so much play back in the day."

Donnie poked his head from the hall. "Don't listen to him. I got hardly any play back then."

"They used to call him The Playground," Frank yelled back.

"What does that even mean? No—nobody ever called me that." Donnie turned to leave again.

Frank winked at Cliff and whispered, "Yeah, they did."

Cliff finished what was left in his mug. "You decide where you're going today?"

Frank pulled a map out of his pajama pocket and laid it on the table. Several spots had been marked in red. Frank lowered his voice to Cliff. "I'll check these places out to bury those bones the guy didn't buy. And since he wants to meet again, I figure this time I'll make the transaction in LBL. That way, if he does the same thing, I can just go bury what he doesn't buy somewhere close. Probably don't need to be riding around with bones in my car."

"What did he want?"

"A couple of the big ones: femur, humerus. And then four smaller ones."

"You already got 'em?" Cliff asked.

"I pulled some off the woman downstairs," Frank replied.

"Donnie won't notice?"

"Only if he takes off her glove or looks at her bottom. I used a mannequin arm and a glove to hide it. You wanna go out there with me?"

"Nah. I'm booked all morning. I'll move those tables for your mom and then get to work," Cliff replied. "You tell your brother about the other guy? The one who wants to cremate his ex-wife?"

"Nah, I had to back out of that. Called him last night and said I couldn't do it anymore. Donnie's all over me."

"So, I take it you don't want another project?"

"What does that mean?" Frank asked.

"I have a friend who might be in the market for having something dug up. I was catching up with him this morning and he mentioned that his father-in-law may have been buried with something pretty pricey—didn't say what."

"You didn't mention anything about what we're doing, did you?"

"Hell nah," Cliff replied. "He was just talking. I thought if you were interested, I'd try and see what the item was, and if everything checked out, I'd find a way to introduce you two in private."

"I better not. The chef is in the middle of his menstrual cycle so I need to lay low. I've still gotta figure out how I'm gonna finish this limb transaction without him knowing."

16

Frank threw on a pair of old jeans and work boots and drove out to LBL for the second time in twelve hours. Even in the daytime the narrow lanes of the Lake Barkley Bridge cast a menacing image to approach. It made Frank subconsciously hold his breath as he drove over. He would roll his window down—even in the rain—in case the bridge collapsed and sent his car into the lake below. It also helped to blare music and sing along to whatever was on the radio at the time.

He made it off the bridge and had commenced with normal breathing by the time he exited off 68 onto Trace Road. He noticed signs for the Visitor Center and thought it may be helpful to ask for directions, but quickly decided against it. He didn't need anyone knowing he was here.

Instead, he laid his map over the steering wheel and navigated south toward the locations he had chosen. The southeast corner of his map displayed a handful of cemeteries along a collection of roads and paths that had been designated as accessible: James, Wilson, Dickson, Gillim, and Shipwell. Just west of that cluster was a road that had been labeled inaccessible; this road led to two cemeteries—Fox and Benton—and would require him to walk.

James Cemetery took him nearly fifteen minutes to find, and only five seconds to realize that it wouldn't be ideal for stashing unpurchased body parts—or anything private. The headstones could be seen from the main road making it more visible than Frank wanted.

Wilson Cemetery was significantly more unkept than James, but also sat close to the main road. He continued to Dickson, but like Wilson—and James—one did not have to enter to see it. The plots were located on two small hills, and high above was a lone streetlight to illuminate the area. "Jeez. Come on people. Give your loved ones some privacy."

The entrance to Gill Cemetery was deceiving. The road was paved and clear for almost a quarter of a mile, but suddenly came to an end. *Finally*. He pulled off to the side of the path and removed the cooler of two limbs from the cab, then, thought it may be safer to check out the spot before carting the limbs to wherever he was about to go.

He closed the door and locked it before tucking his jeans into his socks. "Try and bite me now. Stupid ticks." The stretch ahead appeared to be nothing more than a walking path through mud. A sign, likely blown over, lay in the mud: *Gill Cemetery Ahead*.

The trail led him a short distance through the trees before turning sharply to the right and then straight up a steep hill. Frank paused and sized up the slope. He checked around for a sign to indicate he was going the right way. This would have been a very inconvenient path—if not impossible—for cars or even carts to access. *How would anyone get a casket up there?*

At the top of the hill another Gill Cemetery sign lay fallen over. This one—made of wood and nearly faded—was covered by brush. "This place doesn't like signs," he muttered, walking past it. The mud and dirt path wound to the right once more and opened to a small clearing. "Bingo," he whispered. The first things Frank noticed were the PVC pipes in the shape of crosses sticking out of the ground, that surrounded a large stone monument in the middle of the lot. Frank took a closer look at the middle headstone, but the engravings were almost illegible. Gill was the only name he could make out and a year: 1802.

The surrounding pipe crosses had been inscribed with a name in what looked to be a marker. "No dates," he muttered. Each cross had been situated just above a stone marker—what Frank guessed was the original gravestone. The stones were all worn down.

There were eight graves in all. The word "Gill" was written across the horizontal arm, and just beneath it, on the vertical arm, was a number from one to eight. Frank moved through the clearing, scanning each of the PVC crosses, and noticed a date written on grave eight: 1907. When he stepped back, his foot landed on what should have been solid ground but instead was a large pile of leaves covering a hole over grave seven. Frank cursed and fell on his butt about twelve inches down from the surface into the grave.

He immediately turned onto his side to push himself up and scrambled out of the sunken hole. "Owww!" he growled. "Are you kidding me!" Because of the leaves and overbrush, Frank hadn't noticed that all the graves were slightly sunken in. He stood up brushing the dirt and debris off his pants and examined the holes more closely. "That was traumatic." He rubbed his hip and reached for a nearby stick and began clearing leaves up and out of the grave. "How far do you go down?" After a couple of minutes, he knelt and used his hands to pick up piles of leaves and move them to the side until he hit dirt.

Frank took the stick and poked it in the ground to see how

far down he could go. He turned toward grave eight—also sunken in—and did the same thing with the stick, noting that it too went down a little more than a foot. "This may work," he said.

He trekked back down the hill and laid the map out over the hood of his truck, placing a black X over the cemeteries he'd just visited, then looked at the ones marked by the map as inaccessible: Fox and Benton. "If this was accessible," he said, "what does *inaccessible* look like?" Gill would be fine to bury what he had, but he still had plenty of time. "Let's see what else we have," he said.

Shipwell Cemetery rested—on the map—just along the coast of the peninsula. Like Gill, a sign on the side of Highway 229 announced its location. The entrance to the cemetery felt like déjà vu: the road ended shortly ahead and diverged into a narrow, mud covered path into the woods—with no headstone or sign in sight. Frank switched off his truck and removed both the cooler from the cab and the shovel from the bed. He readjusted his pantlegs, making sure they were still tucked into his socks.

The road of mud and dirt took him nearly a hundred feet in before disappearing altogether into tall brush. Fortunately, there was enough of a path to navigate a direction. He patted his pocket to make sure he had his knife, put in his ear buds, and started walking.

Addy Michaels was a close friend of Frank and Donnie from high school, and a minister for a small church about fifteen

miles north of Murray. When Frank couldn't preside over a service, Addy was the back-up. He had just sat down on the couch
to watch ESPN highlights when he got a phone call from Donnie asking him to sub in for a funeral at eleven. The family's
preferred minister had contracted food poisoning and wouldn't
be able to lead it. "No problem. Send me the guy's notes if he
has any. I'll head over in an hour or so." Addy felt no need to
rush. He clicked off his phone, and turned Sportscenter back
on while he finished his breakfast.

Addy turned the front doorknob to go into the Burgers
house. It rattled forward once he released, then clanged onto
the ground. "Oh," he mumbled. He picked up the pieces to set
them on the side table, and walked inside, down into the preparation room to check in with Donnie.

"Something's up with your doorknob. Just fell off."

"Don't get me started," Donnie said.

"This guy really has food poisoning? Or was he hung over?"
Addy asked.

"I doubt he was hung over; he's nearly eighty years old."

"Amateur. Where is Frank?"

"LBL. Don't ask."

"Family already here?" Addy asked.

"Yeah. I'll introduce you and let you take it from there."

"Anything I need to know?"

"The projector's broken so there's no PowerPoint."

Addy's head tilted in intrigue. "Was there supposed to be a
PowerPoint?"

"No, I just didn't want you to be caught off guard in case
you prepared one. Usually it's just pictures running throughout
the service, but we have them playing in the lobby. Oh, and the

speakers are messing up—they were going in and out the other day."

"Still? I thought he got those fixed." Addy laughed. "It's alright. The room is small. I'll just talk louder. You have any water?"

"You can grab a bottle of water from my office. Or, you can grab one of the expensive sparkling waters that Frank hides in the back of his fridge."

"If you're offering me one of Frank's fizzy waters, I don't want to be rude." Addy smiled. He made his way through the house like it was his own and introduced himself as if he was family. He offered quick introductions, short lines of condolence, and depending on the individual, a light-hearted comment to ease the awkward tension of meeting someone new.

By the time the funeral started he was acquainted with the nephew of the deceased, the wife, and several out-of-town friends. He knew a few local guests from his softball league and recognized others from the brewing ministry put on by the local Lutheran congregation which Addy had been inducted into as an honorary member.

After Addy's prayer and short message, the nephew—barely holding it together—leaned over and asked if he wouldn't mind reading the eulogy he wrote. Addy accepted.

On Frank's tier system, this was a bottom-tier funeral: a small service and a committal ceremony at the cemetery. At the close of the service, Donnie instructed the pall bearers to load the casket into the hearse and wait for the officers on duty to begin the escort. The nephew caught Addy by the arm as he was walking back inside and asked if he wanted a ride.

"That's okay. I have to go back in to get my Bible, but I'm right behind you."

"Oh hey!" the nephew yelled back. "Can you give this to Mr. Burgers?" He reached into the breast pocket of his coat and pulled out a piece of paper. "I forgot to hand it to him this morning."

"Sure," Addy said. "I'll put it on his desk if I don't see him." Addy stepped back into the house and jogged toward the parlor. He noticed Cliff in the kitchen rummaging through the refrigerator and yelled "hey" as he ran past.

"Sup, brah!" Cliff yelled back, throwing up his hand.

Addy grabbed his Bible from the parlor and walked into the kitchen. "You seen Donnie anywhere?" Addy asked.

"Yeah, he's downstairs. What's up?"

"Can you give him this?" Addy held out the paper.

"What is it?"

"I don't know. Someone gave it to me and said give it to Frank or Donnie."

Cliff nodded his head. "Coupon."

Addy laughed. "They still use those things?"

"No, there's no *they*. Frank uses them. Donnie doesn't know they're still up, apparently. I'll hold on to it and give it to Frank when he gets back. We still goin' to eat tomorrow night?"

"Yeah, that Ethiopian place in Paducah. Seven, right?" Addy asked.

"I got clients until like six-thirty, and then I'll need to shower. Seven should be good."

"Awesome," Addy replied. "Your sister coming?"

"Nah, she's busy!" Cliff answered.

"That's too bad." Addy winked.

"You're stupid," Cliff said.

"Later, man." Addy started to text Frank as he opened the front door. "Whoa!" Addy yelled in surprise. "I'm so sorry. Excuse me."

"No problem, Preacher."

Addy's mind took a moment to register who was in front of him. He wasn't used to seeing Monty in a cop uniform. "Mr. Suthers. I didn't recognize you."

"I try not to wear the uniform in church." Monty smirked.

"I was referring more to the fact that I don't see you very often *at* church," Addy said playfully.

"Well, had you been at the work day l-l-like the rest of us this morning, you w-would've seen me."

"Yeah, I got called in last minute for this funeral. Everything go okay?"

"Went fine," Monty replied. "They didn't need much help so I just fixed the faucet in the women's bathroom and got the hot water working again in the kitchen. Y-y-you headin' home?"

"Actually, no. I'm supposed to be at the graveside, but I'm running behind."

"Y-y-you need an escort?"

Addy smiled. "You serious?"

"Why not?" Monty replied. "Where to?"

"Murray Cemetery, next to the theatre."

"Let's go."

"Were you coming for a funeral?" Addy asked, unlocking his car.

"N-No. I was coming to see Frank or Donnie. I'll come back," Monty said, getting into his cruiser.

17

Monty knocked on the door and took note of the colorful stick-er—a skeleton holding a sign to advertise the hours of opera-tion—on the windowpane, adjacent to the Burgers' home front door when no one answered. He clicked the doorbell, and after several moments, knocked again. This time the door creaked open. According to the sign, the funeral home was open—and it was a place of business—but he still felt awkward walking into someone's home. He tried the doorbell again and stepped over the threshold looking around inside. He knocked again, louder. "Mrs. Burgers?" Monty called. "It's M-M-Montgomery Suthers, Murray Police. Donnie?" He stepped in and closed the door. The house was quiet—minus the faint hum of music play-ing from a room somewhere in the house.

Monty dialed the house number on his cell, and let it ring. Donnie answered. He was in the middle of trying to finish the preparation on a client before a two o'clock service and asked if Monty wouldn't mind chatting downstairs.

"Is it legal for me to be down there?" Monty asked.

"I won't tell if you won't."

Donnie called up the stairs when he heard Monty open the preparation room door. Donnie had never noticed how loud those stairs creaked until the cop walked down them. Monty held out his hand for a shake but Donnie held up his gloved hands taking a rain check. Monty glanced over at the table with the deceased and took a seat on a nearby stool.

"You're cutting it kind of close, aren't you? Shouldn't he b-be already good to go?"

"Ugh. Yes and yes. Everything *should* be ready, but his daughter changed her mind about the outfit last minute. In the process of changing him, the makeup got a little messed up, so here I am."

Monty peered around the room.

"You ever been in a preparation room before?" Donnie asked.

"Never have, surprisingly."

Donnie felt a little embarrassed at the décor: movie posters of *Top Gun, Beetlejuice, Tombstone, Adventures in Babysitting,* and *Who Framed Roger Rabbit* hung on the walls, amid several odd-looking—and at times inappropriate—family photos. Monty walked up to a few of them for a closer look. He pointed at the *Tombstone* poster. "That's a g-g-good movie. One of my favorites."

"A classic."

Monty turned to see a plastic skeleton sitting at a desk wearing a Saint Louis Cardinals visor and a faded Power Rangers t-shirt. The skeleton was angled down to look as if he was reading. Monty walked over to the side of the desk and flipped up the book: *How Pet Funerals Saved My Funerals.* Monty made an audible "hmm".

"Not my idea," Donnie offered, noticing Monty.

"You offer funerals for pets?" Monty asked.

"Not yet. That's all Frank's thing. He thinks it'll be another way for us to make income." Donnie continued to work. He felt a bead of sweat crawl down his eyebrow. "Was there something I could help you with Mr. Suthers, or did you need to talk to my brother?"

"Well, maybe. I'd prefer it if the both of you were here, but I can always call him. T-T-There was another robbery last night at the Frazier Cemetery."

Donnie forced himself to continue working, trying not to let his anxiety take over. "Oh, no."

"Yup. The funny thing is that the r-rob-robbery took place right next to where the last one did."

"You think the person made a mistake the first time?" Donnie forced a chuckle.

"I don't know. They started an exhumation of the plot this morning around ten. I think a family member is going to check and see if anything was stolen."

"How did someone rob two graves from the same cemetery, right next to each other? Willie needs to rethink that camera, huh?" Donnie asked.

"Even if it was on, it w-wouldn't have made out who was doing the robbing. It's on the other side of the lot." Monty moved back to his chair. "Y-Your brother still go on walks through that cemetery?"

"Maybe." Donnie's cell phone started to ring on the desk behind him. "You'll want to ask him. Excuse me for just a second, sorry." He pulled off his gloves and answered the call.

Donnie reentered the preparation room after a few minutes. "I'm so sorry about that. Good friend of the family just passed away. That was her husband."

"Oh. That's terrible," Monty replied.

"Yeah. Wow. I haven't seen her in . . . gosh . . . years. It was my and Frank's second grade teacher—and our babysitter, oddly enough. She was the sweetest old lady."

"Sorry to hear that."

Donnie stood silent for a moment staring at the screen on his phone. "Man, crazy."

"When's the last time you talked with her?"

"About a year ago. We used to chat all the time, she was a big part of our family. After college we talked less. I think Frank still visited with her actually—at least I hope he did. I remember when we were kids, maybe kindergarten and first grade, she came to stay with us for a weekend while our parents were gone and brought us all the toys she'd confiscated from her second graders that year."

"No kiddin'." Monty laughed.

"Game Boy games, Mighty Max, Transformer toys, a Walkman. Of course, I made the mistake of wearing that Walkman the next year to school where the former owner pointed out that it was *her* Walkman. It had a Polly Pocket sticker on the back that I never thought to take off." Donnie laughed. "Mrs. Jennings was pretty awesome."

"I'm sorry to hear about the loss," Monty said. "Y-You want me to come back later?"

"Thanks. No, no that's okay. You mind giving me another second though?" Donnie asked, already dialing the number on his phone. "I need to call Frank and let him know."

"Oh, sure. Go ahead."

Donnie held the phone up to his ear and took a seat back at his desk. The line rang once and went right to Frank's voice-mail. "Hey man. Hopefully you get this before you get home. Just got a call from Carlin Jennings—Mrs. Jennings' husband. She passed away last night at the hospital. I'll give you the sto-ry when you get home. It was expected but he was still a little shaken up over the phone. You may want to give him a call on your way home, just to check in—see if he needs anything. I'm still working on our two o'clock but I wouldn't mind going over there later to say hey. I'll see you back at the house." He clicked off the phone and looked at Monty. "I tell ya, I've been around death all my life. You'd think it gets less awkward and easier to handle when it happens to someone you know. It doesn't."

"I know what you mean."

"Sorry. Where were we?"

"I don't r-r-rem-remember. I just wanted to update you on last n-night. The county is going to have some of the p-patrols check in during the evenings for the next couple of weeks. Doesn't make a whole lotta sense that s-someone was able to rob two graves, side by side and not be seen."

"I'll have Frank give you a call, and I'll stop by later to see Willie. I'm sure we can help keep an eye on it. Drive by in the evenings or something."

"Thanks Mr. Burgers."

When he stepped onto the front porch, Monty reached into his side pocket and pulled out a card. "I don't know if I gave you o-one of these last time we spoke, but if not, here's a number to c-c-call me on if you hear or see anything."

Donnie took the card. "What surprises me is that grave

robbing should be nearly impossible these days. Most all coffins go into a vault at burial."

"Is that mandatory?"

"No. Like I said, just surprising they weren't in one. Hopefully it was just a one-time thing—or a two-time thing I guess, but a one-time total kind of thing."

"Do people get buried with expensive items in this area?" Monty asked.

"Sometimes, but nothing that's worth all that work. There are some cases where the will states for the client to be buried with an heirloom, or a piece of jewelry, or some particular possession, but in most of those cases—if the item is valuable—someone in the family will pull out the item last minute and not tell anyone."

Monty got in his cruiser and closed the door, resting his arm on the open window. He sat in silence for a moment and then said, "This isn't p-pu-public knowledge so be careful who you tell this next p-p-part to. I don't think this person is after money."

"Why's that?"

"Willie had the first grave, from the other night, d-dug up. The coffin was all tore to pieces, lining was ripped out, and the b-b-body was gone."

"Hunh," Donnie said. "The whole body? That is strange."

"You're tellin' me. I'll let you get back to it Mr. Burgers. You take care."

Monty pulled out of the driveway and Donnie stepped back inside, immediately attempting to call Frank again—his voicemail picked up "Come on, man." He tried again, walking into the kitchen. When the phone went to voicemail again, a knock sounded at the front door. Donnie clicked the phone off and turned the knob.

"You forget some—" Donnie started. "Oh." It wasn't Monty. "What do you guys want?"

"Hey, Donnie. Good to see you too. Welcome back," Vince Koch replied.

"Frank's not here."

"We're actually here to see you," Randy Koch said.

18

Frank stepped out of his truck and walked up the front steps of the Jennings' home. He was cutting it close to his two o'clock service by making the stop, but he hated having conversations like this over the phone. He knocked on the door and checked his cell phone once again for the time: 1:02.

The dead bolt shifted just before the door creaked opened.

"Hello, Frank."

"Hey, Mr. Jennings. My brother called me about your wife. I'm so sorry. I didn't even know she was in the hospital."

"I appreciate that. Yeah, she went in last week for a check-up on her heart and . . ." He paused, shaking his head. "Never left."

"I wish I would have known. I would have come by to see her before all this happened."

"Be honest, everything happened so fast once she got in. You never think it'll take a turn like that, and then when it does, you got fifty things you're trying to do all at once."

"Can I ask what happened?"

"Well, I hate to say it, but that woman was stubborn as a mule. She'd been puttin' off a needed heart surgery for a couple years. Doctor told her to come in 'bout two months ago for another check-up. She let that go until last week. And, you know, put it off too long, I guess."

"You got family coming in this week?"

"They're here. When I figured things weren't going to go our way—bout two days ago—I called everyone in. They're all out to lunch."

"You didn't want to go?"

Carlin exhaled "I did, but I about didn't make it on the drive home. I needed to get some rest. You wanna come inside for a bit? I'm awake now."

"Actually, I can't. I've got a funeral service in less than an hour. I just wanted to come by and see you and tell you that I'm sorry. She was an incredible woman. Donnie and I still laugh about stories with her and us as kids. I'm gonna miss talking to her."

Carlin's lip trembled as he took in a breath and looked out over the yard. "Yeah. I'm gonna miss talkin' to her too." After a brief pause, he smiled. "I'm *not* gonna miss having to yell at her because she wouldn't put her hearin' aids in." Both he and Frank let out a laugh. "But that woman was the greatest experience the Lord ever gave me."

"Anything I can do? Donnie said he might come by later."

"That'd be fine. I think we're doing okay though. It's a full house."

"I'll pass the word along to my parents. It was good to see you again, Mr. Jennings."

"You too, Frank. Hey, by the way, I tried to get the hospital to call you all but I guess I spoke up too late."

"What do you mean?"

"She got sent over to Life Memorial Funeral early this morning. I asked why they sent her there and they said it was the only funeral home in town."

"What?" Frank asked.

"That's what I said. I told them that you all were still in

business, but the woman in charge said she didn't know any Burgers Funeral Home and told me that Life Memorial was the default. She also said it was a deal for us because they don't charge for pickups from the hospital, but if I wanted to have her moved to a new home, I'd have to pay for that myself."

"Are you kidd—the hospital has them as a default? How does that even happen? The family has to pick where they want the person sent to." He paused, sensing his agitation. "They're not charging for pickups?"

"I'm sorry, Frank. I would have paid to have you all take care of her, but by the time I thought to tell them where I wanted her sent, they'd already done it. I had it in mind to call and have you all go pick her up from the other home, but I just got too sidetracked with everything goin' on."

Frank stood still in disbelief. "No. It's okay. I'm just . . . wow . . ." He looked up at Carlin. "Hey as long as she's taken care of, I'm happy. I'll keep an eye out for details and we'll see you all at the visitation."

"Thanks for stopping by. Tell Donnie to come by anytime."

Frank pulled out of the driveway and only made it a mile down the road before he pulled over to the side, and slammed it into Park. He sat for several seconds, staring at the road in a daze. "Free pickups?" He repeated the phrase a couple of times more to himself, before pounding his fist onto the steering wheel. "Are you *fucking* kidding me?" Finally, Frank jerked the knob on his radio to the left, cutting off the music. A horn blazed past him to let him know that he was not fully on the side of the road, but Frank ignored it. He continued to sit and look out over the dashboard, tapping his thumb on wheel. "Unbelievable." The alarm in his phone started to buzz, signaling a funeral in forty-five minutes. He clicked it off and dialed Cliff's number.

"Hey, I'm on my way. Quick question: you remember that job you were telling me about this morning—your friend's dad? You think that's still doable?"

19

Donnie walked into his office and took a seat on top of his desk. When Vince tried to close the door, Donnie told him to leave it open. "This isn't a private meeting."

"Okay. We'll get right to it then," Vince said. "You mind if we sit?"

"Yes, I do."

Randy laughed. "I'm really glad you got your dad's politeness. I was worried this was going to be awkward."

Donnie didn't smile. "What do you guys want?"

"Alright, look," Vince began. "About a month ago we offered your brother some money to buy this place: your clients, supplies, name, the house—all of it. He told us no."

"Okay."

Vince and Randy exchanged glances. "Something makes us think he didn't talk to you," Vince said.

Donnie stayed quiet.

"Did Frank tell you how much we offered? Or that we made an offer?" Randy asked.

"Actually, he did," Donnie replied

"Hunh," Vince said. "And you weren't interested?"

"Not my call."

"Aren't you half owner?" Randy asked.

"Forty-nine percent," Donnie replied. "If he told you no, then, I guess the answer is n—"

"I know what's up with your brother—but I don't with you. You ain't got no job anymore. You're gonna turn down over a million dollars?" Vince asked.

Donnie's eyes reacted to the large number before he had a chance to control it and Randy caught the response.

"That's what I thought," Randy said. "He didn't tell you, did he?"

"You offered him a million dollars?" Donnie asked.

"No. We offered him one point one million," Vince said, giving Randy a nod. "I guess you were right."

Donnie's gaze had fallen to the floor.

"I imagine you'll want to talk to your brother now that you know the whole story."

"Yeah," Donnie mumbled. "You definitely have my interest. I don't know why he'd turn that down."

"We get it. It's the family business. Priceless. He'd have said no to ten million. To him, it's not for sale, but to you, we think it is."

"Maybe it's worth checking with your father? It would be a shame for him to find out after the fact, that his closed down funeral home was at one time offered over a million dollars . . ."

Donnie looked up and met their gaze.

"Surely he's more trustworthy than the partner who doesn't share an offer like that."

Donnie stood up from the desk, and sighed. "I'll see what I can do."

"Are you interested?" Randy asked.

"All I'm going to say is I will talk with my brother and let you know."

"That's a better answer than we got from Frank."

"How soon you want to know?" Donnie asked.

"Soon as possible. This isn't an ongoing offer either. We're coming to see you because Randy had a hunch Frank didn't talk to you. So, we figured we would try again."

"Why so much? I mean, a million dollars, for a small-town funeral home?"

"We're not jerks, Donnie. We know this place has value to your family. You've got an immaculate name in the community still, and a history in this town of over a hundred years. We'd prefer to keep a strong relationship with you—and communicate that relationship to the town—rather than publicly stand and watch as you all fall on your face. And so, we've made an offer that tells you we're serious."

"But we're not going to beg," Vince cut in. "If you guys don't see how good the offer is, we won't lose any sleep over getting the business for less than half that later on."

"You think about it. Get back to us soon," Randy said.

Donnie walked behind them toward the front door. When Vince extended his hand, Donnie took it. "I'll talk to my dad, then I'll talk to Frank and I'll see what I can do about taking that deal."

20

Frank sprinted up the driveway and in through the door knowing from the cars on the street that guests had begun to arrive. He peeked into the parlor and saw that Donnie had already brought up the body, but Donnie was nowhere to be found. Frank walked over to the stairs leading to the basement: "Donnie!" No answer. He then called Donnie's cell phone and heard the vibration in the kitchen. "Of course," he whispered.

Frank hurried upstairs and jumped into the shower to get the sweat and smell of dirt off—and check for ticks. It was exactly 1:30 when he bounded down the stairs to greet family, with his hair still noticeably damp. Donnie was now sitting in his office talking with a couple of the guests when Frank poked his head in. "Hey, I'm still doing the two o'clock, right? I got a voicemail from Addy—something about him doing the funeral?"

"I hope you're doing it." The guest laughed.

"That was earlier. I'll explain later."

"Awesome," Frank said, shooting a thumbs up. "You seen Mimi?"

"Yeah, she's in the family room. I didn't open the top of the casket yet. May want to do that before someone tries."

"On it." Frank made his way through the main lobby and greeted some of the incoming guests. No one was in the parlor yet. He placed his notes on the front pew and then moved to open the casket when he noticed it was backwards. Frank started to turn it around when Donnie came running in.

"Hey!" he whispered. "Sorry, it's backwards. Mimi got me in the hall when I was wheeling him in, and I got sidetracked."

"Did you get him changed?" Frank asked.

"Yeah. We're never doing that again. I don't know why you told her we'd do that."

"I do it all the time."

Donnie shook his head. "One outfit from now on."

Frank smiled. "Rookie."

The brothers maneuvered the coffin around and Donnie opened the top portion to make sure nothing had shifted on the ride up from the preparation room. Frank was immediately distracted by the pinkish liquid that had stained the inside padding.

"Dude. What is that?" Frank asked.

"What's wrong with him?"

"Not him," Frank replied, pointing down toward the man's lower section. "That."

Donnie saw it. "Shit," he whispered.

"He's leaking," Frank said.

"I see that, Frank. How the hell is he leaking?!"

"Don't yell at me. You prepared the guy. Did you block him up?"

Donnie looked at Frank as if he'd just been told to plug in a busted appliance. "Are you kidding me? Of course I blocked him up. I probably screwed something up when I was replacing his clothes." He closed the lid.

"What are you doing?" Frank asked.

"I need to go check the plugs."

"Oh no we don't! Ain't nobody got time for that." Frank opened the lid back up. "Look. See? It's not that bad. It's just a little bit of juice." He opened the bottom portion and ran his hand along the interior lining. His hand was visibly wet when he brought it to Donnie's face, who immediately shoved it down out of sight. "Alright, it's a little wet, but it's not flooding out."

"What's wrong with you! I am not risking a tidal wave of embalming fluid to come pouring out of this coffin," Donnie said.

"It's not going to be a tidal wave. You plugged him up, it's just a little loose. He's fine. Plus, we don't have time. This thing starts in thirty minutes. The last thing this family needs to think about right now is their dead father leaking pink liquid out of his anus. I don't want word getting out around town that we're a bunch of anus-leakers. People will start saying we don't know how to run a funeral home."

Donnie attempted to interject, but Frank cut him off. "I swear if you mention my funeral coupons, I'm going to punch you in your dick right here in the parlor. Do me a favor. Go downstairs and look in the closet. You'll see a trash bag of red pillows I bought for our Valentine's Day party this year. Bring it up here."

"Your what?"

"Just do it."

Donnie rolled his eyes and held back what he was about to say. He exited toward the hallway while Frank stood beside the casket, holding the lid open. He examined the stains and tried to imagine how he might explain if he had to. Thankfully he was still the only one in the parlor. Frank moved his right arm around to give the impression to anyone who may walk in that he was straightening things up on the inside.

"Hi, Frank."

Frank closed the lid and turned around. "Hey, Mimi. Anything I can do for you?"

"I'm okay."

Frank had his hand out for a shake, but Mimi went for the hug. He started to rub her back. "I'm sorry about your dad."

"Thank you." She released Frank and dabbed at her nose with Kleenex. "It's crazy. I haven't cried this whole time and now that it's here, I haven't been able to stop. Is that normal?"

"Sure. You lost your dad. It wouldn't be normal if you weren't crying."

Donnie walked into the parlor with a black bag over his shoulder and promptly jumped back out of view when he saw Mimi. Frank took Mimi's hand and led her the opposite way. "You want some coffee?" he asked, moving her down the aisle away from the body.

"I just got some from the lobby, thank you."

"That stuff sucks. I keep the good stuff in my kitchen. We just got a new espresso machine. It'll knock your heels off, come on."

Inside the bag were small red pillows embroidered with cupids and hearts. Donnie tried to imagine what a Valentine's Day party in a funeral home would look like—and why Frank would

have one—but incoming guests broke his concentration. He placed the trash bag behind the coffin out of sight and positioned two of the pillows inside toward the bottom to soak up whatever liquid may be coming out, and then placed one of the pillows under the arm where the liquid was starting to show. He rested the arm on top of the pillow, and then realigned the suit to conceal it as best he could.

"The hearts are a nice touch," a voice said behind him.

"Jeez!" Donnie yelled in a whisper, turning around. "Holy crap." He laughed.

"Long time no see," Lexie said. "Told you I'd see you soon. Did I scare you?"

"Little bit, yeah. Sorry, just didn't think anyone was in here and I didn't expect to hear a voice," Donnie replied. "Hang on one second." Donnie made sure the lid was latched and backed away, scanning to make sure no more liquid was visible. He could feel that his hand was wet and rubbed it casually on the handkerchief in his pocket. "Lexie Porter."

"Donnie Burgers. You remember me this time."

"I'm so embarrassed. I don't know how I didn't recognize you. Can I start over?" Donnie looked down and then back up to meet her eyes. "Lexie! What are you doing here? It's been so long! You look great!"

"Okay, okay." Lexie laughed. "Calm down."

"Sorry about earlier," Donnie said.

"Eh. No worries. It's been twenty years. I'm sure I've changed a little."

"Yeah. Hard to believe it's been that long. You left before high school, right?"

"After my freshman year. I went to live with my mom. She was going through some stuff and it made things easier to be closer."

"What brings you back?"

She tilted her head as if he should know the answer.

"Obviously the funeral," Donnie said. "I mean, who do you know in the family? Were you close to Mitch?"

"Kind of, yeah. He was sort of a coach for me growing up. I was friends with Mimi in elementary school, but her dad taught me how to play guitar and coached me in chess for a while."

"You played chess?"

"And competed. Oh yeah! I was the epitome of cool back then."

"Still play?"

"Yeah, occasionally," she answered.

"If he's free, I'll introduce you to Cliff. He runs the gym next door. He's the one who got me into it a while back, he's really good. Like, he has chess trophies, good."

"Cliff Samson?" She asked.

"Yeah. You know him?"

"No. I remember his name from competitions. He was a lot younger than me but his name stood out because it's my favorite Bible story," she replied.

"Man. Small world. Are you living in the area—"

"Oh wow," another voice said. Donnie turned to see a tall man beside him, looking into the coffin. The man nodded and reached out to grasp the dead man's hand. "Who had the idea for the hearts? That's incredible. Valentine's Day was his favorite holiday."

"Yeah . . . we wanted to add that personal touch. Sorry, we haven't met. I'm Donnie Burgers—one of the owners. Are you family?"

"Yeah. Peter Markham. I'm his son." Peter extended his hand to shake. "Hey Lexie." Peter wrapped his arms around Lexie. Donnie couldn't hear the conversation being muffled between them. Peter finally let go and stared at his father. "I told my sister last night that this is the best I've seen him look in a long time. That shit ate him up toward the end. You guys did an awesome job."

"Thank you. I appreciate that."

"Anyway," Lexie whispered, waving a hand to Donnie. "I'll let you get back to work, I'm going to go find Mimi. It was good to see you Donnie."

"Wait, are you still in the area?" Donnie asked.

"Oh, no. I live in Nashville now. Moved there from Malibu about seven years ago. Own a bookstore slash bar slash coffee shop."

"Really? A bookstore and a bar?"

"And a coffee shop. Been running it for five years, going strong. You should come see me sometime. *It*. Come see *it*. The bookstore. Come see . . . me . . . at the bookstore."

Donnie laughed. "I know what you mean. Are you on social media?"

"Nope. My bookstore is. Here's my card." Lexie reached into a purse shaped like a black dachshund. Donnie hadn't noticed it at her side. She turned the card over and wrote her number on the back. "If you ever come to Nashville just text and let me know. I'm always at the store. It'd be nice to catch up and of course have you contribute money to my store, or bar, depending on your mood."

"How long are you in town for?"

"Depends on how long the funeral goes?" Lexie replied. "I don't stay in Murray longer than I have to." The playfulness on Lexie's face faded. "I'll head back before the graveside."

Donnie looked at the card. "As You Wish Books."

"That's me."

"I take it by the black sash around the B that this is a *Princess Bride* reference?"

"Inconceivable!" Lexie smiled.

Donnie lowered his voice: "Anybody want a peanut?" He chuckled to himself. "Man, it's been a while since I've watched that. Such a good movie."

"Yeah, your Fezzik sounds more like Napoleon Dynamite," Lexie replied.

"Hey! Come on." Donnie laughed. He turned to see Peter still standing at the coffin.

"Okay. Back to work. Seriously, if you get a day free, come see the store." Lexie started to back away.

"I will," he replied, placing the card into his coat pocket. "It was great seeing you again."

"You're damn right it was," she whispered back, smiling.

Donnie moved beside Peter. "Anything I can do?" He could see Peter's face begin to tense. His gaze was fixed on what remained of his departed father. Peter shook his head slowly, and tightened his lips, working to hold back tears. "I'm going to go speak with some of the other family. In about twenty minutes, I'll have you and your sister meet me in the first parlor room across the hall so I can run you through the ceremony and make sure we're all on the same page, okay?"

Peter nodded in agreement, not taking his eyes off his dad. He exhaled through his lips.

Donnie put his hand on Peter's shoulder and whispered, "I have an office back near the entrance if you need some place private. If there's anything I can do, give me a wave, okay?"

"Thanks."

Donnie reached the hall as Frank and Mimi were exiting the kitchen. He flashed Frank a thumbs up. She was holding one of Frank's *Burgers Brothers Family Funeral Home* promotional mugs full of coffee. *Of course.* He flashed a thumbs up back and joined Donnie to stand by the main door to greet guests as they arrived.

The attendance was small—as Mimi and her brother had predicted. Except for the leaky corpse the service went smoothly and, to Donnie's surprise, none of the electronics malfunctioned. Afterward, the small group of family and friends gathered for half an hour in the other parlor for snacks: cheese cubes, meatballs, and small ham sandwiches. Frank spoke with everyone who attended—they were all potential clients! A cousin living just outside of town noticed Frank's coffee mug and asked if he had any for sale. For ten dollars, Frank was happy to oblige.

After the internment, Frank stayed behind to wish everyone off and offer safe travels until he was the last one remaining—a service his father insisted he upkeep. He sat with his arms folded, leaning against the side of his hearse as Mimi sat in one of the blue chairs alone under the shade of the tent, next to her father's grave. The setting brought to mind a memory:

> *Frank had been waiting by the hearse nearby as the deceased's wife, an elderly woman, stood beneath the tent talking to her late husband in the casket. Eventually, when all the family left, she walked to her car as if she was going to follow them out. But when everyone drove off, she stepped back out, hobbled on her cane over to the grave, got onto her knees, and rested on the ground. She began tossing handfuls of dirt onto the casket. Frank could hear her talking. At times he would see her laugh, or wipe tears from her eyes with a handkerchief. Frank waited patiently, resting against the hood of his car, and playing an old Game Boy he kept in his vest pocket for moments like this.*

When he noticed the quiet and looked up from his game, she had fallen on her side. Death entered Frank's mind, but he noticed her arms moving as if trying to pull herself up. Frank hurried over to her.

"Mrs. Thompson. Are you okay?"

The woman let out an uproarious laugh and stopped trying to get up. She looked at Frank. "Well, I'm better than he is," she answered, pointing to the hole beside her.

Frank smiled. "That's true. Would you like some help?"

"You know, it's probably been over ten years since I sat down on the ground like that. I had forgotten why I stopped doing it until now." She let out another laugh.

Frank positioned himself toward the ground and wrapped his arms around her back to help her sit up before assisting her to her feet. He held her hand while gently brushing the blades of grass off her back.

"Thank you."

"No problem. You purchased the Elite package which actually includes a body lift." He handed her the cane. She held on to his hand while she looked at where her husband now rested. After a few moments she gave a nod as if to signal that she was done, patted Frank on the hand, and walked with him back to her car.

He still occasionally saw Mrs. Thompson around town. She always offered a hug and reminisced about that afternoon. Fortunately, he mused, should Mimi choose to sit down, she wouldn't have a problem getting up. Mimi turned back to Frank and made her way over to him. He stood up from the hood of his car sliding his Game Boy into his pocket.

"You okay?"

"Yes. Thanks for staying," she replied.

"You planned a great service," Frank said.

"Thank you." She looked back at her father's casket. "I'm really gonna miss him. I know that he and my brother didn't get along, but he was a good man. And he really loved his kids. I just hate that he could never show it."

"How long are you staying in town?" he asked.

"A couple more days; mostly to figure out his estate. Then probably once every other month until we can get it all settled."

"Well, it was nice to meet you. There's plenty of food back at our place if you'd like to come and take some back to your hotel—or wherever you're staying."

"Yeah. I'm in a hotel now, but I don't have a place to keep any of it; no fridge," she replied.

"That's fine. Just come by whenever you're hungry. I'll keep some leftovers for you and let my brother know that you may be stopping by. How's that?"

She smiled. "You are without a doubt the most interesting funeral home I've ever heard of."

"Hey, whatever gets you thinking about us." Frank offered his hand. "Anything else I can do?"

"No. You did a great job and I can't thank you enough for being so patient with me and my family as we put everything together. I mean that—you read those words perfectly. It's almost like you knew him." She took his hand.

"You're welcome. And I wish I *had* known him. You said a lot of great things about him. I'm sure he's proud."

"Thank you," she said. Mimi let go of Frank's hand, embraced him in a hug and kissed him on the cheek. When she stepped back she dug out an envelope from her purse. "And thank you for the help you gave me with this. I hope this covers everything. Those Koch guys couldn't have been more wrong about you and your family. You all really did an amazing job."

"I appreciate the—" Frank stopped. "Wait. The Kochs? What do you mean?"

"Oh, it wasn't a big deal. They were actually the ones who told me about the coupon. He said it reflected the unprofessional style of service you all offered—or something like that—I don't remember. But my brother and I were totally satisfied. You guys were more than professional."

"Hmm," Frank mumbled. "That's a little bit uncalled for, but I guess it worked out for me, right? Just make sure you write us a good review online, okay?"

She laughed. "I promise."

He stayed behind while she got into the car and watched her drive off. "Man, she's hot."

21

Frank was at his computer going over bank statements when he heard the front door open. "Frank!" Donnie yelled from the lobby. "You here?"

"Nope," Frank replied. He clicked out of the screen and pulled up a Word document.

"Did you get a chance to call Mr. Jennings?"

"Yeah, I stopped by to see him. I mentioned you may drop by later."

"Thanks. I'll run by there tonight. Did he mention doing the funeral here?"

Frank grunted. "About that . . ."

"What happened?"

"The hospital has those bastards as the default," Frank said. "Someone from over there showed up to arrange for his wife before he knew what was going on. Some receptionist actually told Mr. Jennings that she didn't know we were still in business."

"That's a kick to the balls," Donnie said.

"Tell me about it. Just when I think those tampons couldn't get any worse they go and pay off the hospital."

"I'll call up there Monday and see what's going on," Donnie said.

"I saw you talking to Lexie, by the way. You weren't kidding; she looks great! She came and said 'hey' after the funeral on her way out."

"Yeah, she gave me her number." Donnie pulled out her card from his pocket. "And told me to come see her in Nashville."

"Whoa. She moves quick." Frank smiled.

"Nah, not like that. She runs a bookstore up there; asked if I'd come check it out, catch up . . ."

"Pick up where you left off . . . ?" Frank nodded and winked.

"Yeah. We left off with *nothing,* so I won't get my hopes up. You busy right now?"

"Not really. What's up?"

"Look." Donnie closed the door. "I feel awful about what happened earlier and I just wanted to say sorry that I screwed it up. That was pretty embarrassing."

"No worries. We got through it," Frank replied.

"That's what I wanted to talk to you about." Donnie took a seat across from his younger brother. "You should have let me go downstairs with him."

"Come on man, that would have tak—

Donnie cut him off. "If he erupted, we'd have been screwed. That stuff would have poured out everywhere. I'm surprised it didn't get worse. I know you don't like to disappoint the customer, but we can't operate like that. If something is wrong we *have* to fix it immediately."

"I agree, but this guy wasn't that bad. I've seen some leaky anuses in my day. This guy's was nothing."

"There's gotta be a better way to say that," Donnie replied, shaking his head.

"If it was that bad, I would have absolutely said take him downstairs."

"Right, but you can't predict that. If one of those plugs comes fully out, the juices come out of there in a matter of seconds. The smallest bump as we were rolling him down the aisle, or if one of those guys accidentally set the casket down too hard, it'd have been over." Frank was looking at him as if he'd already heard this speech before. Donnie sighed and shook his head. "I know you think you know more than me about this, and you probably do, but I'm not new to this. And when I say that we need to take it downstairs, I need you to trust me and let me do my job. Okay?"

"Okay," Frank replied.

"I'm serious, Frank. That was stupid to have that funeral with a leaking corpse. We're operating on next to nothing, and if we had to refund that girl, and lose face in the town, that would have been the end."

"You're right. It was stupid. The girl was already a wreck, and I honestly thought if we delayed then she would've gotten more upset. I felt like the risk of embarrassment was less if we just played it cool and didn't jar the body too much."

"I'll make sure that doesn't happen again. Just, next time I say let's do something, trust me, okay?"

"Yes, Chef." Frank took a sip of his coffee.

"Is this payment from Mimi?" Donnie noticed an envelope with the name Markham laying on the desk.

"Yup."

He pulled out the cash and thumbed through it. He counted it again. "Is this it?"

"Yeah," Frank replied. A folded sheet of paper fell out, onto a stack of books.

"Did she pay in installments?" Donnie asked.

"No. That's what she handed me today. That's the price we agreed on."

"Who agreed on it?"

"She and I did," Frank replied.

"You didn't think to check with me before you agreed on a price that's nearly, what, *half* what we normally charge?"

Frank narrowed his eyes and clicked his tongue. "Well, no. I didn't. I've been running this place for six years without you here; never checked in with you about prices before. I don't quite see what the problem is now."

Donnie waved the money at him. "This. This is the problem. I get it, I've not been here, but I'm still part owner of this place. I'd appreciate it if while I'm here you clue me in to what's happening. Like what you're charging and what people are offering you for our business."

"What does that mean?"

"You got an offer from the Kochs and you didn't tell me."

"I did tell you. And, I told you I didn't take the offer."

"You didn't tell me they offered you over a million dollars," Donnie said.

"Who told you th—wait . . ."

"Why didn't you tell me about the million?"

"Did they come here and talk to you?"

"What does it matter if they talked to me or not? I know about the offer. Why didn't you talk to me?"

"What a couple of jerks! I told them we weren't interested—"

"Forget about them! You spoke on my behalf without even clueing me in."

"I didn't tell you because I'm not taking the deal."

"Look, I get that you own fifty-one percent. But I'm still your partner—and your brother. I deserve to weigh in on whether that deal is a good one or not."

"Good one for who, Donnie? For you or for the family?"

"What's that supposed to mean?"

"Come on, man. Everyone here knows why you came back. I didn't want to believe it, but it's all you talk about—money, the offer, starting your own place. Isn't that why you're really home? Isn't that why you left your job so that you can talk me into selling this place to get your money? Have something to show your backers?"

"Actually, no. That's not why I came home, but when I got home, and saw that you're doing funerals for pocket change, I realized that we wer—" He saw Frank trying to move a folded piece of paper away from the desk. "What is that?" Donnie quickly snatched it from him and unfolded it. It was the coupon with an illustration of a skeleton, and the caption: "You've found a killer deal!" The skeleton looked a lot happier than Donnie.

"What the hell is this?"

"That's the . . . that's the coupon she found." Frank knew he was dead as soon as he said it.

"I thought I told you to take those things down."

Frank raised his hands in surrender. "Honestly, I thought I did."

"Obviously not! Why the hell did you even take this?"

"Because she gave it to me when she came to see me. I told you she gave me a coupon. You don't remember this?" Frank replied, staring back at his brother.

"Yes, and I remember telling you that we can't afford to do charity cases. I thought you got the hint."

"Dude! It's not like she didn't pay us—"

"She may as well not have!" Donnie dropped the envelope of money back on the desk, which made a louder sound than Frank expected.

"Don't be a dick, man. The girl didn't have any money," Frank said.

"Neither do we!" Donnie took a deep breath and turned to leave, but stopped. He put both hands on his hips and shook his head, staring at the floor. "How many of these coupons have people used?"

"I don't know. A few." Frank lied.

"How many?" Donnie crumpled up the paper and threw it at his brother.

"Dude, I. Don't. Know. Not many. They're hidden. Not everyone finds them."

Donnie sat down. "When Dad left he gave us the option to sell and told us if we didn't to make sure we worked to keep the place alive. The one thing Dad didn't want was our family name being attached to some struggling—"

Frank smiled and held back a chuckle.

"Gimme a break—are you serious?"

"Oh, what?! Come on. *Keep the place alive*? You didn't say that intentionally?"

"Gosh, it's not enough that you make us lose money, you can't even take this business seriously."

That did it. "Excuse me," Frank said. He straightened the coupon back out and laid it flat on the desk, tapping his finger over it as he spoke: "Please explain how this makes us lose money? I'm pretty sure it's what gave us Mimi as a customer in the first place. She had the Muggle-Tard brothers bury her mom and thought they charged too much, so she came to us."

"Well, sure, you practically gave it to her for free. Who wouldn't do a funeral with us?"

"It's not free, Dingus! We still made a profit," Frank replied.

"Not as much as we would have made had you not given her a break!"

"If I didn't give her the break, she wouldn't have come to us!"

Ginny charged into the room. "Would the two of you shut up? I'm trying to watch my stories."

"Sorry Mom," Donnie offered.

"Sorry," Frank replied.

Donnie waited for his mom to leave and closed the door behind her. He stared back at Frank. "Again, I know you think you know everything there is to know about this business, and that you've got it all under control. But this!" Donnie pointed to the coupon, "And what happened today proves to me, you don't! The money, the irresponsible decisions; you really wonder why I want that deal? It's not about the money—though it is a good deal, and you're an idiot for not taking it. I want that offer because I can't trust working with you!" He paused and got up. "It's almost like this is some game to you. The choices you make and the gimmicks all seem like they're just designed to get a reaction out of people."

"What are you talk—"

"I'm not done. Disregard the fact that you embarrass us with most of your ideas, you're careless about them. Frank, my name is attached to this place. It's more than just our family business on the line. How am I supposed to be taken seriously as a business owner if one of the businesses I'm attached to ends up in the papers over a grave robbing scandal? And what is this? Did you really think it was a good idea to put *you've found a killer deal* on the cover of a coupon? For a funeral? How is that appropriate?"

"I thought it was cute. Mimi liked it," Frank replied.

"That's what I mean, it's all about fun and getting a rise out of people—never mind that it makes everyone in this family look unprofessional. Tell me honestly: do you really care if the place goes bankrupt?"

Frank held Donnie's gaze and said his next comment slowly, and clearly for his brother to understand: "It's not going to go bankrupt because I'm taking care of that."

Donnie stared at him and nodded. "Okay. Okay. I guess I have no reason to worry then." He moved to the door. "I want the coupons off the website. And, from now on, all final prices are decided by the two of us. Don't go behind my back again." Donnie exited the room, closing the door.

Frank listened to the footsteps pounding up the stairs. He tossed the money and coupon into the desk drawer and slammed it shut. "Well, that sucked."

SUNDAY

22

Ethiopian Bistro, the only Ethiopian restaurant in a two hundred-mile radius, opened in the historic district of Paducah, Kentucky—a small town north of Murray—near the water. Paducah had begun to carve a name for itself in the arts and food industry in the early two thousands. The Quilting Museum was the Mecca of quilters nationwide, while the downtown, historic district experienced a boom from local artists to display their work, and chefs hoping to bring new culinary experiences to western Kentucky. Despite the unique style of cuisine for the area, the Bistro had garnered a positive response from the both residents and tourists since its opening.

Frank, Cliff, and Addy had been meeting once a month for dinner since Addy had moved back to Murray and switched off the responsibility of choosing each time. Ethiopian Bistro was becoming the favorite. Frank, unbeknownst to the others, always called ahead to reserve the same table.

"I think we've sat at this table the last four times we've been here," Cliff remarked as the waitress walked away to put in their drink order.

"Crazy, right?"

"I'm pretty sure Charlotte has been our waitress each time too," Cliff said.

"What are the odds?" Frank said, offering Cliff a wink.

"You realize she's like nineteen, right?" Cliff asked.

"She's twenty-one."

"Mmm-hmm. That's my cousin's baby sister man. Be careful with that."

"What are you talking about? I'm just as surprised as you are that we're sitting back here." Frank checked his cell phone. "But just to be sure, you think your cousin would be cool with me asking Charlo—oh hey!" Charlotte approached the table carrying their drinks. "Um... yeah... guys, we ready to order?" Cliff's lips tightened as he shook his head. A snorted laugh escaped Addy's mouth as Frank opened his menu to hide his blushing.

Within an hour the three of them had eaten to the point of exhaustion. Cliff was already starting to sweat. "Cliff," Frank said, scooping the remainder of the platter onto his injera, "I'm beginning to think your body doesn't like spicy food."

"Yeah man, you are sweating pretty profusely," Addy added.

"Think of it as happy tears from my body," Cliff said. "But yes, I'm pretty sure my body hates me right now. I'll go walk off the searing internal burn in a bit." He took the final bite from his plate.

Charlotte brought out a pot to refill their coffee and pulled up a chair next to Cliff—out of view from her manager.

"Do we need to go?" Cliff asked.

"Nah, they won't kick you out," she replied.

"I feel like we just got here," Cliff replied.

"I mean, you can pay me so I can cash out—that'd be great."

Charlotte left and then returned to the table and handed each their card tucked in a black check holder. When her shift officially ended, she ordered a drink from the bar and returned. "I've never asked, but how do you all know Cliff?"

"I own the funeral home where he operates out of," Frank replied.

"Your gym is in a funeral home?" she asked.

"Kind of. I rent out their garage."

"It helped us tremendously; we'd been trying to get that garage cleaned out for years," Frank said.

"Yeah, that thing was trashed when I worked there over the summers. We couldn't even walk in," Addy said.

"Cliff interjected, "I didn't know you worked there?"

"Oh yeah. Around high school, early college days. What was that, fifteen years ago?" Addy took a sip of his coffee. "I wouldn't call it working. I would come back for the summers and because I was getting my bachelor's in biblical studies, Mr. Burgers would let me step in as an on-call minister. Plus, he'd pay me to do some odd jobs around the house—like clean out his garage after he realized Frank here wouldn't do it."

Frank laughed. "It was all Dad's stuff! He should have cleaned it out." He looked at Cliff. "Thank goodness you showed up."

"I'll drink to that," Cliff replied, holding up his bottle. "You guys gave me a cheap space. I'd have cleaned two of those garages to get the rent I'm paying now."

"Speaking of payment, Frank, don't forget to add the emergency fee from yesterday to my check," Addy said.

"Oh, thanks for reminding me." Frank reached into his pocket, and then extended a closed fist toward Addy. "I picked this up for you on my way home earlier." He opened his hand

and let out a fart that easily could have been heard at the front of the restaurant.

Cliff got up and muttered a curse as the waitress choked on her drink. "Very generous, thank you," Addy replied. "Hey, by the way, why were you in LBL yesterday?"

"Who told you I was in LBL?"

"Donnie. Why? Was it a secret?"

"I was just up there hiking. I have a thing for old cemeteries."

"Find anything interesting?" Addy asked.

"Yeah, actually. I found a couple that were pretty creepy."

"Creepy how?" Charlotte asked

"All the markers in one were worn down and had been re-placed with white PVC pipes in the shape of crosses. But in the other one, some of the graves had those breathing pipes coming out of the ground."

"What's a breathing pipe?" Addy asked.

"Exactly what it sounds like. A breathing tube. They used to shove a metal pipe down in the ground—through the casket—in case the person buried was actually alive."

"No way," Addy said. "That can't be real."

"Just telling you what I saw," Frank answered back.

"Is he serious?" The waitress asked Cliff.

"I'm serious. It's a real thing. Look online."

"There's no way that's real," Addy replied.

"Plus, all the graves were sunken in. I was trying to read one of them and stepped back right into the hole," Frank said. "It was at least a two-foot drop."

"Oh no!" The waitress said, placing her hand over her mouth. "I would have died right there."

"Probably not two feet, but it was a pretty good size drop."

"Where was it? You remember?" Addy asked. "Easy to get to?"

Frank paused and thought for a second. "Southeastern tip, I think. I don't remember the name; they're on my map. I drove to a couple that were easy to access, but I saw a sign for the one with the breathing tubes and turned down the road to see if I could find it. That road ended and I got out and started walking."

"Nope," the waitress said. "That's how you get killed."

"I'm pretty sure whatever is back there is already dead. We should go hiking out there tomorrow." Frank smiled at Charlotte.

"There is no amount of money that could get me out there."

"Why not?" Frank asked.

"Cause LBL is haunted. Bethel Cemetery. You all grew up here, you should know about it."

"That place isn't real," Frank replied.

"Yes, it is. My dad has pictures of it," Cliff added.

"Dude, I'm telling you, your dad took pictures of an old cemetery and said it was Bethel," Frank downed the rest of his beer.

"I've seen a picture of it," Charlotte offered.

The table went quiet.

"I told you there are pictures!" Cliff exclaimed. "Bunch of graves in an overgrown field, right?"

"No. I don't think so. It was just one gravestone," Charlotte replied.

"See," Frank said. "The whole thing is just an urban legend now. Everybody has their own version. Our dad used to take us camping up in LBL and tell us about that place."

"I think it's real. We at least know that *she's* real. There was a whole class discussion on her in, what was that, ninth grade?" she asked Cliff.

"Everybody has that discussion in ninth grade. Around Halloween," Frank continued, "when Principal Atlas gets everyone in the cafeteria and tells the story, right?"

"Yeah!" Charlotte replied.

"Those stories about her and that cemetery have been around since my dad was a kid," Frank said. "Isn't it a little convenient that no one knows where the place is?"

"Alright, well, my parents must have actually cared about my psychological upbringing and I must have been sick on that day in school because I have no idea what you guys are talking about," Addy said.

There was an audible mixture of 'what!' and curses from the group.

"You've never heard of Bethel cemetery? Or the witch-lady" Frank asked.

"Nope," Addy said. "Sounds like it'll make a good sermon though."

"How did you grow up in Murray and not hear about it?" Frank asked.

"The only haunted cemetery in Murray I know of is Asbury," Addy replied.

"What's Asbury?" Charlotte asked.

"Asbury is an *actual* cemetery that everyone in town believes is haunted," Frank answered. "Unlike the made up one of LBL."

"It's one of Murray's top haunted attractions—that and the Sig Ep house."

"The Sig Ep house I know about. What's with Asbury? Have you been there?" Charlotte asked.

"Tons of times," Frank replied. "It's in the middle of nowhere and oddly, it's probably the prettiest cemetery in Murray. It goes back into the woods, tons of trees with hanging vines—lots of overgrowth and headstones. Some of the graves are as old as late seventeen hundreds. But if you go there at night, supposedly there's a creature that chases you out."

"You've seen it?"

"Hell no! I'm not going at night." Frank laughed.

"There's no creature," Addy said. "It's the old man's dog who lives next door."

"How do you know that?" Frank asked.

Addy took the final swig of his beer. "I met the guy who owns it at a funeral. He told me that when he sees kids pull up to the lot, he'll let his dog out. He said he trained the dog to go to the back of the cemetery and wait for trespassers to get a little ways in before he starts moving around. Said it was much cheaper than getting a camera—and more fun." He chuckled. "Wait, so what's the deal with Bethel? And who is the woman?"

"Bethel is the headless horseman tale of Murray, Kentucky. A cemetery in LBL that no one can find," Frank said.

"Except my dad," Cliff said, sipping his coffee.

"As I said, that no one's ever seen. The lot has only one grave: a woman named Avilla Bethel."

"A woman who lived in LBL years ago and did a bunch of weird stuff to the kids that lived there," Cliff said. "She haunts the cemetery where she's buried but no one knows where the cemetery is, so, it's almost like a reverse buried treasure story—it's best to just stay out of the *whole* area in case you stumble upon *her* area."

"Or what?" Addy asked.

There was silence over the table. Each looked at the other and then Frank said in a serious tone, "Isn't it obvious?"

Addy leaned in and asked in a quiet voice: "Does she tickle you?"

"Bingo," Frank said.

Cliff and Charlotte both laughed.

"You've seen pictures, huh?" Addy asked Cliff.

"My dad has them."

"Your dad has a picture of Tupac after he died too," Frank said.

"Right," Addy said, mimicking the voice of Dr. Evil.

The bartender stepped out from the kitchen. Charlotte jumped up and quickly grabbed the dessert plates off the table, making it look as if she was clearing dishes and getting the customers out.

"I need to go pee. Is that cool?" Cliff asked.

"Yeah, that's fine. But you guys probably need to look like you're leaving," she said.

"We'll be in the car. Hurry up."

Addy reached over and turned down the radio when Frank started the car. "I meant to tell you earlier about something that happened this morning."

"At church?"

"Yeah. There's an older guy who comes on and off on Sunday mornings—Tom Middleton. You know him?"

Middleton. The name rings a bell," Frank replied, tightening his grip on the steering wheel.

"Nice guy. His wife passed away just before I took the job—maybe seven years ago. Tom still talks about her all the time, though, and he doesn't have a filter so most of what he says is pretty inappropriate. I think she cheated on him. Anyways, ever since I met Tom, he's talked about this necklace that he gave her. It was a family heirloom from his great, great, *great* grandmother—crazy old. Tom told me years ago that the necklace went to the daughter, who I'd met a couple of times, and there was a big falling out between them. He's been trying to get it back, but earlier this year Tom's daughter passed away—before they were able to patch anything up, unfortunately. He and I went to lunch a while back and he told me that his daughter's husband admitted to him that the daughter never had the necklace. It was actually buried with the ex-wife."

"That was mean," Frank said. He noticed his mouth had gone completely dry.

"Yeah, but get this: this morning, Tom looked unusually cheery and I noticed he had something shiny around his neck—which he never has. Always has his top button undone, but other than gray chest hair, nothing has ever caught my eye like that chain."

Cliff opened the car door, surprising Frank. "Yo, yo, yo. Sorry for the wait. Wanted to find Charlotte and tell her bye."

Addy continued, "I asked what the necklace was and just as he was about to pull it out from under his shirt with his thumb, he looks me in the eyes, hesitates, and says 'It's nothing—an old necklace.'"

Frank swallowed. "Was it—was that it? The necklace?"

"I think it was," Addy replied.

Frank looked in his rearview mirror at Cliff, who was on his phone.

"I heard this afternoon that Tom's wife's grave was robbed. Did you hear anything about that?" Addy asked. Cliff looked up and connected eyes with Frank in the mirror.

"Yeah we had a police officer come by yesterday and talk with us about it. Told me and Donnie to keep an eye out, but didn't tell us much else."

"Physically, there's no way Tom could have dug up a grave by himself. He would have had to hire somebody," Addy said, looking at Frank.

"It's not that hard. No different than shoveling a long drive-way. You really think he robbed his ex-wife's grave? Maybe he just didn't want you to see his necklace. Could have had an embarrassing pendant or something—like a Playboy bunny symbol."

"It seems too coincidental that his wife's grave gets robbed and Tom is wearing a piece of jewelry he told me got buried with his ex-wife. Crazy, right? Anyways, figured you'd find that story interesting."

The silence went just over ten seconds before Cliff broke it: "So, who's up for a movie? *Baywatch* is playing!"

Donnie opened the office door and stepped into the hallway, stretching his arms over his head. Frank's office door was closed; he could hear someone talking on the other side. The clock over the landing on the stairs showed 11:04. "Jeez. It got late." A laugh in the kitchen startled him. He peeked in to see his mom and dad sitting at the table and walked in.

"Thought you had gone to bed," Dave said.

"I should have," Donnie said. "May have been more productive. I was looking for commercial spaces with a buddy online, then I somehow ended up looking through exotic vacation sites and reading reviews of the best restaurants in New Zealand." He chuckled. "What are you doing?"

"Just looking through these photos."

Donnie picked up two of the pictures. "Man, haven't thought about this place in a while."

"What picture is that?" Ginny asked.

"The lake house. It'd be nice to have that right now, huh?"

"Speak for yourself. After four floods, I was happy to be rid of it." Dave yawned. "I'm heading up, you two." He offered a peck on Ginny's lips and went in for the same toward Donnie but got pushed away. He gripped Donnie's shoulder and said good night as he walked into the foyer and up the creaky, wooden stairs.

Donnie moved over to the coffee pot and asked if it was decaf. Ginny nodded. He poured himself the rest of the lukewarm pot, reheated it in the microwave, then made a new batch for the morning before taking a seat beside his mother.

"What did you do tonight? I take it no one called," Donnie asked.

"No, not tonight. Your dad and I made dinner, had some

wine, and played Scrabble for a while. I got sidetracked cleaning up when I found these." She handed Donnie a picture of himself standing in a light blue tuxedo beside Frank, who was dressed in a similar orange tuxedo. "You remember this?" She laughed.

"Oh man." Donnie smiled. "How old were we here? Twelve?"

"That was in ninety-six, I think. What about this?" She handed him another picture: Donnie was dressed in a large, lime green shirt under a red-and-black windbreaker with a yellow sideways cap, and baggy pants. Frank stood beside him in khaki pants, a button-up shirt, and a sweater tied around his neck.

"Holy crap! This was seventh grade. I forgot we did this. Don't know how I talked him into dressing as Carlton."

"And then there's this one, my favorite." Ginny slid another picture across the table. Two high school students stood with their hands on their hips staring back at the camera. Donnie, the taller of the two, was dressed in tight green underwear, a red shirt, yellow cape, and a black eye mask. Across his chest was a hand drawn R. Frank stood beside him wearing a light blue Batman suit.

Donnie laughed. "This is going on my restaurant wall."

"I don't know how Principal Atlas let you two show up like that." Ginny chuckled.

"He didn't. We made it to lunch before he spotted us and told us to go home and change. Frank yelled across the cafeteria 'to the Batmobile' and took off running to the parking lot. I'll never get that image out of my head—him running at full speed in that spandex and cape." He shook his head and smiled. "We both had Saturday detention after that."

"Frank said you two got into it yesterday," Ginny began moving pictures back into the box.

"A little bit, yeah."

Ginny looked up. "What happened?"

Donnie told her about the leaky body, and about some of Frank's recent antics: the funeral coupons and the cash he found in the envelope on Frank's desk. "It's one thing to hear these stories over the phone, but when I have to experience it, my God! He's using money we don't have to try these different schemes, and the schemes don't do anything except embarrass us."

Ginny laughed.

"I'm glad you find it funny."

"*You found a killer deal*," she repeated. "Only your brother."

"Oh yeah, it's funny until we get a review written up about us online that actually posts that for people to see. Totally unprofessional. If this was at the restaurant, I would have fired him."

"Don't be so hard on him, Donald. He worked very hard on this place while you were away."

"Oh, I know he worked hard. It's not easy laying concrete for a basketball court. You know I found a mockup of an inground pool for our backyard inside his desk? A professional mockup. Of a pool!" He took a drink. "He's going to get this place closed down, you know that, right? We're either going to go broke or he's going to scare off what remaining clients we have left. Likely both."

Ginny sat quietly for a moment, not taking her eyes off the

photo in her hand, but her mind seemed to be elsewhere. She moved her aqua-colored glasses onto the top of her head. "It was probably a month or so before you came home—just after Franklin put in that basketball court—there was a funeral for a high school boy who died. Car accident. There were several students here from the university and the high school, and even young children—the boy was a swim coach. I was helping with the reception when I noticed I hadn't seen your brother in a while. And then I noticed that I hadn't seen much of the family; thought they may have left. You know where they were?"

"Playing basketball?"

"They were playing basketball. With your brother. He had almost ten of them out there, playing a game. The boy's sister, his father, his two brothers from out of town, and his close friends. We had guests hanging out here until the sun went down: eating food, gabbing away and switching out in the game; must have been twenty-five people out there watching this boy's family play basketball with your brother. It was probably the hardest day of their life, and your brother made it joyful. He provided a distraught family a few hours of peace, and for a little while, held their broken hearts together."

"He didn't tell me that."

"I'm sure you've never asked him about why he got that, or the wall of board games, or the TV, or the corn hole set. He got it for moments like that. For when he sees children attending a funeral for a grandparent. For someone who doesn't know how to handle themselves at a funeral. For the wife who needs a moment to breathe."

"Mom. It's a touching story," Donnie said. "But you can't

sustain a funeral business when you're practically giving them away. We made next to nothing from the Markham family."

"And yet we're still operating. It's okay. This family has multiple sources of income."

"What's that mean?" Donnie asked.

"It means I can help out when needed."

"No way. I'm not taking money from your business; that's for you."

"Donald, it's all going into the same—"

"Mom, this place is supposed to fund your business; not the other way around."

"What things are *supposed* to be isn't always the way they are," Ginny said. "In most cases, you just have to deal with it. Work with your brother. Be patient with him. Trust him—he loves this place."

"I wish it were that easy," Donnie said. "Our ideas of a successful funeral home are pretty far apart."

"Well, that's why your father left it to the both of you. So there would be balance. He sees things in a way you don't, and the same goes for you. While you're home, try to use your knowledge of the business world to help him out. And while you're at it, try to remain calm, and see where he's coming from creatively. Believe me, he *wants* this place to succeed."

Ginny didn't leave any time for Donnie to reply. She instead slid her chair back and remarked that she was off to bed. She piled up all the remaining pictures and placed them in the box. As she turned to leave, she leaned down and kissed Donnie on the head and embraced his head to her chest. "I love you. Good night."

"Love you too. 'Night."

Ginny made her way into the dark foyer and saw light stretching out from underneath Frank's office door. She tapped on the door and poked her head in. Frank was standing up in the back corner going over his notes with his back turned to the door. Ginny picked up her purse off the bench and watched briefly before finally saying his name and startling him.

The two of them chatted momentarily before Ginny said she was going to bed. She asked how the services went earlier and Frank told her the truth about what happened. He did not put any blame on his brother—or himself. "Just have to be more careful about stuff like that. Those wardrobe changes are tricky," he said. "I'm going to run by the bank tomorrow. You want to go ahead and give me your check before you head up?"

"Of course." Ginny reached into her purse, and tore a check from her book.

"Thanks, Mom." Frank slipped the check into his desk.

"Probably best not to tell your brother about this, for now. And I hope you're keeping track of the interest."

Frank winked. "You know it."

23

Monty Suthers sat in a back booth at Sally's Diner, sipping on his fourth cup of decaf coffee, staring at his Kindle. Reading would normally clear his mind, but tonight it was doing little to drown the images of an empty coffin and vandalized corpse in his brain.

Years ago—early in his police work—Monty's niece gave him a copy of Betty Wren Wright's *The Dollhouse Murders* in an attempt to explain why she thought her dollhouse was haunted. Monty had devoured the book and discovered that reading allowed him to escape the anxieties over speech and his work. He helped her find a new home for the dollhouse and, in return, asked her to continue recommending books: she did.

He loved the stories, but couldn't shake a slight embarrassment of being in his fifties reading Louis Sachar and Beverly Cleary—more recently Suzanne Collins and James Dashner—and so he bought an e-reader. He could read whatever he wanted without anyone knowing or making snide comments.

"You've been staring at the same page of that book the past two times I've walked by," his waitress, Sophia Stills, said.

Monty looked up and smiled. "Yeah. Having a h-hard t-time concentrating."

"It's louder than usual in here. I don't know why it's so busy tonight. It's Sunday in the summer. Where did everyone come from?" she said. "You're getting to a good part."

He held his Kindle far away from his eyes, then turned to Sophia: "How did you know what I was reading?"

"Outstanding eyesight. Plus I've read that book a dozen times so it wasn't hard to pick out. I've never used one of those. You like it?"

"Oh, it's wonderful. I was skeptical before, but they get addicting."

"Eh. I don't know. It's hard to beat holding onto a real book. Knowing where you are in the story, how far you have to go, the smell of those pages as you open it for the first time."

"These models actually come with the smell built in. It b-b-blows out a puff of air when you start the book to simulate the real-book feel."

Sophia laughed.

"D-D-Do you like to read?" Monty asked.

"I love to read. Read all the time. Mostly fantasy. I've got a book in the back to read during breaks, a book in my car I listen to on Audible, by my bed, my living room chair."

"How d-do you keep up with all that?"

"You get used to it."

"Then you'd love this. All the books you have in o-one place, and inc-credibly light," Monty moved his hand up and down to emphasize its weight.

"I'll have to look into it. Of course, I'd have a hard time justifying a hundred-dollar e-reader when I can get books free at the library." She refilled his coffee mug.

Monty shrugged. "Not to b-beat a dead horse, but you can check out library b-books on this."

Sophia eyed the device. "Hunh. I may have to reconsider." She smiled. "What about you? What do you read?"

"I read when I can. Mostly—" He looked around. "M-Mostly young adult stuff. I know, I'm too old for it—"

"I wasn't going to say that. A good story has no age limit. Any recommendations? I'm always looking for something good."

"I'd have to think about that. I'm sure I c-c-could c-come up with something," he said.

"You want something to eat?"

"No thanks. I won't make it home if I eat." He chuckled.

She made her way around the U-shaped diner refilling coffee mugs before coming back around to the server's station next to Monty's table.

"Did you hear about those grave robbings? I heard tonight that someone's grave got robbed twice."

Monty looked up, instantly snapping out of his daze. "W-Who told you about that?"

"Some college kid from earlier tonight. I overheard it in a conversation. Is it true?"

Monty sighed. "It wasn't r-r-robbed twice. There were two graves, right next to each other."

Sophia laughed. "Don't trust everything you hear."

"They say anything else?"

"Like what? Is there more to it? Do you know anything about it?"

"I do."

"What'd they take?"

"Can't say quite yet. Still w-w-waiting to hear back."

"Do you know who did it? Did you catch them?" Her face lit up as if he'd given her a gift.

"Not yet." He took a sip of his coffee and swirled it around in his mug, looking around the café. "I did find something, though."

She sat down on the other side of him and scooted in to face him. "What'd you find?" she asked.

He hesitated, unsure if it was because of a coming stutter or because he knew discussing this case was unprofessional. "I can't say yet. It m-may be nothing. Just a c-couple of pieces around the inside of the gravesite."

"Can you trace it to anyone?"

He looked at her. "I'm p-pretty sure I wasn't supposed to tell you that."

"Oh, don't worry, I'm only going to put it on Twitter when I get home. Not a big following there."

He laughed. "In that case, I'm going to n-need you to get me an application. H-How's the health insurance here?"

Sophia snickered as she looked up toward the door when a couple of young men walked in. She stood and grabbed two glasses from the server station and filled them with water. She patted his hand. "Be right back."

He felt his body tense at her touch; something turned in his stomach. He took a deep breath. "Too much coffee," he said. Monty dug out cash from his wallet and laid it on the table before clicking off his book and waving goodbye to Sophia. She winked and waved back.

MONDAY

24

Frank struggled to press the barbell up from his chest and Cliff started yelling "push" and placed his hands underneath the bar. "Come on, not even touching, not even touching! You got it!" Frank blew air through pursed lips and placed the bar in its cradle, at last letting out a deep groan. The radio signal intro to Skee-Lo's "I Wish" came on over the speaker and Cliff began nodding his head: "oh yeah!" He threw up his hands and started to rap along.

Frank attempted to follow but started coughing and shaking his arms. "I'm too out of breath. Can't rap." He heard his cell phone chirp and crawled over the grass to look at the message. "Oh."

"What's up?" Cliff asked.

"Donnie told us to turn the music down."

"You want me to turn it up?" Cliff asked.

"Of course."

When Frank caught his breath, he told Cliff about what the Koch brothers were doing with the hospital.

"Free pickups? That's a game changer. I take it that's why you had me call that guy back about the job?"

"Yeah," Frank muttered.

Cliff laid down on the bench and grabbed onto the bar overhead. "You know the name Joe Jackson?"

"No. He go to Murray High?"

Cliff smiled and lifted off the bar. "No. Baseball player. Early nineteen hundreds."

"Nope."

Cliff counted out ten and dropped the bar onto the cradle. He sat up and took a breath. "He was a part of the White Sox in the 1919 World Series."

"You do realize I'm not a sports person, right?" Frank asked.

"Everybody knows who Joe Jackson is. *Shoeless* Joe Jackson?" Frank shook his head.

"Nothing? Wow. Okay." Cliff laughed and moved to get his water. "I'll skip all the sports stuff since it's not going to matter. Joe Jackson is probably one of the most well-known baseball players. You've never heard of the Black Sox scandal?"

"Nope."

"Come on, man." Cliff sighed and motioned for Frank to get on the bench. He stood behind to spot. "I wouldn't say he's as famous as Babe Ruth, but he's up there. Unfortunately, he and some others got accused of throwing the World Series and got blacklisted from baseball."

"I'm not digging this guy up, am I?"

Cliff looked at him and shook his head. "What? No."

"Then I take it that what I *am* digging up has something to do with him?" Frank lowered the bar down and began to press up.

"I hate that you won't get excited about any of this. This guy Michael that we're talking to, his ex-wife's *dad* apparently had an item of—if it's real—considerable value. Six figures, easy."

"I'm already interested."

"The ex-wife's great-grandmother, who got the item from Joe Jackson himself, wanted to make sure the item stayed safe. Her husband died early on and their only daughter got in a bad marriage, so, instead of willing it to their daughter, thinking her husband would take it, she willed it to the daughter's son privately in her will—the ex-wife's dad. He got married and had five daughters. Now, supposedly, all the kids knew about this thing and its value, but when the dad died two years ago, he had never told anyone where it was: nothing in the house, nothing in the will, nothing in storage. Gone. The thing just vanished."

Frank finished his set.

"Two weeks ago, I met up with Michael—my buddy—and we're talking about baseball and somehow the Black Sox scandal comes up. He tells me this story and ends by saying he thinks he knows where it is."

"The guy's buried with it, isn't he?" Frank asked.

"Bingo," Cliff said.

"Does Michael know for sure?"

"He's almost positive. Get this, no one outside the immediate family knows about this thing. The daughters have supposedly never told their husbands. Michael didn't find out about the item until after his wife left him. A few years back he attended the wedding of the youngest sister who was a close friend of his, and he and her dad start talking outside—just the two of them. The dad brings up the item and Michael says he knew nothing about it. Michael has nothing to lose so he asks if the dad will ever sell it. The guy says, 'No. I'm gonna keep it in the family, but I think it'll be safer if I hold on to it rather than give it to my girls.'"

"Yeah, he's buried with it. What's the item, then?"

"Technically, it's two items, but they aren't as important as the signature."

"Joe Jackson's signature is worth six figures?" Frank asked.

"An *easy* six figure signature," Cliff replied. "Shoeless Joe was illiterate. He hardly ever signed anything unless it was for someone he knew well because it was embarrassing for him. There are hardly any pieces with his writing on it."

"Why do they call him Shoeless Joe?" Frank asked. "Did he not wear shoes during games?"

"No, he wore shoes. There was one game where he took them off. Someone called him Shoeless Joe, and it stuck."

Frank stood up. "So, your guy is offering thirty grand to dig up this item?"

"Thirty grand. Fifteen up front, fifteen once we give him the shoes."

"Man. That's a lot of money." Frank breathed. "What if it's not there?"

"He's positive, it's there."

"Something that valuable—he's sure no one took it at the funeral?"

"He said they're in a spot no one would look—on his feet."

25

Donnie came down to the kitchen a little after seven-thirty a.m. and poured himself a cup of coffee before making his way to the table where the morning paper had been read and refolded. Donnie turned the front page around to read the headline when he noticed his father standing outside on the back porch.

"Hey. What are you doin' here?" Donnie said, walking out. The screen door slammed shut behind him, startling him.

"Well, good morning to you too," Dave replied.

Donnie smiled. "Sorry, I just thought you were already gone. Don't you have a meeting near Fort Campbell?"

"Not until nine-thirty. I'll leave in a little bit; just wanted to enjoy the breeze before it gets too hot."

Donnie snorted. "It's already here. I forgot about this humidity. It feels like ninety degrees now."

"This ain't humidity." Dave laughed, taking a sip. "Where's your brother? With Cliff?"

Donnie nodded toward the gym as he took a sip of his coffee. "Yeah, they're in the garage." Donnie pointed. "You didn't hear them singing this morning?"

"I guess not. I probably didn't have my ears in." Dave took a seat on the swing. "Your mom said you were pretty ticked last night."

"Yeah, well. Part of the territory, I guess."

"You and Frank gonna be okay?" Dave asked.

"I mean, I think he's running your business into the ground. Other than that, yeah, we're fine."

"Hey, not my business anymore." Dave chuckled.

"Yes, it is. You can distance yourself all you want, but it's still your name on that sign."

"If I wanted to distance myself from this business, I would have packed up your mother and me and left for cooler climates years ago. And I believe the sign conveniently says Burgers *Brothers'* Family Funeral Home. I don't have a brother."

"Dad, I'm serious. You've gotta talk to him."

"I offer to give him advice all the time."

"He doesn't need advice. He needs you to tell him he's doing a crap job. Come on, Mom is considering giving him money from her business. She can't spend—"

"Let me give *you* some advice about your mother that took me nearly twenty years to learn: your mother is gonna do with her money whatever she wants."

"Yeah, but Mom started that business to *make* extra money, not pay for the funeral home."

"Donnie, we didn't keep the home open all these years with hopes of grandeur and financial freedom. We kept it because it's been in our family and because we do it well."

"Unfortunately, doing something well for *free* won't pay the bills, family legacy or not."

"Is he really taking coupons?"

"Yes!"

Dave laughed.

"This is why you left isn't it, you knew you couldn't work with him." Donnie smiled.

"Hey." Dave's tone sharpened. He turned to look Donnie

in the eyes. "I didn't leave. And I'd really like it if you wouldn't say that I did—to me or anyone else. Don't make it out in your head that I gave up control of this business because of anything other than wanting to spend more time with your mother. I understand that everything turned out fine, and I could have continued working, but after her surgery I decided—we decided—that it was fine for me to step back and hand the place over to you all. Okay? It had nothing to do with a failing economy, or me thinking I needed to get out from under this place before it tanked. My decision was purely personal."

Donnie sighed and sat in silence for a long moment. "Okay."

"I'd even venture to say it was a little selfish of me to hand it over to you both so early. Or, to Frank, I guess. Neither of us ever thought you'd actually stay in Murray." Dave elbowed Donnie's arm. "I had already started consulting by that time, which was going okay. Your mom's business has always done well, and then we had this place with you guys! We were going to have three incomes!" Dave chuckled.

"You'll have two when he squanders all your money," Donnie said.

"Why do you do that?" Dave asked.

"Do what?"

"Make him out to be completely incompetent."

"Because he is. The speakers in parlor one have been out for almost two weeks and he can't fix them because he's still paying off a pool table. One of the projectors is out—and apparently has been out for some time. That front doorknob falls off whenever you touch it and I'm almost certain the electrical tape on his desk is what he'll use to fix it. We had a leaky corpse and he wouldn't even let me take it downstairs to correct it. This is all just in the last two weeks."

Dave sat quietly for a moment then finished his mug of coffee. "Did you know that I did some consulting for Randy and Vince Koch a while back?"

"Yeah, I heard about that from Mom. You haven't been doing it the whole time have you?"

"Heavens no. The Koch family has been in that home since before you and Frank were born. I wouldn't have consulted back then. I started after Life Memorial bought them out. It wasn't for them; the owner of Life and I are old friends. He wanted Vince and Randy to have some guidance while they managed under the new name."

"If I were you, I wouldn't tell Frank you did that," Donnie said.

Dave chuckled. "Oh, no! I like living in the house. But my short time with those two guys showed me something about the funeral business and your brother. You know what your brother understands that most funeral homes—especially the Kochs—don't?"

"What?"

"What does Frank love doing the most?"

"I don't know if you want to hear some of these answers." Donnie grinned.

"You're probably right. Let me put it another way. He's in his thirties and still lives in the town he grew up in. What keeps him here?"

"You guys? I don't know. Family?" Donnie answered.

"You're close. What is your brother good at?"

Donnie paused. "You mean, like, overall?"

"I mean exactly what I asked. What is your brother good at?"

"Nothing," Donnie replied.

"Oh, come on. Yes, he is. What's he good at?"

Donnie thought for a moment. Frank played a lot of sports when he was a kid. He definitely wasn't good at those. He did theatre all through high school and college and won some awards doing that. As annoying as Donnie at times found him, Frank was exceptional at conversing with others—especially older crowds, and even more so with those who were experiencing grief. Finally, he looked at Dave and said, "People. He's good with people."

"Right. What else?"

"He's good at . . ." Donnie paused. "Talking? Writing?"

"He does give a good speech, doesn't he?"

Donnie realized where all of this was going. "He's good at making people feel comfortable. He puts them at ease when they're anything but . . ."

"Sure, that was a nice stock answer. How about this, what job do you think your brother wants when he leaves here?"

"I didn't know he had any intention of leaving—" Donnie stopped. He got it.

Dave raised his coffee mug after a moment of quiet and stood up. "Exactly."

Donnie had never thought about it before, but his dad was right. Frank had never once mentioned a desire to do anything else. The funeral home was all he talked about.

"Even when he was a kid," Dave said, "this place is all he wanted to do. You on the other hand . . ." Dave didn't finish that sentence and Donnie didn't say anything. "Your brother understands more than most others that a funeral home's job is to not only give people a chance to remember their loved ones, but it's to facilitate bringing people—families—together. The Kochs treat it as a business, and it is—you have to—but that's *all* they are. They're a service. And, they do offer some great services. Frank wants to offer an *experience*. He sees the funeral as an opportunity to mend wounds in families, get people talking who normally don't, and to make a tragic occasion something that people can remember fondly. He gives people something positive to cling to. He makes it a celebration of life rather than a mourning of it."

Donnie stared out into the yard as his dad walked back toward the door to the house and patted him on the head. "He does have some goofy ideas, you're right."

"He's got bad ideas." Donnie laughed.

"Fine, maybe he's got some bad ideas, but this place is all he has. It's all he knows. And, despite the bad ideas, it's what he's good at. You know it. And I know it. And because I know that, no matter how bad things get, I know that your brother—as spaced out as he can be—will fight to keep this place alive."

Donnie and Dave then softly said together, "Pun intended."

Dave continued, "I know the basketball court, and the gym, and the bar, and the cornhole sets, and the game chamber as he calls it, are weird and unconventional, but he's tapping into something unique for this town—and for funeral homes. The Kochs don't have any interest in stuff like this—they just want money. Trust me: this place isn't going anywhere. We've seen our share of rough patches and always made it through. Don't worry so much. I don't. And it's practically my legacy."

"What about Mom's business?" Donnie asked.

"Your mom started that place knowing that it may have to be a source of income for the family sometimes. She understands. There are still plenty of people in this town who want a family-owned funeral home to take care of their family—they don't want some corporate shmucks like the Kochs doing it. This place is going to be fine. Question is, are you?"

"Meaning?" Donnie asked.

"Meaning, why are you still here? What do you want to do when you leave the home again?"

"Who said I was leaving?" Donnie asked.

"You mean you're staying?"

Donnie was quiet. He could see Frank in the yard lying on his back as Cliff was stretching his hamstring. Donnie didn't hear it, but he could tell from the sudden movement—and how Cliff kicked Frank's leg—that Frank had likely farted mid-stretch. Donnie smiled. "I don't know. Honestly, I don't know what I'm doing."

"And you still wonder why I gave your brother the controller's share?" Dave asked.

Donnie nodded his head. "Touché."

"I gotta go."

"You coming home for lunch?" Donnie asked.

"Not for lunch but I'll be home this afternoon. Your mother gave me a list of things to get at the store. Fish sound okay to you for dinner?"

"Yeah, that's fine."

Dave left Donnie on the swing and made his way to the car, but not before they both said, "I love you."

26

The preparation room door swung open and Frank swiftly shoved the information about the shoes into his desk and clicked off Wikipedia's Joe Jackson page.

"I take it you're not down here to ask if I'll play you in Goldeneye," Frank said.

"I wish," Donnie said. He came and sat across from his brother. "I actually came down to start working on the girl that came in earlier, but I wanted to talk to you for a bit, if that's cool. You busy?"

Frank sighed. "Honestly, it's not the be—"

"Just two minutes," Donnie interrupted.

"Look. I know you're pissed off about what I'm doing, and about the house, and I know you want to go over the offer from the Kochs, but right now I'm swamped with stuff to finish up be—"

"No, no, no. It's not that. I just . . . had something I needed to say."

"Okay," Frank said, scratching the back of his neck. "What's up?"

"Wanted to say that I'm sorry for being a dick. Not just earlier today but in general."

"It's alright. No worries."

"No, I'm serious. I know I just got back, and I know that I've been . . ."

"A dick," Frank offered.

"Yeah. A lot of it is just frustration over what happened in New York and being back here, but that's not a good excuse. I don't listen to you. I come off as if I'm not interested in this place. I haven't trusted you, and I've basically just been a lousy partner—and brother."

"Like I said, no worries. I'm just glad you're home. Dick or no dick."

Donnie's eyes narrowed in confusion.

"I can see how that sounded awkward," Frank said.

"Yeah, anyways, please know that I'll do my best to relax and work with you instead of shutting down your ideas—even though they are pretty weird at times and legitimately freak me out. It's likely that I'm just on edge because of everything that happened in New York and coming home to all this. I have this irrational fear that you're gonna bring the whole place down, and I shouldn't think that. You love this place. And, as irresponsible as I think you're being—"

"This apology is awesome," Frank said.

"I'm trying to say I know that you really *do* want to keep this place goin'." He paused. "I don't like the illegal stuff—you should definitely stop doing that. But, overall, you're doing what you can, and I need to do a better job of trusting that you know what you're doing. I would like us to talk more about how we make decisions and where the home is going, but that's not what this conversation is for. I'm only here to say I'm sorry. And that I was pretty proud the other day."

"Proud of what?" Frank asked.

"I bumped into Bill Cobb on Saturday while I was getting

donuts. He said he offered you a lot of money to do a job, but you turned it down."

"Oh yeah?" Frank replied.

"I really thought when I told you to stop whatever ideas you were cooking up that you were going to try and keep doing it behind my back, but him coming over and saying all that surprised me."

Frank nodded. "Yeah, I mean, you're an owner too. I don't want to do something unless you're fully on board, and with that stuff you weren't on board. So—"

"Which brings me to the next part. I'm going to tell you something, but I don't want you to get excited. I'm not asking this because I want you to do it, or because I'm interested in taking it. What did that guy want you to do?"

Frank squinted at his brother. "It doesn't matter. I told him we weren't interested."

"I know, but humor me. What did he want?"

"I'd rather not. It's stupid."

"He offered double the price if you'd do it," Donnie said.

Frank's eyes gave a brief expression of surprise. "He offered *double*? Double what he told me?"

"Yup," Donnie replied. "So, what did he want you to do?"

"Are you asking me to see if it's worth doing?"

"No, because I'm sure it would land us in jail. I just want to know what it was for my own peace of mind."

Frank took a second to think the situation over, and then, "He asked me to cremate a body." He paused and tried to take in Donnie's expression. "A body that, for lack of better words, didn't belong to him."

Donnie stared at Frank, his face showing no signs of anger or even surprise. "Like, someone we already buried?"

"Nope. Someone who hadn't died yet."

"And he wanted us to cremate this person and do what?"

"Give it to him."

"Instead of who they belong to?" Donnie finished.

"Yeah. He told me the name of someone who was, at the time, on hospice care and asked how much I would charge to switch the bodies for burial so her husband wouldn't know, then cremate the remains and give them to him." Frank didn't take his eyes off Donnie. "I quoted him a price that was way too much, and he accepted. I really didn't think he'd say yes."

"And now he's offered you double for the same task."

"I guess. If that's what he told you," Frank said.

"Jeez."

The two of them sat in silence for long moment, Donnie staring at the top of the desk. "Who in the world would pay that much money for something like that?"

"I mean, it's super illegal," Frank replied.

"Yeah, but is it really worth that much money?"

"It is to him. I told you man: people get weird for sentimental stuff. Plus, it's his ex-wife. Supposedly, she cheated on him with the guy she was married to before she died. He still loved her and, well, to make a long story short, felt that he should be the one to keep her, not her husband. Plus, I guess he wanted payback. Like a, 'ha-ha I stole *your* wife' kind of thing."

Donnie's face registered attention. "What do you mean 'guy she *was* married to'? She's dead?"

Frank's eyebrows lifted, and he shifted his eyes to look

behind Donnie at the wall where corpses were kept in refriger-
ation. Then he looked back at Donnie. "You're about to work
on her."

"That's her?" Donnie asked.

"Yup. Cooler 2."

When Frank turned to the filing cabinet and swiped a paper
off his desk to file, Donnie got up and walked over to inspect
the body. Frank heard the door open and the bed roll out. Donnie didn't say anything for a few moments.

"You're running those numbers in your head aren't ya?"
Frank asked. "Thirty-grand for a cremation and slightly decep-
tive switch. Not a bad deal, huh?"

"This is her?"

"Yeah," Frank said, looking up. "Oh! Wait!" Frank rushed
to the wall and pushed the bed back into the cooler, closing the
door. "Wrong person, sorry."

"Who was that?" Donnie asked.

"Nobody. Different client that I'm workin' on."

Donnie wasn't buying it. "Frank, who was that?"

"It's another client."

Donnie put his hand on the handle and moved to open it,
but Frank put his hand out to stop him. "I recognize that woman! Who was it?"

Frank paused. "How about this, if you don't look in there,
I'll take Saturday donut duty for the rest of the year."

"Dude."

"This year and next year?"

Donnie opened the door and pulled out the bed all the way.
The woman's makeup and dress looked surprisingly fresh with
the exception of her arms and legs below the knee which had

been removed and were sitting neatly on towels at the end of the bed. "What the . . ."

"Alright, listen, before you get upset—"

"What did you do?"

"About a week ago—"

"Frank, we buried this person."

"Good memory." Frank arched his brows and pointed a finger at Donnie, smiling.

Donnie's eyes were piercing.

"Can I explain?" Frank replied.

"No, no, no. Tell me you didn't dig this person up."

"Just hang on, hear me out."

Donnie couldn't take his gaze off the corpse. "I can't believe you did this."

"Would you stop? Just listen to me."

"Damnit!" Donnie slapped the counter with his hand, knocking a limb onto the floor with a sickening *thud*.

"Okay. A while back Cliff came to me with someone who was interested in buying human parts—bones mainly. They didn't give me a name, just a list of four bones they wanted. He offered two grand for each, but ended up buying only two of the four that I brought him. That's what I was doing in LBL— burying the ones he didn't buy."

Donnie sat down and put his head in his hands.

"A few days ago, Cliff got *another* email from him; he wanted more parts."

"Oh my God," Donnie whispered.

"We'd gotten this woman in the day before and she wasn't going to have a funeral. There was no family in the area, no visitation. Her son just wanted a burial, and so once he signed the paperwork, technically he wouldn't see her again. The problem was that all this happened so fast that I didn't have time to drain the fluids and remove the limbs before the burial, so I weighed down the coffin and hid her in *here* until I could bury her. I'm still waiting to hear from the bone guy to schedule a drop off."

Frank could sense Donnie's increasing anxiety: he was taking deeper breaths and seemed to be massaging the temples of his head with a lot of force.

"In my defense, you told me to stop doing this *after* I'd made this deal. She's only still here because I haven't met up with the guy again or had a chance to bury her."

Donnie was quiet. He let out one final, long breath and stood up to move toward the stairs. "I don't even know what to say. Like, my mind is so confused at this moment that I feel as if I could go into a panic attack. This is unreal." He stretched his head back and laughed to himself, then spoke to the ceiling: "And the best part is, I came down here to apologize for giving you such a hard time. To say, 'you know Frank, we don't agree on your illegal, dumbass, ill-thought-out, retarded ideas, but you know what, you're trying.' And even though you run this business about as effectively as you ran our high school bake sales, there's no doubt in my mind that dad giving you controlling interest was the best.possible.fucking.idea." He took another deep breath, letting out the air slowly.

"Thank you?"

Donnie turned to go up the steps. "I'm leaving."

"And there it is. Of course you are," Frank said.

"What did you say?"

"Sorry, I probably mumbled that last part. I said, of. course. you. are. That's what you do. I hold everything together—"

"You mean you screw everything up," Donnie interrupted. "Don't make this about me."

"I hold it together," Frank corrected, in a serious tone. "And you . . ." He paused. "Leave. It's what you do. You're always in it for *you*. Dad gives me controlling interest, you leave and start cooking. Your restaurant gets some bad press about the owner, you get embarrassed and come back here. You don't like my ideas, you leave again. I get it. When you're not in control, you bail instead—"

"You know *nothing* about what happened in New York, first off," Donnie cut in coldly. "And how dare you say I'm only doing stuff for me! You don't think you're in this for you? At least my selfish attitude doesn't hurt anybody. Look at what you're doing! If you get caught, you're in jail. Lotta good you're doing the funeral world in jail. But really, nevermind what happens to you: what do you think is gonna happen to Mom's place if you get caught? What about Dad's name in this town? Did you think about what'll happen to Cliff's gym? Or my restaurant? You think I'm going to be able to open a new place after all this goes down? Don't talk to me about 'being in it only for me.' Look in the mirror dumb ass; you're not doing this for anyone else but yourself. Because *you* don't want to lose *your* business. Nevermind everyone else."

Frank stared at his brother for a moment in silence, and finally breathed out a "hunh."

"Just so we're clear," Donnie continued, "I'd rather not leave, but your desperation is driving this place into bankruptcy, and I'm not going to wait around for the police to figure out what you're—"

"Why do you think that? Do you think I'm that dumb to

concoct something this sensitive without considering precautions? We're not gonna get caught! And we're not going bankrupt!"

"Oh please. I know that Mom is giving you money to keep this place going. When she starts writing checks from her company to keep you afloat, I'd say that's an obvious sign of the end."

Frank glared back at his brother for a long moment before he turned toward the rows of gray filing cabinets against the wall and opened a bottom drawer. He pulled out a folder and a small folded paper from his pocket and handed it to Donnie.

"What is this?" Donnie asked.

"This is Mom's check." Frank dropped the folder of loose white papers on his desk. When Donnie asked what it was, Frank replied: "You're smart. You tell me."

Donnie stepped over to the desk and opened the folder. There were dozens of spreadsheets. Donnie lifted the top one and skimmed through it.

"You think Mom *just* started helping with this place?" Frank asked.

Donnie sifted through the other papers which documented that Ginny had been giving money to the funeral home from her business for nearly twenty years. Frank was still talking but Donnie wasn't listening. Frank asked his question again.

"What?" Donnie asked.

"I said, look at the difference between what she was giving now versus five years ago. She's not paying as much."

"How much is Dad contributing?"

"He's not."

Donnie didn't respond.

"Yeah, big shocker, huh?" Frank said. "Your screw-up brother is actually doing a decent job."

"Why is Dad not contributing?" Donnie asked.

"Because his money is for retirement. Mom's is too, but she's *always* given money to this place—it's the family business. It's not making a ton, but we're pulling in more than we were five years back; things are a little better." Frank took a seat at the desk.

Donnie set the folder on Frank's desk. "I'd question your definition of things being a little better. You may be pulling in more, but how much are you spending?" Frank began to respond but Donnie continued: "It doesn't matter right now. All I care about is what are you going to do about *that*?" He motioned to the cooler.

"I'll bury her tonight—once Cliff finishes up with his client."

Donnie walked back over to her and sighed. "If you get caught, that's it—we're done!"

"I know," Frank said. He opened the front drawer of the desk and pulled out a large envelope and opened it, holding it out toward Donnie. "But if we *don't* get caught—which we won't—then we can make some needed updates a lot quicker."

Donnie squinted. "I can't see that. Is that money?"

"Four grand. That bone guy bought a hand and a tibia. For two grand a pop, I can't pass this up. I don't want Mom paying for the home any more than you do, but I don't see another way out. The ass hats have money, and they have pull in this town. You know they're doing free pickups from the hospital?"

"What are we charging?"

"I was charging two hundred, but now I've gotta do it for

free to have a chance. Look, I can be the best funeral director in the world, but if we don't get money coming in here soon to spice this place up, we're screwed. As much as I hate to admit it, those guys look better than we do, their foyer smells like cotton and honeysuckle, and their landscaping is on point. On top of that, they just hired two really hot receptionists. The hottest thing we have is Cliff—and we can't even afford to hire him. We can't compete without the money. And unfortunately, this is the best option we're gonna find," Frank said, tapping the envelope. "Mom and Dad put us in charge, so, I'm doing whatever I can to keep it that way. I know you don't agree, but to be honest, I don't trust that you're going to stay here. I wish you would, but I know this isn't your thing. It's mine because it's all I know. So, help out if you want, get involved if you want, but I'm fixing this my way."

His phone buzzed.

CLIFF: Where be?

FRANK: Downstairs. You done?

"Alright, I gotta run." Frank moved toward the corpse. Donnie didn't say anything. Frank's phone buzzed again.

CLIFF: Yee yee, comin in . . .

"Frank. I want the body out of—"

"I know. You want it gone. We'll ta—"

"Don't interrupt me," Donnie said. "If I see another body in here that doesn't belong, or an arm, or a leg, or even a vertebra that has no business being here, I'm calling the police."

Frank stood motionless. Silent.

"That cop was here the other day—did you know that? All he would have had to do is open that drawer, and that would have been it. I can't go down with you on this. And I won't. So, if you want to roll the dice go ahead, but I'm not going to let you ruin my future, or Mom and Dad's name for that matter."

There was a creak on the steps: "Should I come back?" Cliff asked.

"No," Frank said. "No, we're good."

"I hope so," Donnie mumbled. "Seriously. Don't let this ruin our family."

Frank motioned for Cliff to come and help him. The two bagged up the remains of the woman's body into a plastic bag and placed the four separated limbs in coolers. They put the coolers back on the tray and slid them inside the refrigerator.

"I'll come back for those later. We okay?" Frank asked.

Donnie shrugged, then sighed. "I've said all I have to say."

27

Donnie spotted Addy across the bar. The bartender asked if he wanted his usual and he said yes, then made his way to the table. There was someone sitting across from Addy who turned toward Donnie and got up from his chair. "Hey, Donnie," the guy said.

"Donnie, you know Nick Stills?" Addy introduced.

"Yeah, we've met a few times. What's goin' on, man?"

"Just catching up with Addy. Welcome back to town." He shook Donnie's hand. "See ya later, Addy. Hit me up if you wanna grill this week."

"You got it," Addy said. Then under his breath to Donnie: "That guy's a piece of shit."

Donnie gave him a confused look. "That's a little harsh for a preacher, isn't it?" Donnie smirked.

"You *actually* know him?" Addy asked.

"Kind of. I know his wife, Sophia. She and I go way back."

"Yeah, well, he and I go way back. I don't have a lot of tolerance for bullies." Addy continued staring at Nick at the bar. "I'm pretty sure he beats up on his wife. I can't prove it though. They come out to where I preach sometimes." He took a sip of his water. "How do you know Sophia?"

"She was a manager at the place I worked at in high school. She and I would drive out to Paris to get beer all the time."

"What? And you two never hooked up?"

"Nah. She was gorgeous, but I think I was a little young for her. We still talk quite a bit, actually. I need to go see her." The waitress brought over two bottles of Shock Top and a plate of fried ravioli.

"I went ahead and ordered for us," Donnie said and passed the waitress his card.

"Day drinkin', huh?" Addy asked.

"Yeah. Needed a break," Donnie replied. "Thanks for coming."

"Fortunately, my job encourages meeting with depressed individuals like yourself." Addy raised the bottle and clinked Donnie's. "Of course, I may leave out *this* little detail should anyone ask where I was."

"I'd say more frustrated than depressed."

"Your brother?"

"Eh. Mix of stuff—mostly Frank, but I got my own stuff, too."

"You tell your parents about what happened in New York?"

"Told them as soon as it happened. Only person who doesn't know is Frank. And about every time I want to tell him, something happens that completely derails the conversation." Donnie took a sip. "I can't really go into details right now, but he's gotten into some weird stuff."

"Weirder than his Mardi Gras party back in February?"

"That testicular cancer event he did?" Donnie asked.

"No. This was an actual Mardi Gras party at the house."

Donnie's mouth dropped. "You're kidding me."

Addy laughed. "I'm not. To his credit though, it was a good event. And surprisingly, very tasteful . . . once you got past the invitations. He even put a little skeleton inside the King Cake."

Donnie sighed and rested his head in his hands. "Did people actually come?"

"Oh yeah. Probably fifty or sixty people came through. He told me recently that it got him a new client—did a funeral just last month for someone's mom."

"Wow. Yes, he's gotten into something weirder than that."

"Like, something illegal?"

Donnie's eyes connected with Addy's. "Can't really say."

"It'd probably be best if you didn't include me on whatever you guys are do—"

"No, no. There's no 'you guys' in this. It's strictly Frank."

"Whoever it is," Addy said, making sure he had Donnie's attention, "I can't get involved. My record's too sensitive. God was gracious enough to have this church to take a gamble on me after what happened at the last place. So, no offense, but I'm not losing this job over you guys."

"How were they taking a gamble? What happened wasn't your fault—that guy had it coming."

"That's debatable." Addy took another sip. "It's church politics. Even if it was his fault, it doesn't look the best to have a guy who was publicly arrested preaching your sermons."

The waitress came back by and cleared the plate. She offered another beer but Addy declined. "Anything I can do that doesn't involve getting involved?" Addy asked.

"I really don't know. I just feel like he's going off the rails and if I don't do something, he's not only gonna get the place shut down, but he's gonna get arrested."

"Tried talking to your dad?" Addy asked.

"Not about this."

"So leave. That's what you wanted to do anyway, right? You

came back here, took a break—you've apparently found a few backers who will take a gamble on you. You've got money saved up, right?"

"Yeah," Donnie replied. "And I've still got shares in a few restaurants—my money to live on is fine."

"Then go get your restaurant."

Donnie sat quiet.

"Where you thinkin? Nashville? Louisville?"

"Yeah. For this one, I think Nashville."

"Alright, so there ya go. You have shares in the other places, and you've got your consulting work, right?"

"Yeah." Donnie finished his beer.

"Problem solved. If your brother is involved in something serious, and you can't get him out of it, then it's probably best if you let him fall."

Donnie took a breath. "I can't do that."

"If things are as shady as you're making them sound, then your choice is to either let him fall on his own, or fall with you."

"If it was your brother, what would you do?" Donnie asked.

"And he wouldn't listen to me?" Addy swirled the remaining beer in his bottle and took one final gulp. "Whatever I could to protect him."

Donnie gave the response a thought. "So, you *wouldn't* let him get busted."

"I didn't say that. I said I would do whatever I could to *protect* him. Truthfully, you can't distance yourself from your brother—he's family. It's not the same as walking away from say, me—or New York. Frank will always have some connection to you regardless of what you do or where you go—unless you shut out your whole family. Whatever happens to him will inadvertently impact you because it impacts the entire family: discussions, finances, anxieties. Letting him get away with it may hurt him, and, turning him over to the police may in fact protect him—I don't know. Like I said, if it was my brother, I'd do whatever I could to protect him in the long run. If that's what you want, then you have to figure out what that means for Frank."

"So, what should I do?"

Addy laughed. "Hell if I know."

"That didn't help," Donnie said, standing up.

"You didn't ask me here to help; you just said you'd buy me a drink." Addy stood up. "You ready?"

A hand came down on Donnie's shoulder and pulled him closer: "We need to be careful Donnie, otherwise this town'll think it's funeral directors are a bunch of drunks." The voice let out a raspy laugh.

Donnie turned to see Vince Koch's hand extended in front of him. "Hey Vince," he said. "What are you guys doing here?"

"Same thing as you, it smells like," Vince replied.

Randy extended his hand to Addy. "Hey, Addy. This where you get your inspiration?" He laughed.

"Nah, the inspiration has a blue label and sits in my desk at work," Addy joked, shaking Randy's hand. "You guys doin' alright?

"Doin' fine. Just meeting a client for happy hour. Y'all wanna join us?"

"Nah, I can't. I gotta get back," Donnie said. Addy said the same.

"You had a chance to think about our offer?" Vince asked, as Donnie was inching backwards.

Donnie looked at Addy to see if he was paying attention; he didn't want him asking Frank about the Kochs or an offer. Addy was scrolling through his phone, walking toward the door. "Um . . . sort of. Frank's hesitant. It's a little difficult for him to give up something like this, no matter what the money is."

"Well how 'bout this," Vince said. "You tell your brother that if he'll sell at the price we agreed on, we'll let him manage the place—practically keep the same job he has now. The only difference will be that it's under a new name."

"And he can't keep making those coupons," Randy added.

"And he'll need to get rid of that truck," Vince continued. "But, mostly, it's the same job."

"Hunh," Donnie mumbled. "That's a pretty good deal."

"What if we make it *damn* good deal then?" Vince asked. "You sell to us, we'll give you the money that we offered, Frank can run it, and we'll tack on a little something extra for your restaurant."

Donnie's eyes narrowed; he thought he misheard: "What did you say?"

Randy stepped in: "We'll write you a check to help with your restaurant. No equity needed. Your dad told us you were looking for backers so we thought it may be something to put you at ease about the whole thing. Consider it a signing bonus."

"How much?"

Vince grinned. "Let's just say you won't be disappointed."

Addy called from the door. "I gotta run. I'll call ya later."

"Wait, wait. Hang on, I'm leaving." Donnie turned back to the Koch brothers. "You guys have got a deal. I need some time to get things together, but if that's what you're offering, I can get my brother on board."

Vince extended his hand. A glistening white smile spread across his face as he muttered the words: "Sounds good." The two shook hands. "You talk to Frank and get back to us—as soon as you can."

Frank didn't say a word for much of the drive to LBL. He crossed over the bridge and exited off the main road before passing Cliff a map from the glove box. He pointed to a cross circled in red and asked him to navigate to it.

"The cemetery should be on this road in maybe a mile? Two? Looks like the third right," Cliff said.

Frank reached into his pocket for his cell phone and attempted to make a call before cursing that there was no service. "Hey, do me a favor. Hit *recent* on my calls and send a message to Bill Cobb."

"He's the guy with the ex-wife?"

"Yeah. Just text him and say, 'Talked to my brother, sorry for the delay in response. I'm happy to help. Let's touch base soon.'" Frank spotted the cemetery's sign and turned down a dirt road leading into the trees.

"Sent. I take it from the conversation I heard that Donnie is fully on board?" Cliff asked.

Frank's truck came to a sudden stop and he turned to face Cliff. "Sure." He looked back up at the windshield toward the sign suspended on a chain between two trees blocking access to the road ahead: ROAD CLOSED. "This can't be it."

Cliff turned around and looked behind him, then back at the map. "Yeah, did you take the third right? Was there a sign?"

"Yeah," Frank agreed.

"The map shows that it's still a ways up. What do you wanna do?"

"Walk, I guess."

"We could just move the sign," Cliff said.

"If the road is bad up there, we may not be able to get very far."

"Or get back out."

"Or that. Yeah, let's walk. You wanna grab the shovel and I'll grab the bag?" Frank reached over and took bug spray out of the glove box, then removed the trash bag from the truck's cab. He covered himself in repellent as Cliff complained about the incessant heat. "I got waters in the back; grab a couple if you want."

Frank clicked the automatic lock when he heard the passenger door close. He started walking up the rocky path but soon realized that he was the only one walking. He turned around to see Cliff still standing by the truck, staring in Frank's direction. "What are you doing?"

Cliff didn't respond.

"You alright?"

"Something doesn't feel right," he said. Frank couldn't hear him, prompting Cliff to yell it back, and then confirm that he wasn't sick.

Frank started back toward the truck. "You mean you don't feel right about burying her here?"

"No, I mean . . . something here doesn't feel right."

Frank turned and examined the path, and then back to Cliff. "Those witch stories got to you, huh?"

"I was trying not to think about that. Thanks," Cliff said.

Frank laughed. "It's the middle of the day; I'm sure we're fine. What ghost story happens in broad daylight?" He walked over to the truck and pulled out a golf club from the back seat. "Here. Totally safe. Come on, let's do this and get back before I get freaked out too."

Cliff picked up the shovels and began walking alongside Frank. The path led them through the trees and turned, putting the truck out of view. Frank tried to make conversation to keep Cliff's mind from wandering, but the answers were one worded in between Cliff's nervous whistling of Disney songs. Suddenly, Frank came to a stop. "Wait a second," he said.

"What?"

"What is that?" Frank said, pointing up ahead.

"Yo, man, stop playin'," Cliff said dropping one of the shovels and holding up the other, ready to swing.

"I'm serious. It's right there," Frank whispered, his eyes wide in surprise.

"I'm out," Cliff said, turning to leave.

"What are you doing?"

"I'm not playing with this stuff, man. I told you this place was haunted."

"Dude, it's not a person. Look! It's a fox!" Frank's voice sparked the brown fox to start running over the grass and brush. Cliff turned to see it disappear. "You thought I saw a ghost?"

"Why didn't you lead with that, then?" Cliff said. "Why you gotta act all freaked out over a fox? I didn't know what you were seeing."

"I've never seen a fox before. I was excited. Come on, if I saw a person standing out there I would *not* be standing here telling you to look too. I'd have been in that truck before you knew what happened." Frank laughed. "You really think those stories about that woman are true?"

"Yeah. That's why I don't like being out here."

"So, if I were to start whispering 'Cliff' in a raspy, old lady's voice—"

"Yo, for real . . . not even funny to talk about," Cliff said.

28

After dinner that evening, Donnie settled into the preparation room and began working on the client for the next day. Pandora started playing Justin Timberlake's "Can't Stop the Feeling" when Donnie heard footsteps coming down the stairs. "Donald?"

"Yes, Ma'am?"

"You have a second?"

"Yeah, what's up?" He stepped back and washed his hands. When he turned around, Ginny was holding out a folded piece of paper—a blank check!

"What is this?"

"It's a down payment."

"I don't understand." He handed the check back to her.

"I can't offer a lot of money, but I have enough to at least get you going. I know what having your own restaurant means to you, and I want to help."

"Mom I don't—"

"I also know you're frustrated here. Your brother told me you're looking into opening up something in Florida. I don't like you moving that far away from us, but I also don't want you to go through something like New York all over again. Let me help. You're an amazing chef! Whether it's here, Florida, or South Dakota, I want you to have your own place."

"Mom." Donnie paused. "Thank you, but I've been talking

to a few guys, and I think I've got a couple who will put up what I need. Plus, your money is for your retirement."

"Donald. First off, my money is my money. And I spend it how I want. Second, while I appreciate your concern over my retirement, I fully believe I'm helping my retirement by investing in you. I expect to make some profit, and I expect for this down payment to be returned to me." She waved the check in front of him. "I just want you to get on your feet. If you have other investors, just add this in with theirs." She took a pen off the work desk. "I'm glad you came back—we all are. Your brother especially. I know you can't see it, but boy did he miss you. But even he knows you aren't happy here. And you *won't* be." She grabbed his hand. "This business—this house—it isn't for you anymore. Take the money. Get that place opened."

"I really . . . I mean this is . . ." He paused to look at the number she'd filled in. It was for twelve thousand dollars. "I can't take it. Not like this."

"You need more?" she asked.

"Mom," Donnie said.

"Please don't misunderstand. I want my money back one day, but for now I just want you to get started being happy. Call those backers of yours and get it started." She turned to go as Donnie stared at the check in disbelief. Finally, he spoke out, "Mom." She turned around. "Listen, I can't take this now."

"Why won't you let me do this for you?"

"Because you've done something else for me—and it was more than financial; you inspired me. You started your own business when you were my age and I want to show you that I can do the same, that I can follow your steps. And I can't do that if you back me. I'll let you back the next one."

"I'm not just giving you money because you're my son, you know that, right? Deep down this is entirely selfish. I need a bigger retirement income if I'm going to travel every month. I wouldn't be giving you this money if I didn't think you could pay me a profit."

"I know. But, just this once, let me get it on my own," Donnie said.

"Okay. You're on your own." She kissed him on the cheek.

"Thanks, Mom."

"You're welcome. Now, tear that check up before your brother finds it and cashes it for an air hockey table."

TUESDAY

29

Frank left the house early to assess the cemetery holding Joe Jackson's signed shoes. It would be a stretch to call what remained of Almo, Kentucky a town. Almo Road, just five miles north of Murray on Highway 641, led to the remnants of a community by the same name. Frank drove past a brick church that looked nearly a century old and spotted the entrance to the cemetery. He continued driving, out of curiosity for what remained in the town's province. Past the church he followed the road and spotted the ruins of a general store, a family diner, and what looked to be the structure of a filling station. Then he circled around into a small community of trailers, and double-wide homes, all within walking distance from a small post office. Unless one knew where to look, the trail to Marlowe Cemetery—situated across from the old church—went entirely unnoticed.

Frank had accompanied his dad to this cemetery on a couple of occasions when he was younger. The grounds were as he remembered: off the main road, in an area of town that saw little to no traffic, and in a very unlikely spot for anyone to just stop by for a visit. There were just 23 plots being used, making it easy to find the resting place of Myles Hamm—and his thirty-thousand-dollar Joe Jackson shoes. Frank took a few pictures of the gravesite, walked around the lot to get a feel for the layout and any vulnerable spots for visibility should they need flashlights, then returned to his car.

Frank pulled out of the cemetery entrance path back onto Almo Road and drove toward the intersection of the main highway. The few cars on the main highway at 7 a.m. slowed to a stop as the light turned yellow. Frank was scrolling through a review of night-vision goggles when he heard a car horn blast. He glanced in his rearview mirror; no one behind him. He set his phone in the cup holder and pulled out to make a left on the highway when he spotted a police cruiser stopped on his right at the red light of the cross section. It was Monty Suthers. And he was making eye contact! Frank casually looked away toward where he was turning and pretended like he didn't see him.

Excuses raced through his mind to justify why he was in that part of town at seven a.m. The cruiser pulled up next to him. He turned his radio on and started singing, still acting as if Monty's presence wasn't causing his heart rate to skyrocket. Frank accelerated for a moment and then released the pedal, but Monty's car stayed even with his. Eventually Frank gave in and turned to glance; Monty's eyes met his again. Frank raised his eyebrows and waved, adding a smile. Monty smiled back and waved.

The cruiser fell behind Frank's truck and switched lanes to follow behind. Frank avoided eye contact through the rearview mirror—he knew Monty would notice—and finally after two miles of anxious driving, turned into the Walmart parking lot and idled in a spot near the front. Monty's cruiser didn't follow. *What am I doing?*

He nervously eased back up to the main road's entrance and scanned the highway, irrationally believing that Monty would be waiting on the side of the road. *Calm down. You didn't do anything, you didn't leave anything. He doesn't even know you were at that cemetery.*

When Cliff arrived to open the gym Monty was already there sitting on a large tire, dressed in black running shorts with a faded, gray Atlanta Braves t-shirt. The morning humidity was already manifesting in pockets of sweat on his back. Had it not been for the cruiser, Cliff wouldn't have recognized him. "Mr. Suthers?" he asked.

Monty swallowed the rest of the water from his bottle and shaded the sun with his hand as he turned around. "Mr. Samson. How are you?"

"Great. You here to get that pump on?"

"I'm here to t-t-take you up on your offer. You said to come back anytime for a w-wo-w-workout, so, here I am."

"Awesome."

"You have air conditioning in there?"

"We got fans." Cliff pointed to the door. "Let's go inside and I'll give you an evaluation and work you through some exercises."

"I'll be honest, I've n-n-never really had a trainer before and I haven't been in a real gym for probably f-f-fifteen years," Monty said.

"They don't require you to be in the gym?"

Monty looked down at his stomach, grabbed it on each side, and moved it up and down. He arched his eyebrows at Cliff.

"Alright." Cliff laughed. "Fair enough."

He and Cliff talked a bit about his medical history and what his goals and expectations were. Monty mentioned he wanted better overall health but when Cliff prodded further, Monty said he wanted to look better.

"To feel more confident naked?" Cliff asked.

The comment took Monty by surprise. He didn't know how to respond, and his embarrassment seemed to be stopping him from saying anything at all.

"I mean, that was my goal," Cliff said. "I wanted to look good naked. And actually see my ding-dong when I looked down."

Monty stifled a laugh and nodded in agreement. "Yeah. Okay. I w-w-want to be confident."

"Can I ask you a personal question?" Cliff asked.

"Sure."

"Have you had a stutter all your life?"

"As long as I can rem-re-re-rem." He stopped and took a breath. "Recall. Yeah. It comes and goes."

"You have anything that helps?" Cliff asked.

"You m-m-mean do I take anything?"

"No. I mean are there certain times it's worse? Or do you have exercises you do to help?"

"Sometimes. M-Most of the time it's when I'm nervous. I've l-l-lear-learned to deal with it. I know some words I can't say, so I change them out for others."

"Okay." Cliff stood up and moved toward some mats in the middle of the empty gym. "Go ahead and get up and come down here. I'm going to run you through a series of exercises to get a better idea of where you're at: form, breathing, how you work out, etcetera. So, just have some fun, give me about forty minutes, and let's see what we can do."

It was difficult for Monty to talk through his exercises and

Cliff finally had to tell him to just focus on breathing. They moved through basic movements: push-ups, pull-ups, and sit-ups; Cliff would periodically correct his form. About halfway into the session, Cliff noticed that while Monty may have been having a hard time breathing, his stutter was gone when he spoke.

"Don't respond to this because I don't want you to pass out, but you haven't stuttered for almost half an hour," Cliff said.

Monty paused as if listening for thunder. He knew what he wanted to say next and had no mental feelings of restraint. "Didn't notice."

He ended Monty on what he called a "finisher": three exercises with a ten-second break in between each. At the end, with Monty on the floor gasping for air, Cliff knelt beside him. "But did you die?" He smiled. Monty was too focused on getting oxygen into his lungs to acknowledge him.

Cliff opened the garage doors and was sitting at his desk when Monty finally came over to sit down. A dozen people had come in since he arrived. "Is it usually this busy?"

"It varies. Because I'm a small gym, and I help over at the house, my hours are a little weird. Everything is by appointment only. Mornings are consistently busy though, as are evenings."

They talked about price and Cliff suggested holding off on a gym membership until Monty became comfortable doing a routine of at-home body-weight exercises. "For now, just do these at home three times a week and come see me once a week. Four days of working out. If you can do this, then I'll start introducing you to weights and we'll talk about gym time. Fair enough?"

"I can handle that." Monty put the duffel bag over his

shoulder and noticed a map of Land Between the Lakes and several pamphlets on Cliff's desk. "LBL, huh?"

Cliff looked toward the stack of brochures. "Yeah, I was out there earlier this week."

"I used to go out there q-qu-quite a bit for hiking—helped relieve some stress." He paused. "Of course, if this workout stuff k-ke-eeps my stutter away, to hell with hiking." He chuckled.

"Keep it up. Let's see if it helps."

"I used to teach over at Murray High. Did you know that?" Monty asked.

"I did. You were actually my history teacher in ninth grade. I don't remember you having a stutter back then, though." Cliff lied about that one.

"Then you m-must've b-been asleep. Everyone called me Mister Stutters."

"What? I definitely never heard that," he lied again.

"Well, I appreciate that. Bunch of l-little bastards." Monty winked.

"See if you can pay attention to your workouts and how they affect your speech: is it better, worse, or the same? We'll watch it over the next few weeks and see what happens. And hey," Cliff added, "you'll actually *want* to do those exercises I gave you, otherwise the next session with me will suuuuuuck."

"Will do," Monty said. He turned to leave and glanced around for Frank's truck. "Is Frank here? I didn't see his truck."

"He should be." Cliff scanned the driveway. "His calendar shows two appointments this morning. He usually parks his truck on the street for advertising. You need something?"

Monty shook his head. "No. Just askin.'"

30

Cliff was right—Frank had two meetings that morning. The first was an early meeting with Bill Cobb at seven-thirty. Frank wanted to get it in before Donnie woke up, but when he saw Monty's cruiser parked in front of Cliff's gym, he called Bill to meet at Virginia Jan's Café instead.

Bill asked to review the process for cremating and returning his ex-wife, but Frank felt like all the man wanted was a role in planning the woman's funeral. Frank ran him through what had been planned by the current husband and assured him that the cremation would be taken care of after the Friday service. He promised to have the ashes back to him as soon as possible.

The next meeting was with an older woman—now widowed—who wished to meet with both brothers and requested no one see her husband once he entered the casket—not even her. As she talked, Frank could feel his body tensing with excitement over the potential income from this new corpse that no one would ever see again. "Mrs. Clark, I completely understand your request," Donnie began. "If that's really what you want to do, then we'll honor your wishes, so please don't be offended at what I'm about to ask."

"You're going to ask if I'm sure?" she replied.

Donnie nodded. "Yes. I only ask because you're not the first to make this request, or even the fiftieth—"

"It's his request, not mine."

Donnie paused. "This is his request?"

"Yes," she replied. "And I intend to make sure it gets kept. I promise, I have no intention of seeing my husband again. It is not because I don't want to—I do—but he made me promise I wouldn't look at him again after he died so that *that* memory of him wouldn't be my last."

"Because you wish to waive the viewing, what should we do with clothes and makeup? We can forego everything and save you some of the cost, but if you change your mind it may be . . ." Donnie paused, thinking she knew where he was going.

"Embarrassing?"

"Yes ma'am," Donnie continued. "In some form or another, it may be a little embarrassing if you change your mind last minute and your husband isn't fully ready for a viewing. If this is the request we honor, then it puts us in a weird position because we don't want to become the bad guys for standing in the way of you seeing your husband."

"Mr. Burgers, I do thank you for the concern and being so understanding. I know it's going to be . . ." She stopped, and shifted her gaze, then lowered her head for a moment. She took a breath, then continued. "It is very hard to face that I'm not going to see my husband again. But I am going to honor his request. He was right; as much as I want to see him, I don't want to see him like that. The last time we spoke his eyes were open, his smile was bright, and his hands were holding mine." Her eyes met Donnie's. "That's the image I want to complete our married life together." She looked at Frank. "Don't you start crying now." She laughed.

"Sorry," Frank said, sniffing and wiping a tear from his eye: "That was sweet."

"Okay, Mrs. Clark," Donnie said. "If that's what you want, the service and viewing will be a closed casket, even to you. What about burial clothes? Do you have anything specific?"

She opened her purse and pulled out a t-shirt with the image of the Lone Ranger. "He loved this shirt, and said he wanted to be buried with it."

"This is all?" Donnie asked.

"Yes. We don't need to do makeup unless it's a requirement."

"Not at all," Donnie said. "Like I said, that'll save you some money."

"I appreciate your integrity for not taking advantage of an old woman." Mrs. Clark grinned. "Your attitude confirms why my husband chose your family to handle the arrangements."

"Did someone else try and take advantage of you?" Frank asked.

"Well, I know about the financial issues you all are having. I received a call from one of Walt's friends warning me that you all might try and talk me into a bunch of add-ons to increase the cost, but you've done nothing of the sort. I've been very pleased with your professionalism."

Donnie looked at Frank who was biting his lips. "I'm not sure what financial—"

"You mind me asking who told you that?" Frank interrupted.

"Not at all. Do you know Randy Koch? After Walter passed, Randy called me with an offer to do the service. He said he and Walt knew each other from the driving range over on 121. I told him that Walt had a connection with your father and Randy—in a very polite way—told me to watch out for price gouging. I don't think he was intending to be mean about it. He did have plenty of nice things to say about you all."

"Of course he did." Frank forced a smile.

"He didn't explain why he thought you all were experiencing financial problems but I never asked. Once I said we'd made our choice, he was very kind and complimentary."

"Hunh," Frank mumbled.

Donnie finally broke in: "Why don't we go ahead and get your husband's memorial planned out. Frank, can you pull up some of the casket models and I'll walk her through some of our service package options."

After making the necessary arrangements for the service, and selecting a casket from Frank's virtual viewing room on his laptop, Mrs. Clark grabbed her cane and pushed herself up off the couch in Donnie's office. She offered both boys a kiss on the cheek, and thanked them generously for their time. She mentioned recently hearing about Donnie's reputation as a chef and asked about his experiences. Before Donnie could finish, she went into some of her own culinary practices in California and even Puerto Rico. As excited as Donnie was about his accolades, Frank could tell he was not going to take the obvious opportunity in front of him. So, he strategically directed Mrs. Clark to the brochure in her hand, indicating the option for a meal after the service—cooked by Donnie himself! She didn't think there would be many in attendance and liked the idea of having a meal afterwards for family. Donnie gave her some options he could cook up, and Frank offered to preside over the service unless she had another candidate; she did not.

When she reached into her purse again, Frank expected her

to pull out a coupon, but she came out with her check book instead and requested the total. She paid everything up front.

"Do you have a date in mind?"

"What family we have are already here, and all of our friends are retired. They can make any time. When can you all be ready?"

"Thursday?" Frank asked.

Thursday morning was perfect.

"What a jackass," Frank said, sitting down at the table. He pulled his paper plate and sandwich toward him.

"What?" Donnie said. "That he bad-mouths the competition? You do that."

"Not to clients."

"Frank. Yes you do!"

"Alright, fine. But I don't go out of my way to do that. I might ambulance chase, but I'm not gonna call potential clients to slam the Kochs, or anyone else."

"Because you have class?" Donnie grinned.

"Whatever. Plus, the guy's a liar. You know that's the fifth or sixth time someone has said that Randy knew the person from the driving range? I've asked—Randy doesn't play golf."

"So, he does his research and makes up a connection. It's working, apparently."

"Still. Don't tell someone we're having financial troubles. Not cool." Frank opened his bag of chips.

"You know she's going to ask to see him again, right?"

Donnie asked, mixing his chicken salad at the kitchen table with a fork and then taking a bite.

"I think we're fine. She seemed genuine about the whole thing." Frank made a swirly design of mayonnaise on his turkey sandwich. "Besides, she made a promise; she's not going to break that."

"They always ask at the graveside," Donnie said.

31

Monty Suthers had been thinking about Frank all morning. He sat at the stoplight on his way home—the same intersection he saw him at earlier—remembering the bizarre interaction they had: Frank making eye contact and suddenly turning away, acting as if he couldn't see him. That anxious look, coupled with being in a practically deserted part of town at seven a.m., had been poking at Monty's gut since he left Cliff's gym. *Oh, what the hell.* He switched on the light bar atop his cruiser and sounded the siren to get the attention of the drivers to his right. Seconds before the traffic light went green, Monty eased out in front of the cars at his side, cutting over toward Almo Road. *Just have a look around.*

His cruiser moved slowly down Almo Road trying to make sense of what Frank would be doing all the way out here. He drove by the community's post office, through the narrow streets of double-wide homes. He had not been through this part of town in years. A middle-aged man was sitting on his porch wearing a bathrobe, holding a beer. He held up his can to acknowledge Monty's presence; Monty waved back. *Maybe Frank was visiting someone. Maybe he was picking up mail from the post office?*

He turned back down the main road and drove past the old brick church. "You could just ask him," he said to himself. "Just say you saw him in Almo earlier, ask what he was doing all the way out there." He stopped his cruiser abruptly when he saw the sign, after checking to make sure no one was behind him. Beside him was a path into the trees he had never noticed. The sign read *Marlowe Cemetery*. His gut stirred.

The road took him up for what seemed like half a mile into the trees at a small incline to a clearing with several headstones. Monty put his cruiser in park and opened his door to the warm dusk air. He stood and walked around the lot. He didn't know what he expected to find: something out of place or disturbed. *Maybe he didn't come up here.*

Everything seemed normal: no vandalized graves or special markers. Not even a sign of tire tracks in the grass. There were a handful of Marlowes but no names that stood out. He wiped away the sweat that was already forming on his head with his hand and took a breath. *What were you doing, Frank?*

Frank's truck crept up the path to Marlowe cemetery's entrance and came to a stop. "I think we're okay with flashlights up here."

"Oh," Cliff said. "I didn't bring any. Did you?"

Frank sighed. "Nevermind."

The two began digging. It was the biggest payout for a dig and neither had the energy to be excited about it. "How is it this late at night, and still this hot?" Cliff asked.

"We're in Kentucky. Go get a water," Frank said.

"I've already had four of those bottles."

"Have you peed yet?"

"Nope." Cliff shoveled a pile of dirt over his head and

emptied it on the ground above onto the mound. Some of the loose dirt trickled back into the hole, onto his head. "I'm wiped, man."

"Tell me about it. I've been up since six-thirty—and no nap!"

"How long have we been digging?"

"Two hours," Frank replied. "We're almost there."

Cliff stuck his shovel into the ground and stepped up the ladder out of the hole to go and pee while Frank continued digging. "Almost there . . . almost there . . . thirty grand . . ."

"Talking to yourself huh?" Cliff asked.

"You're not peeing on the dirt we just dug up, are you?"

"Shit . . . my bad. I'm not even thinking."

"Come on, man, it's running back down here."

"Sorry. I didn't want to pee on a grave."

"So you pee on the di—never mind."

"Hey, you do realize that if someone were to come up here and see that truck, we're screwed."

In all the details that Frank had outlined and planned, never once did it occur to him that his truck was a dead giveaway to his involvement. That truck was known by nearly everyone in town—especially the police—and its appearance next to an open grave would no doubt be the end. "I do now. We gotta hurry, come on!"

Frank was the first to notice the mud; a result of Cliff's pee was his first thought. But at almost four feet down he could see—and feel—that the dirt was getting wetter and heavier to throw and before long, he and Cliff's shoes were becoming engulfed by it.

"Why's it so muddy down here?" Cliff asked. "Is this normal?"

"Sure . . ." Frank sighed. "Maybe. I'm sure it's not abnormal."

"Good thing I wore boots."

Both were too tired to even be upset at the pooling water beneath them. Their minds had switched to autopilot, neither one speaking to the other, and neither hearing anything but the recurring sounds: chirping of the crickets and katydids, the slicing of the shovel into the dirt, the *plops* onto the ground above where they threw it, and trickles of it falling back into the hole.

Cliff slowly raised his shovel and set it into the earth. Subconsciously, he expected to hear *sllaahhp* when he punched it in the mud with his foot, but the sudden crunch of something below with a subsequent crack snapped him back to attention. He let go of his shovel and looked at Frank, who was already on alert. "Whoa!"

"What was that?" Frank asked.

"Did that come from down here?"

"Yeah. I think so."

Frank slid his shovel into a spot near Cliff's and mashed it with his boot—*crack!*—sending Frank falling forward as the shovel sliced through more of the earth than he anticipated.

"You okay?"

"Yeah," Frank replied, steadying himself. "Is that the coffin?" He stooped down and began grabbing handfuls of mud, throwing them to the side. Cliff used his shovel to drive water and chunks of dirt away, being careful not to break anything else.

"What the . . ." Frank muttered. "Dude, look at this."

"I can't see anything. What is that?" Cliff asked.

"Get your phone out."

Cliff shined the flashlight on his phone. Frank's raised and muddied hands were holding fistfuls of earth . . . and something else. "What is that?"

"I don't know. Some sort of plastic—or wood. It's everywhere, look." Cliff shifted his light to the ground where several shards were speckled through the disturbed soil. Then suddenly, with the sound of another *crack*, Cliff begin sinking down into the mud and tumbled to the ground, cursing in a panic. He scrambled to push himself up, but the weight from his arms broke into another part of the coffin's exterior letting out another loud snap. Cliff screamed, flinging mud and water—now bubbling up from beneath—everywhere!

"Calm down, calm down! Stop moving!" Frank stepped along the edge of the coffin and grabbed his hand. "You're fine."

"I'm not fine! Half my body is inside this thing with a dead guy. Pull me out!"

"I gotchu. Just don't pull out too quick or you'll cut yourself on the wood."

Cliff eased his hand out and instinctively braced himself with the other—instantly breaking through another spot: *snap!* "Are you kidding me!" Cliff yelled.

"Shhh!" Frank whispered back.

"Dude. Get me out of here! Now!"

Frank took hold of Cliff's hand and arm just behind the elbow, as to not let him slip back, and cautioned him once again to step out lightly—and to not step anywhere else. Cliff scurried out and pressed his body against the wall of dirt while Frank knelt and shined Cliff's light into the punctured holes. He put his hand inside. "Yup," he said, breathing heavily, "there's the body. Didn't you say this guy died like two years ago?"

"Not even. You sure we got the right grave?"

"Positive. I double-checked before we started; not making that mistake again." Frank felt along the edge of the newly made hole in the coffin and took hold of a jagged edge. He pulled up on it, easily snapping off another large piece of the box's exterior. "I've never heard of wood rotting this fast—especially on a coffin. This is a mess."

"It's wood that's been sitting in water and mud. Of course it's going to start rotting," Cliff said.

"Coffins don't rot that fast. And I don't think it should be this muddy down here. This is . . . I don't even know if this real wood." Frank inspected one of the shards.

"Shit, we gotta get those shoes out. We busted everything up and now mud's getting in," Cliff cautioned.

"I'm pretty sure water was already in there." Frank poked the shovel's end back into where the corpse's feet would be, sliding smoothly down into the dirt and causing more water to bubble up. "That's why it's muddy. Whatever this coffin was made of rotted and let a bunch of water pool inside." Frank pushed the water and dirt away and shined the light. "Unbelievable." Frank sighed.

No doubt what could be one of the most expensive pieces of sports memorabilia to be sold was now sitting just an arms-length from Cliff and Frank. Myles Hamm wasn't wearing them; they were nestled between his legs. Cliff held his breath as Frank lifted them out, and finally breathed out a curse when he shined a light on them. They were completely ruined.

Frank ran his hand along the sole to remove the sludge. He was holding a pair of old baseball cleats. One of the fewest—most unique—items that Shoeless Joe Jackson ever signed had been resting in a pool of water underground for who knows how long and was now stained black with mud and decay.

32

Frank had not been gone more than twenty minutes when Donnie heard the front door close from the family room. He squared his shot and struck the cue ball, narrowly missing his target. He hollered for his brother, certain Frank had forgotten his wallet or phone. He examined the table and called again, listening to footsteps move in the foyer toward him.

Vince appeared around the corner, followed by his brother Randy, both wearing jeans and a red polo with the Life Memorial insignia on the breast of the shirt. "Your dad told me you all bought a pool table." Vince said. "You should think about adding in Skee-ball and a couple of arcade games if you really want to bring in business."

"Please don't tell Frank that," Donnie said, taking aim at another shot. *Crack!* "What's going on?"

"You thought about our offer?"

Donnie looked up. "You stopped by to ask if I've thought about your offer? Are you serious?"

"It's a time-sensitive deal." Vince smiled.

"Why the hurry?"

"Our offer, our timetable."

Donnie took pause, his eyes narrowing at Vince. "It's been twenty-four hours . . . I don't have an answer for you."

"Have you mentioned it to him?"

Donnie took another shot. "Nope."

"Then our deal drops ten percent," Vince replied. "Frank can still manage, and we'll still put up for backing your res—"

"Excuse me? You didn't give me a deadline."

"Well, I expected you to at least talk with him by now. We did stress that we were in a hurry."

"So, what? You're gonna drop it ten percent every day I don't talk with him?"

"Maybe. Do you plan on delaying it past today?"

Donnie laid the pool stick across the table and leaned on the edge with his hands. He started to say that convincing his brother to sell his life away couldn't be done in a week, let alone a day. But he went in another direction. "How long you guys been bad-mouthing our business?"

"Define bad-mouthing." Randy smiled.

"Calling clients and convincing them not to choose us," Donnie said, coldly.

"Who said we're doing that?" Vince asked.

"The clients who chose *us*," Donnie replied.

"I didn't come here to get into it, Donnie. I only stopped by to—" Vince began.

"I'm still interested in your offer, and I will talk to my brother, but I want you and Randy to stop interfering with clients, okay?"

Randy walked over and picked up the pool stick. "You mind?"

"Actually, per my brother's rules, yes," Donnie pointed to the sign on the opposite wall. AMENITIES ARE FOR FRIENDS AND FAMILY ONLY.

Randy smiled and muttered something under his breath.

"I'm not gonna critique how you and Randy do business. You want to provide free pickups from the hospital, and ambulance chase, that's your business—you're doing it well—but if I hear from one more person that you've told a client our home is going under, or that we're scam artists, or that Frank has leprosy—anything—the deal's off."

Vince said, "It's funny that you think you're in a position to dictate the terms of this deal."

"You want our business, don't you?"

"No, no, no. Donnie, you're misunderstanding this: we're *taking* your business, and it's regardless of whether you and Frank are on board. This place is done." Vince tapped the felt with his ring. "Randy and I are offering you a deal because we're nice and respect your dad. We don't want any hard feelings. But to be honest, we're tired of waiting on your brother to quit dicking around with this place and accept that this town is not going to have two funeral homes."

Donnie replaced the pool stick in its holder on the wall and turned to face Randy with his arms folded. "I think you need to go." Vince started to respond but Donnie cut him off. "And I'd appreciate it if you'd wait on me to contact you. Don't come back here again."

Vince took a deep breath through his nose and looked down at the floor. "Okay." He put his hands in his pockets and turned to walk out toward the foyer. Donnie heard the front door open and turned the corner to see Vince standing in the doorway jiggling the loose knob. He looked to Donnie. "If I don't hear from you soon, we'll cut our offer in half. Of course, if you think your brother would rather take his chances, we're happy to sit back and wait for the inevitable." When Vince released the doorknob to gesture, it detached from the door and slid out onto the floor with a loud *clang*. "Now *that* was good timing."

WEDNESDAY

33

Cliff struggled to keep his eyes open that next morning; he was running on only a few hours of sleep. Fortunately, the dull pain in his arms and back were helping him not to pass out in front of the clients already working out in the gym.

After getting home the night before, Frank sent a text to Cliff asking if he could get in touch with the bone/limb buyer ASAP. Apparently, storing them was no longer an option, and he needed to quickly get rid of what he had. He texted back he'd take care of it.

Cliff preferred not to clue Frank in on too many of the details of finding a buyer for human limbs and bones, mostly because it involved one of his closest friends, and he wanted as few connections back to Matt Griffin as possible. The two became friends over several matches in state chess tournaments, and after learning of their acceptance into Murray State, arranged to share a dorm. Cliff and Matt moved into an apartment beginning their junior year and lived together until Matt dropped out that spring and bought a place in Nashville to run his internet security company full time. One of them would occasionally make the two-hour drive to meet up for dinner or a concert, and but several nights a month they would face off in online chess matches. After Cliff purchased the lot next to the funeral home, Matt called him with an odd request.

Matt's work in internet security had introduced him to a sector of the online world he never imagined. In time, he had acquired a handful of clients whose activity—he speculated—was on the other side of legal. Matt had met many of his clients through online chess portals and a few months before Cliff's purchase, Matt stumbled upon a request for specific body parts. When he approached Cliff with the idea, Cliff declined and never even brought it up to Frank, until nearly two years later when Frank asked if he might know anyone who was interested in buying some bones.

When he arrived at work, Cliff sent a text to Matt and asked when they could catch up—code to set up a private chat room. Matt replied he could meet in an hour and provided Cliff with a picture of the invite address and the password.

Cliff explained to Matt that Frank had another batch of bones needing to be sold but that the buyer who requested them—the same one who purchased the first batch—had gone MIA. Matt confessed that buyers of illegal materials could be flaky but assured him that he would check around and report back within twenty-four hours or find a new buyer.

Cliff logged off and called Frank's cell: nothing. Same with his office phone. Frank's truck wasn't in the driveway, but his calendar showed no off-site appointments. He tried the cell again, but it switched over to voice mail after two rings. "I guess he's in a meeting," he whispered.

Cliff was wrapping up a training session with a client, watching her pound a sledgehammer onto the large tire in front of them, when his cell phone rang. He stepped back toward his desk. The screen displayed UNKNOWN. He told the young woman to take a break and walked outside to answer the call.

The buyer did not introduce himself when Cliff picked up. Instead, he began talking as if he and Cliff were already mid-conversation. The Russian accent and the short sentences were a dead giveaway that the caller was the original buyer from several days ago. Matt had previously instructed Cliff to listen and not talk too much with this guy; the buyer wanted to get off the phone quickly. Cliff peeked his head back into the studio and mouthed *get some water* to the woman. She was sitting on the tire panting.

After the buyer listed off the parts he wanted to view, he indicated that, similar to before, he would not buy all the parts. He wanted to view six of them, and he would purchase no more than four. He then provided the meeting place and time and wished Cliff a good morning. Cliff had to interrupt him because he knew that one of those parts they weren't selling.

The man's voice grew irritated and sharp. He swore that he was told the part was available; Cliff calmly reiterated that it wasn't. The man told him to recheck, and Cliff once again declined—he knew the brothers had no intention of getting rid of someone's skull.

The man cursed and went quiet for a moment. Cliff asked if he wanted the rest and the man agreed, though, he made clear, he was not happy with this deal and would not be doing business with him again

"Your customer service is disgraceful," the man said.

"I will communicate your concerns to management," Cliff replied.

The phone went dead.

Cliff quietly rapped on Frank's office door, in case he was meeting with a client.

"Come in."

Frank was sitting alone at his desk typing on his laptop. Cliff took a seat: "Where've you been?"

"Nowhere. I've been here all morning," Frank replied.

"Oh. I tried calling."

"I was in the bathroom when you called. I was in the middle of a game and didn't want to switch over," Frank replied.

"Thanks for calling back."

"Sorry. I got sidetracked."

"Our guy called," Cliff said. "He set up a meeting time."

Frank checked his watch. "Awesome. Hang on, I'm supposed to meet with Donnie about something in two minutes." Frank leaned to the side and shouted past Cliff: "Donnie!"

"Yeah?" Donnie yelled from behind the closed door of his office, across the hall.

"Can we push back that meeting for ten minutes?"

"What?"

"Our meeting. Can you gimme like ten, fifteen minutes?"

There was a pause while Donnie walked over to Frank's office. "We put intercom speakers into our phones for *literally* this very purpose. Why do you always yell across the house?"

"Sorry." Frank leaned over and pressed the button on his

phone labeled with a small sticker of Donatello from *Teenage Mutant Ninja Turtles*. The phone chirped, and Frank spoke into the speaker, "Donnie, I need to talk with Cliff. Can you meet in ten minutes?"

"Actually," Cliff said, "we may need a bit longer. Maybe an hour?"

Donnie sighed. "I have to meet someone then. We can't meet now?"

Frank started to ask Cliff if he could come back, but Cliff cut him off: "We actually have to do this now." He looked at Donnie: "Sorry man. Kind of time sensitive."

"Fine. But I don't want to keep putting this off."

When he heard Donnie's office door shut, Cliff handed Frank a piece of paper with handwritten information. "Two things. First, we're all set for a drop off." He recounted the phone call to Frank and gave him all the details for the transaction—Friday at 5 p.m. "I wrote out all the ones he wants to look at just to make sure it matches what you have."

Frank nodded, looking at the sheet of paper. "Two grand per part? Man, why didn't we do this sooner? I've made enough for four funerals off two bodies."

Cliff's cell phone chirped. "You realize you'll have to eventually account for all this money, right?" Cliff asked, scanning his screen.

"One step at a time. What's the other thing you have to tell me?"

"Our guy is here to pick up the shoes."

"You said he wasn't coming until tomorrow. Did you tell him what happened?"

"Nope. There's been a change of plan. He just pulled up."

34

Michael Sims was walking up the front steps when Frank and Cliff opened the front door. Michael wore a Tennessee Titans hat with sunglasses. The hunter green polo and dark brown shorts looked to be a size too small for his biceps and quads. Michael glanced up and recognized Cliff, nodding his head, and then shifted his gaze to Frank.

"Frank Burgers?"

"Hey. Mr. Sims, right?"

"Yeah. Call me Michael." The two shook hands. "Sorry for the short notice on the time change. I had a meeting come up in Nashville tomorrow—is this okay?"

Frank looked around the lot and at the clients working in the gym. No one was watching. "Let's go in my office."

Michael put his keys and glasses into his hat and laid the bundle on Frank's desk, taking a seat in the chair nearby. He offered another thanks for meeting last minute and indicated that he did have cash in the car, where he preferred to make the switch. Frank started to sit at his desk but instead moved over to the bookshelf and pulled a shoebox from the top. He could hear Michael mutter something to himself as he watched him place the black box on a pile of folders.

Cliff was still standing by the door when Frank turned around and said he needed to be quick because of a meeting with his brother.

"That's fine with me," Michael added. "The quicker we do this, the better, you know?"

"It's not that easy, actually," Frank took a seat on his desk, folding his arms. "Cliff, you wanna tell him?"

"Nah," Cliff replied.

"What's wrong? Did something happen? Those are the shoes, right?"

Cliff now crossed his arms and shrugged. "Eh. Yes and no."

"We had a bit of a problem—unavoidable, really." Frank saw panic come over Michael's face. "Nothing to do with the police—no one saw what happened—but the shoes were . . ."

"Maybe you should show him first, and then explain," Cliff offered.

"Yeah, show me first, then explain. What happened?"

Michael ripped off the box's top the moment it touched his hands. The shoes were wrapped in a towel as if to preserve their superiority and appearance, but their appearance was anything but superior. Michael stared at the shoes for a long and uncomfortable moment before he reached in to pull one out.

He let the corroded shoe hang from his fingertips as if it were a handkerchief Frank had just sneezed in. Much of the mud had been wiped off, but the shoe's exterior was still slightly damp. Michael lifted the lace with his finger. The moisture apparently registered to his sense of touch. He started patting the shoe with the back of his hands.

"The coffin had a leak. A big leak," Frank said.

"Whole thing had rotted through," Cliff said. "I ended up stepping into it . . . about three times."

"How? He's not been dead that long. How could it have rotted?"

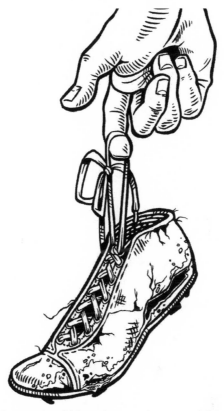

"I don't know. Could have been a cheap model or just a fluke buy," Frank said.

Michael examined the other shoe, feeling over the apparel's surface. "I don't even see the signature."

"It's on the other one, on the sole."

"You can't even see it," Michael said.

"If Joe signed it, it wouldn't have been in a marker. That's probably pen ink," Cliff said. He pointed to a mark on the flat of the shoe. "You can tell that it's got writing on it, but unfortunately there's no way to tell what it says."

"I don't believe this." Michael sighed, dropping the box and the shoe into his lap. He let out a groan as his forehead fell into the palm of his hand, resting on the chair's armrest. Frank and Cliff stood quiet, allowing him time to process what he was seeing, and now realizing. "I almost would prefer . . ." he began and paused. "Man, I feel like it would have been better if they weren't in there. At least I would have had some hope, you know?" Frank nodded. "I mean . . . the shoes are real. I'm holding *shoes* signed by Shoeless Joe Jackson—likely one of the coolest, most sought after signatures in the sports world—on a baseball cleat, no less! A hundred grand, easy. Except . . ." He lifted the box. "It's not what I'm holding, ya know? This is Joe Jackson's signature, but it's not. All I'm holding now are an old pair of stained, ruined, history-less—worthless—shoes. What the hell happened down there?"

"Show him the pictures," Cliff said.

Frank pulled out his phone and passed it over. "So, if you scroll left, there's four pictures of the inside and the mud. The ground was dry until about four feet down, then it was like we were in a marsh. Those yellow, brownish looking pieces all over the ground are pieces of the coffin that had broken off—or rotted—with all that water."

"What's this?"

"Oh, sorry," Frank said, "you went back too far. That was before everything went south, when Cliff was climbing down into the grave. Seemed funny at the time."

Michael handed the phone back and stood up, not taking his eyes off the box. "Man, this definitely ruins a whole-lotta plans. Puts me in a bit of a bind too with some buyers. What am I supposed to do with these?"

"Up to you," Frank said. "Honestly, I'd get rid of them. Just in case police come looking, there's no reason to be a suspect over a pair of rotten shoes."

"Wait. You said no one knew where those shoes were, right? So, no one should know to come looking for them?" Cliff said. "Bodies are buried without shoes all the time. If they investigate, nothing will be out of the ordinary."

"Yeah, he's probably right though. No point in keeping—" Michael stopped and shot a glance to the door behind where Cliff was standing. Cliff's face registered the same surprise.

"What?" Frank asked.

"You hear that? There was a . . . like a creak out there," Cliff whispered.

"Yeah, it's a hallway in an old house. Donnie was probably walking by."

"No. This was something else." Cliff opened the door.

"Nothing?" Michael asked. "We good?"

Cliff poked his head into the hallway, "Yeah. Sounded like someone was standing right outside the door." He stepped out into the foyer and peeked into Donnie's office, which was empty.

Michael picked up his keys and put on his hat. He moved toward the door, tucking the box under his arm when Cliff stepped back inside, and took a seat. "Alright, well, this was depressing." He shook hands with Frank. "Thanks again."

"No problem. If you come across any more family members who are buried with expensive items, gimme a call."

Michael didn't smile at the joke. "This is awkward to bring up, but what do you want to do about money?"

"Not awkward at all. Do you need help bringing it in? Or should I go out with you?" Frank asked.

"Wait, sorry, I'm talking about your money. The fifteen grand."

"Yeah . . ."

Michael looked at Cliff and back to Frank: "The fifteen grand I gave you."

"What are you talking about?" Cliff asked.

"I want it back. The money I paid you before."

"Uh . . . no . . . ?" Cliff said.

"I paid you guys fifteen up front to get a pair of signed Joe Jackson shoes." Michael held up the box. "These aren't it."

"You offered us fifteen grand to *dig up* a pair of Joe Jackson shoes. That was what we agreed on."

"Cliff, I offered that to you believing I would fetch a hundred for the shoes. I don't have that money," Michael said.

"Well, we're not giving it back to you just because you didn't get what you wanted. We still did our job."

"Hang on a second," Frank cut in. "We agreed on *thirty* to dig up those shoes. Are you trying to get out of paying us the rest of our deal?"

"You think I'm going to pay you another fifteen grand for this?" Michael laughed. "You're out of your mind!"

Cliff stood up from his chair. Frank could always tell Cliff's intimidation pose because he seemed to grow about five inches and his neck disappeared. The glare in his eyes was menacing. "Yo. I don't care what your financial situation is, you owe us fifteen thousand dollars. Now, I'm gon' need you to go out to your car and bring that inside—right now."

"Or what? What are you gonna to do? Call the cops?"

Frank could feel the anxiety bubbling in his stomach. Cliff had been challenged, but Michael was right—what could they do? Frank saw him take a step toward Michael, maybe as a last resort of intimidation.

"Cliff, if you touch me, I swear to God, *I will* go to the police," Michael said. "Give me my money back."

Frank nervously laughed. "I'm not giving you that money back. We did our j—"

In a flash, Michael advanced on Frank to grab him by the shirt collar and shove him back toward the wall. "Give me my money back! Give it to me!"

"Hey, hey, hey! Yo! Michael! Yo!" Cliff pulled him off Frank with one arm and moved him back toward the door, standing in front of him like a barrier. "Yo, what the hell is wrong with you?"

"I need that money, Cliff," Michael exclaimed, frantically trying to get past. Cliff effortlessly held Michael back as his arms flailed to break free. In his excitement, one of his hands whacked Cliff across the head—Michael froze. Cliff bit his lip and groaned. Frank saw him instantly drop his arms and take in a deep breath through his nose. His eyes closed as he clinched his fists and exhaled. Cliff opened his eyes, grimly staring at Michael

"Oh, balls," Frank whispered. Despite his size and swollen body mass, Cliff, in Frank's eyes, was one of the kindest and most genuinely caring guys Frank had ever known. But he had one rule: never hit him in the head. Playful or not—the impact on his skull from any sort of hand contact ignited something in his brain that potentially ruined his entire day, and quite possibly the offender's day. Frank moved around to stand in front of Cliff, his eyes had become maniacal. "You alright?"

"*Get the hell out!*" Cliff said, stepping toward Michael.

"I'm sorry man. I didn't mean to h—"

Cliff shoved him, hard, against the door frame sending a shockwave throughout the room—and likely the house. Michael connected with the edge of the door frame and stumbled into the hallway, onto the ground. Two trophies and a collection of Frank's old He-Man toys on a shelf above the window toppled to the hardwood floor.

"Are you out of your mind? What the hell?" Michael yelled, getting up from the floor. Frank could see Michael rearing back to throw a punch and simultaneously yelled "Whoa, stop!" Cliff leaned out of the way to slip the jab. He obviously anticipated the combination because he avoided the cross coming toward his face, and when Michael finally attempted an uppercut—in the blink of an eye—Cliff grabbed his wrist and stretched Michael's arm out into an arm bar. Then, before Frank—or Michael—could react, Cliff whirled him around into a front headlock. Despite Michael's build, and obvious signs of muscular strength, he looked like no more than a child beside the Filipino gym owner. Cliff stood with Michael's body bent over in front of Frank, the head locked in at his side.

"Michael." Cliff paused. "I'm gonna need you to leave. Now."

Michael cursed and then tried to say something to Cliff, but Cliff flexed his arm, cutting off Michael's windpipe for a second. Michael waved his arms and tried to kick, but it was no use. Cliff pulled him into the foyer and toward the front door. "Frank slide him his keys and the shoe box." Frank did; the keys came to a stop under Cliff's foot. "First. I'm sorry I shoved you.

That was rude," Cliff said. Michael tried to respond but Cliff cut him off. "I'm not gonna fight you. Get your stuff and get out of here. Pick'em up." Michael reached toward the floor and grabbed the box and the keys. Cliff then opened the front door and released his grip, forcing him outside onto the porch. Michael took in a big breath and swore again, rubbing his neck.

Cliff held up his hands in surrender. "I'm sorry, alright? I shouldn't have shoved you. But you need to go."

"It was a freakin accident, dick! I wasn't tryin to swing at you!"

"Go home." Cliff went to close the door.

"I'm getting that money from your boy," Michael blurted out.

Cliff held the door open and stepped onto the porch, slowly. Michael immediately backed up and down the steps as Cliff came toward him. He stared at him for a long while and then said: "You sure about that?" Michael looked from Cliff to Frank who was now standing in the doorway. He finally shook his head, cursed again, and got into his car.

The two of them watched his car pull away.

"What are we supposed to do about that money?" Frank asked.

Cliff turned around. "Not a lot we can do. Let me know if he tries anything. I'll take care of it."

THURSDAY

35

The stiff gentleman wearing the Lone Ranger shirt, unconsciously contributing his left humerus and large right femur, brought the limb count to the desired total of six. The items for sale were packed into four coolers of varying sizes, iced down for preservation and hidden behind bins of Christmas decorations beneath the main stairwell until the transaction took place on Friday. The mannequin arm Frank had swiped from the town's Playhouse Theatre—with the shirt's long sleeves—hid the top mutilation well should the wife decide she needed to see her husband again.

To Frank's surprise, Mrs. Clark kept her composure well, as did her two sons who were very polite and well spoken. Their presence brought a noticeable comfort for their grieving mom. Frank could tell she was both pleased and taken aback by the turnout—quite a bit larger than she anticipated. She admitted to him and her children later that some of the guests she had failed to invite because she thought they were dead.

Many guests, hearing about the man's death through word of mouth, traveled in to offer their condolences. Along with extended family, the man's best friend from college traveled from Ashville, North Carolina. He walked into the room with the gusto of a man half his age on the knees of a teenager, wearing a slim fitting black suit and tie: Mrs. Clark hardly recognized him. He'd come alone and stood near Frank and Donnie much of the time, recounting stories from his and the deceased's younger days. Frank welcomed any distraction to help take his mind off the gruesome situation inside the casket.

The man's best friend, and the oldest son, did ask for the coffin to be opened. Donnie deferred to the wife's wish to have no viewing. At one point, Frank thought the youngest son was going to open it himself—he wanted to see the Lone Ranger shirt that his father was wearing. He didn't believe that someone could really be buried in just a shirt. Donnie explained that a suit or gown was normal, but it was something left strictly up to the client.

"On one occasion," Frank recalled, "a man asked me if his wife could be buried naked," The son laughed. Frank said it would have been highly inappropriate and he didn't allow it, but he had buried people in all kinds of attire. "Wife beaters—which is apparently *inappropriate* to say now—superhero costumes, sports jerseys, a clown outfit. Even buried a construction worker in his full get-up with the tool belt and tons of expensive tools."

Donnie made miniature pizzas for the family after the graveside service. Several people commented to Donnie that he needed to open his own place and asked about his history in the food business, which Donnie was more than happy to expound upon. The two Clark boys—foodies—were captivated by the food and stories, of which Donnie had a million. The younger son said he would write about the funeral experience on his blog when he returned home.

"This is the craziest funeral setup I've ever seen. You guys

have food, you have cornhole—and did I see a Nintendo 64
and an NES hooked up to the TV in the family room?"

Frank smiled. "Yeah, man. Goldeneye and Mario Kart still
hold up."

"Plus, this is the best pizza in town," he commented. "You
really don't mind if I write up a review?"

"Nah, go ahead. You're out in Nashville right?"

"Yeah. It's obviously not gonna bring in business but it gives
me something to write about."

"I'll take all the positive press I can get," Donnie replied.

The Clark boys stayed well after everyone had left, playing pool
with Frank and Donnie, until Frank confessed that he needed to start cleaning up. They thanked the Burgers brothers for
their work, and the youngest reminded them to subscribe to his
blog and hit him up the next time they were in Nashville.

Donnie's hand gripped the doorknob, which had managed
to stay in place all day, as he stood on the porch near his brother,
waving. He jiggled it in his hand and looked at Frank, who was
stretching his arms upward and yawning, and gently closed the
door. "Hey. What are you about to do?"

"Go clean up, why?"

"Can we talk?"

Frank sighed. "I'd really like to get everything picked up;
Mom's already started. Can we do this later?"

"We can, I just feel like we're not going to. Kind of like this
doorknob. I asked about getting it fixed a week ago, and it's still
hanging by a thread."

"Ugh. Yeah, I promise, I'll do that tonight." Frank heard the footsteps coming before the front door creaked open. "Hey, Mom."

"Don't 'hey Mom' me. Those boys pulled away five minutes ago. Get in here and help pick up. We have a viewing this evening and I don't want people showing up with the house looking like it does. Cliff's in the kitchen doing dishes and he doesn't even work here." She turned to walk back toward the kitchen, leaving the door open.

"Can we do this later?" Frank asked, stepping inside. "Promise."

Donnie, unsatisfied, put his hands into his pockets and moved toward the door to follow his brother toward the kitchen. "Okay."

36

Monty couldn't explain his sixth sense, and with one exception, he never brought it up. He'd endured enough ridicule from his stutter. Throwing in his sense of premonition based upon something that was probably nothing more than gas could make conversations more awkward.

At first, Monty thought his sensations were signs or symptoms of various illnesses, stress, or—even at one point—stomach cancer. But over time he began to pursue the "song of his bowels," as Sophia called it, and respond when it signaled him. At the first sign of churning, Monty trained himself to act in whatever way his mind encouraged him, whether it was in response to a dangerous situation or simply touching base with an individual.

Monty hesitantly explained the gut feelings to Sophia at her request—and continual nagging—late one night at the coffee shop and was relieved by her positive response. She didn't think it odd at all, believing that it was Monty's subconscious responding to all the thought and research he'd done. Sophia insisted that most people had a similar ability but were likely too distracted to use or understand it.

The feeling normally came at the most unusual—even difficult—of times. Tonight, it was while Monty was filling his cruiser with gas at the station just outside of Murray on 641. A red truck roared past, startling Monty away from watching the numbers calculate on the screen. The truck, alone on the road, sped a little too fast down the open highway away from Murray, and his stomach instantly dropped and gurgled. The gas pump clicked off, but Monty stood still for several seconds holding the nozzle and watching the red truck until it moved out of sight. His mind conjured up Frank Burgers, and his odd trip to Almo.

He replaced the nozzle onto the pump and got into his car, unable to stop the feeling in the back of his mind that his "hunch" was really no such thing. Perhaps it would be a waste to drive back out to Almo. It was the normal two-minute game of mental ping-pong Monty played before he finally, always, decided to follow his gut.

The light of the fading sun struggled to break through the trees as Monty drove up the wooded path to Marlowe Cemetery but shone brightly on the open lot as he came to a stop at the hill's peak. He parked his cruiser and scanned the lots from inside. Nothing appeared out of the ordinary; everything was the same as before. His stomach thumped again, letting out a growl. It wasn't until he stepped out of the car and shut the door that the fresh mound of dirt came into clear view. "Son of a bitch," he whispered.

Monty ran over to the grave marker: *Myles Hamm*. He took out his phone to snap some pictures of the site before calling it in to dispatch through his radio, then began walking the lot looking for any evidence that may have been left behind.

Dispatch came back shortly with confusion regarding Monty's description.

"It's not a new burial," Monty replied. "I was up here two days ago, and the grave was fine. N-n-notify the family and see if we can s-s-start digging." There was more pushback on the idea of digging up a corpse. "We had two incidents this month. If this is another one, I w-w-want to get as much information as we can or at least see what this guy is after."

The Murray Police Department sent over a team to investigate the cemetery disturbance—which Monty had already done—but to his dismay, there would be no talk of exhumation until the following morning. It was nearly ten o'clock that evening before he pulled back onto 641, but not in the direction of home; he was going to the diner. At first, he convinced himself that he was hungry and needed a bite to eat. Then, he told himself that Sophia may be able to tell him something about the Burgers brothers—she had grown up in Murray and knew everyone. Monty told himself whatever he had to in order to outweigh the real reason—he just wanted to see her.

He pulled into the diner's lot and looked down at the shrink-wrapped item laying in the brown Amazon box on the floor-board. *She'll like it. It's not too much. Just give it to her, you idiot.* He picked up the package and stepped out into the sultry night air. He removed his tan, button-down shirt and put on a t-shirt before closing the door. He walked up to the door and instinctively reached out his hand to grab hold of the handle when it opened forward onto his arm, startling him to step back. The young woman leaving in a rush kept her head down, but she was courteous enough to say "Excuse me," as she walked past.

"Sophia?" Monty asked.

She turned around. Monty could see that Sophia was crying.

She snuffled and exhaled as she tried to wipe her tears away with the back of her hand.

"Hey," she said. "Sorry. Didn't mean to bump into you."

"You okay?" Monty asked. He looked behind him to see if anyone was following her out or watching from inside; they weren't. "What's wrong?"

"Nothing. I'm okay. Sorry, but . . ." She turned her head away from him, again drawing her hand up to wipe her face. "I have to run home. Family emergency."

"Anything I can do?" he asked, wishing he could communicate with her telepathically, though unsure of what he would say if he could.

"No, I'm okay. Just a crisis at home. My husband Nick thinks he ran over our dog when he came home. It's a big dog . . . Elvis . . . a Rottweiler. Nick needs help getting him inside . . ." She dug into her purse for her keys.

"Sophia," Monty said. She looked up but kept her eyes away from his. She turned her head away, and then glanced back down at her purse, though no longer fidgeting around inside of it. Something told him that this story wasn't entirely accurate. His stomach was doing cartwheels. "Everything's okay?"

She nodded, but didn't speak at first. Her head turned toward the basketball arena across the street. "I'm okay. I promise."

"Alright," Monty said, hesitantly.

"I need to go," she said.

He reached into his wallet and pulled out a card. He held out his arm to her, but he didn't advance. "Here," he said. She stared at it for a moment, then back down at her bag. "This is my card. If I can do anything, let me know." Sophia nodded and took the card, still not meeting his eyes. "Or if you need help with the dog—lifting it or getting it to the vet—I have a truck. I'm happy to come by."

"Okay," she whispered. "I need to go. Thank you . . . for this." She held up the card and placed it in her bag. "Good night."

"Night Sophia."

Monty's contrived hunger faded as he watched Sophia's car turn onto the main road and disappear into the darkness. He sat down in his car and turned on the ignition, unable to shake the feeling of embarrassment as he stared at the unopened Amazon Kindle box resting in his lap.

FRIDAY

37

The Burgers Brothers' Family Funeral Home averaged roughly one funeral per week. There were times when Frank would go ten days without planning a service, but on rare occasions he could have three in one week. Today there would be three services in *twelve hours*. The first would bring the largest attendance for a young father and teacher at Murray High School who had lost the battle to brain cancer. The wife had ordered Frank's most prestigious package which included a meal for family and close friends—twenty people. Donnie awoke a little after seven to start the meal prep and Frank cleaned the parlor following the viewing the night before and set up for the next service.

Frank assured his brother they could handle the turnout, but confidence did little to keep Donnie's anxiety at bay when the school busses began pulling up with students. Instead of dealing with his questions and doubts, Frank called Cliff and encouraged Donnie to stay in the kitchen and work on getting the grills set up while he ran the service. The parlor sat seventy-five comfortably. Frank—with Cliff's help—crammed a hundred into the pews. In the back and on the sides were another fifty high schoolers standing or sitting in the aisles. He cranked the air conditioner down as far as it would go and kept the service to under thirty minutes. This minimized the discomfort of everyone in the cramped room and allowed the students to pay their respects before they got back on the bus to return to school.

Frank accompanied the family out to their cars for the graveside, making sure to lead them through the back entrance near Donnie, who had the grills running. The aroma from the shortribs and chicken being prepared was already carrying through the house and giving the guests a needed distraction. Frank could hear many of them inhale deeply through their nose and whisper expletives of joy over the smell.

A young woman was standing in the kitchen talking on her phone as Donnie stepped back in from the patio with a plate of meat. He recognized her from high school but couldn't recall her name. She moved the phone down to her neck and asked where she should set up. Donnie figured Frank hired her for help and so he directed her down the hall toward parlor two.

He called Frank for an ETA.

"Already on my way back. Is Addy there?" Frank asked.

"No, why?"

"He's supposed to do the next two services. I can't get a hold of him. I've tried four times since I left."

"Sorry. Mom and I have everything just about set up if you want to bring the side dishes back to the parlor when you get here. See you in a bit."

Addy was scheduled to lead the service for family two, while Frank stayed with family one in the parlor room for lunch, but Addy never showed. Frank had no choice then but to recruit Donnie for assistance and put Ginny in charge of hosting family one. Addy's notes had been emailed to Frank the day before—in case of such an emergency. Thankfully, there were less than twenty in attendance. He and Donnie quickly ran through the order of service with the daughter of the deceased. Donnie ran the songs and slideshow, and Frank led the service and delivered the prepared eulogy. They tag-teamed the graveside ceremony with a prayer and word of encouragement for the family.

By the time they returned, the guitarist was finishing up her final song, "One Headlight" by The Wallflowers. Frank checked his phone for time and loaded a few of the remaining hors d'oeuvres onto a small plate. He pulled up a seat next to Donnie in the back and watched the girl finish out her set. She was noticeably singing to the wife who was sitting at the table beside her, clutching a tissue, and mouthing the words of the song.

"You remember her, right?" Frank asked his brother.

"Yeah," Donnie said. "Tiffanie, right? I didn't realize she could play guitar. I wonder how she knows the family."

"Does she know the family?" Frank asked.

"I guess so. They hired her."

"I hired her," Frank said.

"Are you serious?" Donnie asked. "Why?"

"It's part of the package they ordered; they get a singer for the reception. Have you *really* not read my pamphlets?"

"Guess not," Donnie said. "Probably the only funeral home with an on-call guitarist."

"I hope so," Frank said. Everyone clapped when she finished the song. The singer leaned forward on the stool to bow then promptly stepped over to hug and sit with the wife.

"Addy still isn't here?" Cliff questioned as he walked up behind Frank, gripping his shoulders before pulling up a chair beside him.

"No, did you talk to him?" Frank asked.

"No. Can't reach him," Cliff replied.

Frank could see that Donnie was scrolling through his social media on his phone. He turned away and leaned in close to Cliff. "I need your help with the next one. You free?"

"This is the cremation guy, right?"

"Yeah. Nothing too difficult. I have to make a switch."

"I've got a couple coming in around the time you start, but it's only for an evaluation—probably take forty-five minutes. What do you need me to do?"

"Just a simple diversion. I need to switch the coffin *with* the body for the coffin *without* the body."

Cliff stared ahead and nodded slowly in agreement. "What are you going to do if someone wants to open it?"

"They won't. You got a second to come downstairs?"

Frank walked Cliff through what he had planned: At the end of the next funeral, they would lead the pallbearers out the back entrance instead of the front, where there would be two hearses parked—away from everyone else's vehicles. The body would be loaded into hearse A, and once that was done, Frank wanted Cliff to lead the pallbearers back inside, gather everyone to the front, then give instructions on the procession. Frank would then jump into hearse B—already prepared with the empty coffin of the same style—and drive around front to follow behind the police escort. Cliff would then have to signal Frank to pull around when everyone was ready. From there, at the graveside, Frank would conduct a quick ceremony in Addy's place and by six p.m. he would be twenty grand richer—minus Cliff's cut for helping.

It was not long after the service ended that Frank realized his *simple* plan would not be so easily executed.

On the way out to the parking lot, one of the pallbearers started to make conversation with Frank about his kids, then asked if his oldest kid could ride in the hearse with Frank. In the hundreds of funerals that Frank had been a part of, a pallbearer had never struck up a conversation with him mid-procession to the hearse.

Frank directed the pallbearers as they lifted the coffin onto the hearse, and finally replied to the man, giving him a line about insurance and liability the father seemed to buy. He closed the hatch and gave Cliff a thumbs up, who was standing on the patio. Cliff motioned for everyone to come inside.

Frank moved over to hearse B and jammed his key into the lock, but it wouldn't turn. He was too preoccupied with the switch to realize he grabbed the red keys instead of the green. He groaned and jogged back inside to grab the key off the inside ring but returned to find the father from before standing next to hearse A with a boy that Frank guessed was the oldest son.

"He loves these things. You mind if he just gets in with you?" the father asked. By this point the boy was already sitting in the passenger seat of the hearse that had the *body*. "He wanted to see what the inside looked like."

"Yeah, that's fine. Have at it."

The kid asked if he could sit in the driver's seat. The dad looked to Frank for approval. Frank checked his watch; Cliff still had not come around to give the signal. Frank nodded. "Where'd the interest in hearses come from?" Frank asked.

"I think it's just a curiosity of death. When I told him we were going to a funeral, the first thing he asked about was the long black car. He's only seen this stuff in movies." Cliff appeared and shot a thumbs up indicating that the police escort had arrived. Frank motioned to the father that it was time to head out.

"Would it be okay if he just sat up here with you as you pulled out and then you let him get out at the end of the drive?"

Jeez, guy. Come on. Cliff motioned again. When the father turned his head away toward his son, Frank threw up his arms to Cliff, pointed to the man, then pantomimed a strangling.

Donnie, who was now standing in the driveway up ahead, started to walk over as Frank explained to the father why his oddball son could not ride in the passenger seat, even if it was for a quarter mile. Insurance wouldn't allow it.

"It's the driveway," the man said.

"Hey, the police escort is up front," Donnie said. "Everything okay?"

"Yeah. I'm just explaining why we aren't allowed to let kids ride in hearses anymore." Frank turned back to the father. "Even though it's the driveway, it's still a legality thing. Friend of mine in Nashville had a similar request from a dad. He let the kid drive the hearse up the driveway, not knowing that the guy was a cop. Put the guy under arrest right there."

"What?"

"Yeah, funeral directors are notorious for giving ride-alongs and it's a big insurance deal. States have started implementing secret funeral attenders to test the homes and directors. You know how sometimes the state will have undercover reps show up at bars to try and get them to serve drinks to a minor? Same thing, except for us it's with kids in the hearses. We really have to be careful."

When the father walked away, Donnie was shaking his head,

looking at the ground. "Wasn't easier to just let the kid ride with you?"

"You know I don't like kids riding in the hearse with me. It's awkward."

"Addy's here. He's inside talking; said he'll do the graveside if you still want him to."

"Where's he been?" Frank asked.

"Overslept. He was up all night with some lady who attends his church. That's all he said."

"So, a booty call."

"Probably." Donnie chuckled. "Nah, something happened with her family and he said he had to be there all night. He'll hop in when you pull up."

"Alright, tell him I'm on my way," Frank said, opening the door of hearse A to get in. "Not that I really need him now; the hard part is over." Frank waited for Donnie to turn and start walking back toward the house before he closed the driver's door and walked over to the other hearse. He sat down and turned on the ignition, promptly clicking the down arrow on the AC settings. He clicked his seatbelt into to the lock and shifted into drive before looking up to see Donnie standing in front of the hood. Frank cursed out loud and brought his window down. "What are you doin'?"

"I was wondering the same thing. Why are you driving this car?"

"Because . . . we have a graveside service," Frank replied, as if Donnie was stupid for even asking.

"Body's in that car." Donnie pointed over to hearse A. "You want to explain why there are two caskets sitting out here in our hearses?"

Frank tucked his lips between his teeth.

"Where's the body, Frank?"

Frank turned and looked at the other hearse and back at his brother. "Can we talk about this later? I don't want to keep them waiting."

"Nope."

"Fine, you got me. Okay? It's a weighted coffin. Some-one . . ." Frank sighed. "Someone bought the other body."

"Come on, Frank . . ." Donnie muttered.

"It's not what you think. Trust me," Frank replied. "It's really not that bad when you hear the story."

"I'm done." Donnie flicked his wrists out and held up his hands in surrender. "I'm done. I told you that if you kept at it, I was gonna either leave or turn you in. And, you couldn't have enough respect for me as your brother—let alone a partner—to give it a rest. Or to even talk to me about other ideas."

"I'm going to discuss this—"

"I've asked you like four times to talk with me about this stuff and you keep blowing me off. So, I'm out. You're on your own. If anyone asks why the exterior design on this coffin looks different than the one they *just* saw inside, I'm going to tell them the truth."

"Donnie. I'm not blowing you off. You just never catch me at a good time."

"Well, your time's up. So, good luck in jail . . . or going out of business . . . whichever comes first."

"We'll talk, okay? We'll talk!" Donnie was already walking away, and Frank opened the door to get out of the car. "This isn't a new project. It's he—aagh!" The seatbelt caught him getting out. He unclicked it and closed the door. "It's for Bill Cobb, alright?" Donnie stopped walking and turned back toward Frank. "I did call him and tell him I couldn't do it but when I kept hearing that the Kochs were sabotaging our business, I took the deal. I called him the day after you told me about it." Donnie glanced up the driveway at the assortment of cars waiting to leave. "Look, Bill gave us a lot of money, and he technically did it well before you came home. I already had it planned out before I dropped the job, but when you said he was going to pay more, after what Vince and Randy did, I couldn't pass that up."

Donnie shook his head and began moving away, but Frank continued: "You're right, I don't want to keep putting our family at risk. And you're right, I went behind your back—again. I promise I was going to tell you soon, but for right now, please, don't walk out. Give me another chance: I'll listen to your ideas, I'll drop the body part sales and the grave robbing. Please. I'll talk about the deal with the dick head brothers, whatever you want."

Donnie began moving toward Frank; he approached him slowly, keeping his voice low. "We sit down and talk in the next twenty-four hours or I'm leaving Monday. And if that cop shows up again before I leave, I *will* turn you in."

"You got it. Done. Thank you."

Donnie turned and walked back toward the house.

Frank started up the driveway. His shirt was sticking to his body—the sweat likely from a mix of anxiety and Kentucky summer swelter. He put the air conditioning on full blast. Addy was standing outside and got into the passenger seat.

"Before you start," Addy began, holding up his hand, "don't start."

"I was just going to ask if you wanted some gum," Frank replied.

"Mmmhmm. I am really sorry."

"What happened? Donnie said someone had a family emergency?"

"Nah. Not really an emergency, just a bad situation. I got called over to someone's house late last night to help out with something and ended up being there until after five. Disaster."

"Everything alright?"

Addy let out a yawn. "Not really, but I did all I can do."

Frank inched forward and signaled to the police officer that he was ready.

"You okay to handle the graveside?" Frank asked. Addy nodded, taking a sip of his coffee, and motioned for him to go on.

The final hiccup came just before they lowered the empty casket into the grave. The husband—not Bill Cobb—wished to see his wife one last time. Frank noticed him awkwardly stand up during Addy's prayer, and as Addy was giving his final instructions to the handful of family members under the tent, Frank saw that he was inching closer to the coffin. The moment Addy dismissed everyone, the man reached out to touch the lid and began fingering the lip and around the sides, searching for the latch to open it.

"Mr. King, what's wrong?"

He was startled but not deterred. His response was matter of fact, as if inspecting a product before he bought it. "Just need to get one more look at her before she goes."

Frank said his name two more times with no response before resting a hand on his shoulder, and finally on Mr. King's hand as he tried to pry the top open. He spoke in a low voice, as not to alert anyone else to the scene. He turned his back to the crowd. For all anyone knew, they were discussing last night's Cardinals game.

"I'm sorry Mr. King," Frank said, "once your wife is placed in her final resting place, we try not to reopen her casket out of respect for her." Frank was unsure of how this would go down. Opening the casket again wasn't a big deal—and on any other day he would be more than happy to. But not today. Not when his wife had been replaced by a dark-skinned Asian blowup doll.

The husband didn't draw away from Frank's hand, but instead continued with the other hand looking hopelessly for how to open the lid. Frank tightened his grip, getting the man's attention, but it only exacerbated his efforts. The exchange quickly turned into a struggle as the husband began groaning at the casket, calling for Frank to let him go, and pounding on the casket's top. The man forcibly drew his hand away from Frank's and latched on to the casket as if giving it a hug, screaming for someone to open the top. Frank tried to grab the man by his waist to pull him off before he accidentally knocked over the standing arrangement of flowers nearby. Addy took hold of the arm to urge him off the casket.

Frank registered that someone was screaming behind him, but couldn't make out the words over the man's cries. He felt a hand push him off the husband and saw a woman, not much older than the woman he was supposed to bury, take hold of the man's suit coat and yank him back. Whether it was her voice or the strength of the pull, the husband finally gave up his attempts and stood up to face the woman. Frank now recognized that it was the deceased's sister. Her words were sharp and inaudible. The man looked around at the remaining crowd, panting for breath as she talked, then locked eyes with Frank. Frank could see tears running down his red cheeks.

The sister placed her hand around her brother-in-law's arm and instantly Frank saw his head starting to sway. His eyes glazed over and rolled slightly upward just before the lids closed. His leg tried to step forward but ended up stepping sideways away from the casket—*thank God*—just before giving out, sending him in a dead fall toward the ground. Frank only had to brace himself and hold out his arms to catch the guy.

Two of the sons and their spouses ran over as Frank laid him down gently on the grass and started to fan him with notes from an earlier funeral.

Nearly all the guests had departed before the man came to. His children and Frank helped him to his car. Frank brought him a bottle of Gatorade from the cooler in his car and the man made a joke that he preferred blue and laughed. He confessed that he was ashamed of how he had acted. Frank assured him the heat and emotions over his wife passing were more than enough to cause anyone to faint, though the assurance did little to quell the man's embarrassment over causing a scene.

Frank waved goodbye as the final car drove off. He heard the car door close behind him and the ignition start. Addy was sitting in the front seat, trying to take off his tie. It was done! He did it! Frank put his hands on his hips and went back toward the car, unable to stop laughing.

38

On one hand Frank appreciated that he didn't have to drive to Land Between the Lakes at night to conduct this transaction. On the other hand, he wasn't comfortable exchanging body parts for money in broad daylight at a public campground.

He arrived ten minutes early to a full parking lot with plenty of families and couples scattered around the park. It was way more crowded than the last time they met. Many adults were playing volleyball on the small beach and swimming in the lake's shore. Several kids ran in the open areas—in and out of the water—throwing balls and squirting each other with guns. The picnic tables were full of people enjoying coolers packed full of food. He didn't have a reason to be nervous. Why would anyone suspect he had six body parts in his truck bed on ice, prepped and ready for sale?

It was just about the time for the day's peak heat, and unless he was going for a swim in that lake, which he might, there was no need to get out of the air-conditioned truck. He played a game on his phone until a black Honda Accord pulled into the lot and slowly made its way over. Lock and load, Frank thought.

This time there were four guys instead of the two Frank remembered from before. All but the one in the passenger seat stepped out of the car. None of them said more than "hey." Frank offered his hand to the buyer, but the man walked past, acting as if he didn't see it, and asked where the stuff was.

Frank pulled down the hatch and retrieved the four coolers from the cab. He motioned for the guy to take a look. Two of the others moved in behind Frank and the buyer to cover the examination and act as lookouts, though no one in the campground seemed to pay them any attention. The buyer opened each cooler and signaled the other two to examine the parts. Frank couldn't understand a word they were saying. He guessed they were speaking Russian, but to him Russian sounded no different than French. They would nod, grunt, sometimes chuckle. When the buyer opened the cooler with the left femur, Frank understood a word: "No." He heard "no" again when he picked up the arm to examine the radius bone. The man then indicated which ones he wanted to purchase.

"You mind me asking what you're using this stuff for?" Frank asked.

"Project," the man replied. *Boom!* The passenger door slammed closed *on Frank's truck.* The man who stayed in the Accord was standing beside it, looking back at Frank.

"Did you just look in my truck?" Frank asked.

"He doesn't speak English," the buyer replied. He said something in his language to the man, who nodded and walked back to the Honda.

"Why was he in my truck?"

"This is all you have?"

"This is what I was told to bring," Frank said. "Is that a Russian accent?"

The other two men turned around and looked at Frank. The buyer stared at him for an awkwardly long amount of time before saying, "We wish to also purchase the coolers."

"Those aren't for sale; they're my mom's. She got them like forty years ago from her mom and it's really more of a fam—"

"Shut up," the buyer said. "I would like to purchase the coolers." He handed Frank the envelope and then another fifty. "For the coolers."

"Alright, let me just take these two parts out, and you can have the rest." He removed the individual limbs, wrapped them in towels he had brought from home, and placed them in the cab. He looked around and admired that no one was paying any attention to the highly illegal activity going on around them just yards away. "You guys need anything else? If you want to exchange cards," Frank pulled out his wallet and began looking for a card, "we can do this a lot quicker than talking through my buddy." Frank heard a car door slam and looked up. They had already removed the coolers from the bed of the truck and loaded them into their car. The engine started and before Frank could say "thanks," they backed up and pulled out. "Good talk." Frank held out his hand to wave bye.

Frank walked for nearly thirty minutes before he spotted the sign for Gavin Cemetery. The spot was only a couple inches on the map away from the transaction point. *Clearly, someone was drunk when they made this map.*

The sign brought a sigh of relief. Frank wiped sweat and a now dead mosquito off his forehead with the back of his hand and took a swig of his water. He continued along the trail at the instruction of the sign's arrow.

Had it not been for the *crunch* under his shoe, he would have walked right past the cemetery. Frank jerked his leg back when he felt—and heard—it beneath him and looked down; a shattered white object covered in the grass. It was a seashell. Frank bent down to examine it, curious as to why a seashell was left lying in the recesses of LBL, then noticed sticking out from the overbrush what he'd come to find: a headstone. "Finally," he muttered.

A handful of two-foot cemetery stones were hidden among the trees and practically invisible if one were not searching for them. Knee-high weeds and tangled overbrush covered most everything. He set the shovel and the wrapped-up limbs on the ground and began inspecting the graves; there were only a few to choose from. The tallest stone was covered in moss, hiding what remained of it's faded inscriptions. The names on the smaller stones were all worn down with age and unclear.

He had taken longer to get here—and consumed more of his water—than expected and needed to start digging. He chose a burial spot at random and gave his best estimation of which side of the marker to dig. The sweat seeping out had begun to make his back and arms itch, while the overbrush kept sneaking under the cuff of his pants causing him to frequently swat at his legs.

Frank did not intend to dig very far down—this place was so far back in the woods it would be unlikely for anyone to happen upon it, and daylight would be running out soon. On top of that, he couldn't shake the stories that plagued LBL from his childhood and just few days prior: disappearances, a haunted cemetery, an old woman with a crooked back—tilted to the side—and one eye. He started to hum and then sing softly to himself the lyrics of Bon Jovi's "Livin' on a Prayer," which helped to drown the paranoid feeling that someone was watching him, or, that a long, gray-haired, decrepit old woman would be standing behind him, rasping for a breath.

He was several scoops of dirt into his dig before something broke his concentration. A noise: the *sound* of a breeze cutting through tree leaves above and the rustling of tall grass beside him. He muttered, "finally" to himself, happy about the coming breeze, but when it never came, he paused. Frank turned his head up and looked around at the trees and the ground. Everything was as still as the stones beneath him. *Whhhiiissshhh*. He could hear the wind through the trees and grass, but nothing moved. "That's weird." He put his head back down to continue digging but the sound grew louder, as if rain was beginning to fall nearby and he was in its path. But neither rain nor wind ever materialized. And then he heard the hum—a voice. A person was humming, it was unmistakable. It was soft, almost imbedded in the noise of the trees, not coming from any particular direction. "Um . . ." he muttered. Frank stood still staring out into the woods, feeling his heart begin to pick up rapidly.

"Hello?" He yelled, but he knew no one would answer. There was no one around but him. He reached into his pocket for his cell phone to call someone—anyone—to distract himself, but his mind couldn't focus. He scrolled up and down through his recent calls list, trying to force himself not to listen to what was happening around him—especially whatever was making the sound—*a woman's voice*? And who would he call? There was no service out here. He breathed steadily through his nose, trying to control the shivers going up his back like electric shocks. And then the humming became clearer, and the hiss of the wind more pronounced. "Screw it," he muttered. He picked up the wrapped limbs and shovel and left in the direction he came, not even bothering to cover up the hole he began to dig.

The drone of the wind was the first to go, but the faint humming continued to swirl around him for several yards out of the cemetery.

Frank sat in the driver's seat of his truck catching his breath from the sprint out of the woods and distress from the experience. He pulled onto the main road of LBL, headed toward the bridge, and clicked on his phone. The limbs were now in a hidden compartment behind the passenger seat. Daylight was not yet gone, but the treetops blocked out what little there was left. He wanted out of LBL; he needed a new place to bury the limbs.

Addy picked up almost as soon as the phone started to ring. "Hey, what's up?"

"Quick question: you remember a few days ago, you and I were talking about Asbury cemetery with Cliff and that waitress in Paducah?"

"Yeah."

"You said the guy who lives there has a dog that he lets loose on people when they walk in the cemetery. Is that true? I mean, does he still do that?"

"I'm pretty sure not. That dog was already so old when I met him. If it's still alive, it ain't running anywhere. Why? You going out there?" Addy asked.

"No way. One of the kids was asking about it this morning at the funeral and I told him about it. He was kind of a chode so I was hoping he would get a good scare out of it," Frank lied.

"I think by now the guy relies on the legends of that place to keep vandals away. The bugs are probably the scariest thing in there."

SATURDAY

39

Frank's sleep came intermittently through the night. Every time he closed his eyes, he was standing back in that isolated cemetery in LBL, digging into a grave. In his mind there was something in front of him—something standing in the trees. A disturbing presence. No matter how many times he awoke and turned over or adjusted his pillow, he continued to find himself standing in that grave, being watched by the still, dark, gnarled figure in the trees.

When the alarm went off, he regretted scheduling an early meeting with Bill Cobb at Virginia Jan's about the status of his cremated ex-wife. He moved cautiously down the stairs, looking only through half-opened eyelids, telling himself he could nap when he came home. He poured a mug of coffee, wrapped it in a napkin to catch the spills, and exited the house.

Frank put in an order for a dozen donuts at his mom's café counter and took a seat across from the middle-aged man with a goatee, wearing cargo shorts and a Hawaiian shirt. Bill, a Murray State professor, never appeared in anything less than pressed pants with a shirt and sport coat during the school year.

"Mr. Cobb." Frank smiled, patting him on the shoulder. "Almost didn't recognize you."

"Hello, Frank. How are you?" Bill replied, shaking Frank's hand.

"Great. Sorry I didn't text you back last night, I passed out early."

"I assumed we were still on to meet when I didn't hear anything back."

Frank looked around the restaurant. The bustling crowd was normal for a Saturday morning. A steady stream of hungover college kids filed one by one to the counter and out the front door. Most of the tables were filled with elderly farmers and couples enjoying their morning coffee and sugar fix. "I see you decided to come to the funeral, yesterday. Anybody say anything to you?" Frank asked.

"No. Not a soul. I wasn't too surprised at that though. I barely knew anyone there."

The lady at the counter called Frank back for his order. He had them refill his coffee mug too before he walked back over to Bill's table. "What about the husband? Did he make it as awkward as you expected?" Frank asked, setting his bag and napkin wrapped mug on the table.

"Nope. I bumped into him as I walked in. We both said hello—he asked how my day was. At one point, when I was standing at her coffin, he pulled me aside and introduced me as her *first husband* to someone he knew from church. It was the most civil he's ever been. To be honest, I was pretty taken aback by the whole thing. Kind of made me feel bad for doing what we did." Bill took a sip of his coffee as Frank tried to figure out where Bill was going with this story. "But then I remembered that he used to screw my wife while I was outside swimming in his pool so, those remorseful feelings didn't last too long."

Frank wasn't sure if he should laugh. "Right, well, I just wanted to give you an update on where we were. I was able to make the switch, and she is in fact being cremated. The remains will be delivered to me soon and after that I'll contact you for pickup. How do you want them?"

"What do you mean?" Bill asked. "Are you referring to an urn?"

"Yessir." Frank pulled out a handwritten piece of paper with descriptions and numbers and slid it across the table folded up. "Those are some of the urn models we offer, and the model numbers with prices that I'll give you if purchased through me. Sorry, but I couldn't get my printer to work this morning before I left."

"Wait a second," Bill said.

Frank continued, "You can come by and look at some of the models if you want; we have most of them in the show room—"

"Wait. Hang on," Bill interjected. "I don't get an urn with the money I'm paying you?"

"No sir. That's entirely separate."

Bill looked at Frank, pinching his lips and exhaling out his nose. Frank could see Bill was disappointed. He apologized for the miscommunication, stating that the payment was made solely for the job itself not for the storage of remains.

"Is there a law that states she must be stored in an urn?" Bill asked.

"No sir. That's just the normal procedure. I can have her put her in a Ziploc bag if you want."

"Is that free?" He asked.

"Yeah. It's a little weird, but I guess you—"

"Then let's do that. I'm having those ashes scattered and turned into something else anyway. I don't need the urn."

"Sure. I'll call you in a couple of days and you can just stop by to pick up the package when it gets dropped off."

"Great. And thanks again for doing this." Bill handed Frank an envelope, who promptly made sure no one was watching. He gripped the envelope, and Bill confirmed he would drop off the rest when he picked up his wife.

Neither Officer Suthers nor Frank were paying attention to what was in front of them as they both passed through the open door at Virginia Jan's. Frank, too occupied with checking the donuts in his bag, and Monty with his cell phone. Monty clipped Frank's shoulder, sending some of the coffee in Frank's cup out and onto Monty's uniform and phone, as well as on Frank's arm. Frank swore before he looked up. When he saw that coffee had gotten on the phone, he dropped the envelope on the nearby table and gave Monty the napkin wrapped around his coffee mug. "Oh my gosh, I am so sorry!" Frank exclaimed. "I wasn't paying attention."

"It's alright. I w-w-wasn't either." Monty wiped off the screen with the napkin as Frank went to get more. The envelope got his attention. One of the patrons retrieved a towel from the counter and brought it to Monty. He bent down to wipe up the coffee in front of the door. *Why is he carrying an envelope to a diner? Did he meet someone?*

"Again, wow, I am so sorry," Frank said, returning with napkins. "You're not going to arrest me, are you?"

Not for this. "It's okay. Like I said, I w-w-wasn't watching where I was going. Don't w-walk and read at the same time, I guess."

"I get you anything else?" Frank asked.

"Nope. I'm fine. The n-napkins were all."

Frank picked up his stuff and exited. Monty watched him get into his truck and then he scanned the restaurant as he approached the counter to put in his order. He asked the cashier if Frank Burgers had been there very long before he left.

"I'd say he was here about ten minutes. He always comes in Saturdays and gets a big order. He sat with someone today," the young woman replied.

Monty looked around. "D-D-Do you know who?"

"No, I wasn't paying attention, sorry. But they were sitting right there." She pointed over at an empty table near the wall, and far back from the door. "I guess they left too."

"You didn't see or recognize the guy he was with," Monty asked.

"No, I'm sorry. With so many coming in it's hard to keep track. What can I get ya?"

Monty gave the towel back and threw the soiled napkins away. He moved to the end of the line, where he noticed another napkin on the floor. But this napkin wasn't like the ones he just threw out—it was the one Frank had given him. And, it looked just like the one sitting in an evidence bag inside his glove box.

40

Something clinked inside the cab when Frank took the last turn into the funeral home too quickly and went over the curb. He turned his head to look behind him and saw the corner of a brown cardboard box. "What is that?" he muttered.

A square package, a little thicker than a cereal box, was resting on the floorboard in his cab, just behind his seat. He studied it for a moment, wondering how it could have gotten there. It wasn't there yesterday when he went to meet the buyer, and he always kept the car locked, unless someone broke in last night or at the donut shop.

He threw the truck into park and maneuvered it out from behind the seat. He tilted it and lightly shook the package: several items clinked together inside. Whatever it was was heavy, hard, and tightly packed. He carried the box inside and considered opening it, but when he saw the recliner in the living room, he decided against it. He set the box down in his office and then put the donuts on the kitchen table. No one was awake.

He grabbed the newspaper from the porch and took a seat in the overstuffed easy chair, pulling back the lever to recline. It took only a few minutes to fall asleep with an unfolded Sports section on his chest.

Donnie and his father, Dave, came downstairs just after 8 a.m. but neither one noticed the pair of legs sticking out from beneath a newspaper. Frank stirred when he heard the paper being picked up off his chest and saw Cliff standing over him.

"Mornin' snickerdoodle," Cliff said.

Frank yawned. "What time is it?"

"Eight-fifteen."

"Jeez. I am wrecked." Frank ran his hands across his face.

"You get back late last night?"

"No. I didn't sleep well. I got back in around eleven, I think. But I kept having this repeating nightmare."

"About what?"

"I don't remember. I was burying something in LBL. I think it was the . . ." Frank lowered his voice. "It was the place I went to yesterday. When I was there, I heard this strange noise like . . . wind."

"Yeah, wind *is* pretty terrifying," Cliff said.

"No, it wasn't wind. That's the thing. I was digging this hole and all of a sudden, it sounded like wind. In the trees and the grass. I could hear the stuff moving but there was no wind. It was as calm as this room." Cliff looked around. "But the worst part was that I could hear this soft humming beneath the wind noise."

"Wait, this was your dream?"

"No, this was yesterday while I was digging—it was real."

"And I'm out," Cliff replied, turning to walk into the kitchen.

"No, no. Wait. That's what kept me up. I was back in this cemetery digging, and there was something out in the woods. I couldn't turn to look at anything else. I would wake up and every time I went back to sleep, I was right back there. Except, whatever it was got closer to me each time I was there. Something black, like the trees, but something in my head kept telling me it's not a tree . . . it's something . . . or somebody . . ."

"Yeah, well, I'm not sleeping tonight," Cliff said.

"Anyways, yeah, up all night and then I had to meet Bill early this morning."

"That go okay?"

"Yeah, went fine. We're good. I got part of your money in the office."

"What happened with the wind and all the humming?" Cliff asked.

"Psh," Frank blew through his lips. "I ran. I got down five or six shovels full and left. Didn't even bother covering the hole back up."

"You've still got the parts?"

Frank smiled. "Nope. I found the easiest spot on my way home. I don't know why I didn't think about it before, but I've figured out a better way to hide this stuff."

Cliff took a seat on the couch near Frank's chair. "Where did you bury it?"

"Asbury," Frank whispered.

"At night?"

"I called Addy. He said that dog is long gone. Plus, the guy's too old now. I didn't have a problem."

"Your *better* way to hide stuff is by burying it in Asbury?"

"No. I just needed something quick last night. But when I got there, there was already a hole dug and a tent set up for a burial today. Which means, this afternoon someone is going to lower a coffin over those two limbs, and no one will ever know or think to look underneath it."

The right side of Cliff's mouth turned up, and his head began to nod. "I gotchu. That's brilliant."

"Cuts out the work and removes any trace of vandalism. Should I need to bury anything else, my only work *now* is to look for when and where burials will take place. If I get in there the night before, no one will ever know."

"Plus, you don't need to go to LBL anymore."

"I'm not burying anything else in LBL." Frank shook his head. "Screw that place. You eat breakfast?"

"Nah, I have a client soon. He's running late. I just came in here to grab coffee."

Cliff grabbed a donut on his way out the back door and Frank went to the kitchen and took a seat next to his brother. His father looked up from the comics page of his paper. "Rough night?" He smiled.

"Eh, not really. I had a hard time sleepin."

"The services go off well yesterday?" Dave asked.

Frank shrugged. "For the most part, yes. Had some hiccups." He recounted the story of the dad who wanted his son to ride in the hearse. When his mom asked why he didn't just say yes, Frank lied and said he hated children. Ginny clicked her tongue and went back to working on her Sudoku. "The food was a big hit, though. Probably the best response we've gotten."

"I bumped into Randy Koch the other day, asked me about that—the catering—but I told him to talk to you and your brother about it," Dave said.

"They want to start catering funerals?" Frank asked.

"They have restaurants who will cater sometimes—for small gatherings—but they liked the idea of having an in-house cook. Anything that brings in money and makes them look fancy is interesting to them."

"Is that strawberry or blueberry?" Donnie asked Frank who was about to take a bite of his donut.

"Blueberry. They only make them on weekends. So good."

"Gross," Donnie replied.

"I like the blueberry," Ginny looked up from her puzzle. "There're real blueberries in there."

Frank took a bite into the blueberry glaze, trying to catch the falling chips on his plate. "Hey, did you put a box in my truck this morning? Or last night?"

"No, why?" Donnie asked.

"Because when I got out of my truck this morning, there was a box. A big one. Either one of you put a box behind my seat?"

"Nope. Don't have a key," Dave replied. Ginny ignored him, which was answer enough for Frank.

"You didn't open the box?" Donnie asked.

"Man, I was so tired when I got home. It's in my office. It's not addressed or anything—just sealed."

"Go get it," Donnie said.

Frank got up to get the box, but Donnie followed him back

to the office. Frank pulled out his knife and slit the the tape. "Don't think it's a bomb, do you?" Frank asked.

"I don't know. Did you piss anyone off recently?"

"Not this week." Frank lifted the flaps on both sides and tilted his head at the contents inside. There were five rows of items, each covered in bubble wrap. "Did you order something from Amazon?"

"Not something like that," Donnie said, picking up one of the objects. He undid the tape, holding the wrapping together, and let the piece roll out of its packaging onto his hand. It was a black figurine with a castle tower at its head. "Hunh," Donnie grunted.

"What is that?"

"It's a rook," Donnie replied. "A chess piece."

Frank picked up another and unwrapped it: a taller black piece with a cross on its head.

"That's a king," Donnie said. "These are gorgeous. This was in your truck?"

"Yeah," Frank muttered. He held up the king and took a picture with his phone. "I'll text Cliff and see if it's his set; maybe he left it in there or something."

Donnie unwrapped a white pawn and then a bishop. "Man. These are incredible."

"You play chess?" Frank asked.

"Yeah. I mean, when I have someone to play with. I love it." He scooted the remaining pieces in the box to the side to look at the game board buried underneath.

"Not Cliff's," Frank said, and clicked off his phone. "Man. Where did this come from?"

"I don't know. But it couldn't have been cheap. Maybe

someone put it in your car by mistake." Within the one second it took Frank to give his brother a look that said *really*?, Donnie realized that no one could mistake Frank's skeleton truck for their own. "Yeah. Good point. You don't play?"

"No. Never learned how. Cliff plays. I'll give it to him."

"What! I just said I liked it," Donnie exclaimed.

"Oh. Do you want it?"

"Yes!"

"Okay. Calm down." Frank smiled. "Happy birthday."

"Definitely doesn't count as a birthday gift, but thanks just the same." Donnie put the pieces back into the box and closed the flaps. "What are you about to do?"

"Go finish my blueberry donut and then maybe go play a round of frisbee go—" Frank paused. Donnie was staring at him, with his eyebrows raised. "Ugh. I guess I'm about to sit here and talk with you." He groaned." Let me go grab my coffee. Hold up."

Donnie heard someone walking up the steps of the porch as he was carrying the box across the hall to his office. He set it down on his desk just as a knock rang out into the foyer. "Coming," he yelled. He pushed up on the closed blinds to look outside into the parking lot: a black Lincoln town car was sitting in the driveway. "You've gotta be kidding me," Donnie whispered.

41

Donnie stepped onto the porch and closed the door. "What are you doing here?"

"We came to see Frank," Vince replied. "And to buy your business."

"I said I would talk to my brother and get back to you. I told you not to keep coming here; all you'll do is tick him off."

"I'm afraid we don't have a choice," Vince said. "Is he here?"

"What do you want?"

"Private business."

The door opened behind Donnie. Frank stood, staring at the guests. "Hey, hey! It's the Cock brothers. What brings you out here?"

"Cut the shit Frank, you know our name is pronounced Coke."

"What do you want?" Frank asked.

"We need to talk to you about buying your business," Randy said.

"Already told you; it's not for sale. And if it was, it wouldn't be going to y—"

"You might change your mind after you see this," Vince said, holding up his phone.

Donnie turned around to look at Frank. "What is that?"

"Don't look at me, I didn't do anything."

"Really? Because a file on my phone says you did," Vince smiled.

"What's on there? You got some nudes of me on your phone?"

"What? No. Why would I have—"

"Can we take this inside?" Randy said.

"For what?" Frank protested.

"Because this is going to take bit to get through and Moron over here wanted to wear *suits* in ninety-degree weather. I'm dying in here. Plus, the glare from the sun is going to make his phone hard to see."

"You're not coming in my house," Frank said.

"Then we go to the police, and you don't hear our offer. Up to you," Vince replied.

"Come on, Frank. It's blazing out here," Randy pleaded.

Frank closed the door to his office. Vince and Randy were already sitting on the couch and Donnie stood leaning on the desk, with his hands in his pockets. He spoke first. "What's going on guys?"

"Let me see the phone," Frank said.

"Just hang on there, cowboy. I'm going to assume your brother has no idea what you did last night and so, you may not even want him to see this video."

"What'd you do last night?" Donnie asked.

"Yo, I didn't do *anything* last night," he replied. "You guys are bluffing—they're bluffing. There's nothing on that phone."

"Frank," Randy said. "We know where you were, and we

know what you did. But we don't have to show anyone else, okay? Just listen to the offer."

For the first time with Vince or Randy, Frank decided it would be best to stay quiet. He didn't need to make eye contact with his brother—he could feel his eyes staring a hole right through him.

"Frank and Donnie, we will offer five hundred thousand dollars for your business. That amount is—"

"Wait, wait, wait. Hold up," Donnie interrupted. "Five hundred thousand? You and I agreed on double that."

"You *agreed*? When did you guys even discuss this?" Frank shot Donnie a hard look. "You were hiding that from me too, huh?"

"No, no," Vince said. "There was never a real agreement. We *talked* about it, but that was before we found *this*. Initially, we offered what we thought would close the deal. And, if you remember Donnie, you never gave us an answer. We told you not to jerk us around and it's been nearly a week."

"So, five hundred thousand. That's it?" Donnie asked.

"That's it," Vince said, confidently. "And, fortunately for us, we're confident that once you see what's on the tape, you'll agree to it, regardless of how unfair you think we are. Which, to be honest, I think offering half a mil for this place is more than fair."

"I don't care if you're offering five million," Frank cut in. "I'm not selling this place to you. So, you can go to the police with whatever you think I did, but even if I get shut down, I'll see to it that you never step foot in this home again."

"What's on the tape?" Donnie asked.

"Dude. It doesn't matter," Frank replied.

"If it doesn't matter, then where were you last night?" Donnie asked.

Frank curled his bottom lip under his teeth. *Was it a bluff? They couldn't have followed me to LBL. It was dark by the time I got to Asbury; I would have seen the lights. It had to be a bluff.* "I was out playing darts at Vitello's."

"Show them the tape," Randy said.

"Fine, show the tape," Frank said.

"Okay." Vince stood up and instructed everyone to gather around him as he held his phone. He brought up his gallery app and clicked on the black thumbnail. The screen went dark with a gray triangle. Vince tapped it. The group collectively lowered their heads toward the phone as if they were magnetized toward it.

"I can't see anything," Donnie said. "You sure it's on?"

"It's on. Just watch," Vince replied.

"Turn up the brightness," Randy said.

"Hang on." Vince began raising the phone up and down to try and see through the video's darkness.

"Just turn the brightness up," Randy said again.

"Can one of you turn the lights off?" Vince asked.

"Got it," Donnie said.

Vince clicked play again and began tilting the phone every which way to try and get a clearer picture. "It's a night-time recording."

Frank leaned over toward Vince's ear and whispered, loudly: "I still can't see it."

"Yeah, I got that," Vince snapped back.

"Vince, would you turn the damn brightness up?"

"It's already up all the way, Randy. I know how to work a

phone. It's just so bright in here. I should've brought my laptop over; that screen is fifty times the size of this."

"That's a big laptop." Frank suggested.

"Shut up, Frank," Donnie said. "Can you screen share to the TV on the wall?"

"Yeah, I can do that," Vince said. "What's your Wi-Fi?"

"Why are you helping him?" Frank asked.

"Because I want to see it," Donnie replied, retrieving a Post-it note off Frank's desk and writing the name and password on it. He configured the TV to connect with Vince's phone and in a matter of seconds, Vince's home screen picture appeared— him and his wife in a selfie pose standing on a beach.

"All jokes aside, that's actually a good picture of you two," Frank said.

Vince didn't bother responding. He pulled up his recent apps and clicked on the black screen. The image was still dark, but there was no mistaking the location. Frank's stomach dropped.

42

The video was nearly fifteen minutes long but Vince only showed them two—it was all they needed to see. The picture, at first, looked still—a landscape of a cemetery. Then something moved into view from the bottom left corner. A person—Frank immediately knew it was him *but how would anyone else know*? The shot was too far away and the individual too distorted to see—and then it zoomed in. *Shit.*

On screen Frank crept through the open areas, holding a flashlight in his teeth, and stopped in front of an open grave. He peered down into it, then around him as if looking for someone. A long object was in his hand that clearly became a shovel when Frank speared it into the earth.

"What's in your other hand?" Donnie asked.

Frank didn't answer. They continued watching Frank who went off screen, then Vince fast-forwarded until he reappeared carrying a small ladder with him. He set something down on the ground and positioned the ladder inside the hole. Looking around once more—possibly in response to a noise?—Frank swung his leg onto the first rung, pulled the shovel out of the ground, and grabbed the item. He disappeared down into the hole.

"Your brother was down in that hole for almost ten minutes before," Vince fast-forwarded again to almost the end, "he comes up *without* whatever it was he went down with." They watched Frank climb back up the ladder, pull it and the shovel out of the hole, and begin making his way off screen. "Do you need to see it again?"

"See what?" Frank said. "You have a video of a guy climbing down into an open grave. That's not a crime."

"It is if the guy buried human remains," Vince said.

Frank looked at his brother and knew at once that his panicked eyes betrayed him.

"What?" Donnie said.

"We know all about it, Frank. Randy and I watched the entire thing live. And when you left, we drove out to Asbury Cemetery to have a look at what you were trying to get rid of."

"Frank, tell me you—" Donnie began.

"Now, why would someone need to hide two body parts? And where did you get those body parts? Are you taking them off corpses? Or are you digging them up? Could it be that the person burying these parts is the same person digging up corpses in Murray?"

"You were watching me? Why were you even the—" Frank asked.

"Oh, no we weren't there. We own that cemetery—bought it from Alan Fox maybe three or four years ago. He told us there'd been a problem with kids thinking the place was haunted and trespassing after dark. So, after we talked with other cemetery owners, we figured the best way to stop it was to have cameras installed. To be honest, it's been entertaining for us. Mostly it's just two or three kids walking in, looking around and trying to scare each other. Occasionally, we'll have groups go in there drinking or trying to play games, which, as I'm sure you know, is dangerous in that place. Someone could really get hurt."

Frank's head was spinning. His breathing had escalated without him realizing. He moved over to his office chair and took a seat.

"Sometimes, because we live so close, one of us will drive out there and have a little fun if the kids start vandalizing the place. As soon as you dropped that ladder into the hole, and turned around, I knew it was you. I zoomed in to make sure. There you were, clear as day." Vince disconnected his phone from the TV, bringing it back to a black screen.

"Tell me that was not body parts that you buried down there," Donnie said.

Frank remained quiet once again, eyes locked on Vince.

"Hey! Dumb ass!" Donnie called. "Did you bury human parts down—"

"Donnie," Randy cut in. "He did. We checked. And we have pictures. We did, however, rebury them, and we'll lower a casket on top of them this afternoon, if you agree to the deal right now."

Frank leaned forward and cradled his head onto the tips of his fingers and thumb. "Let's say we sell—take the five hundred grand—then what? You're just gonna ignore what you saw and get rid of this tape?"

"You got it. All we want is the company. And you out of the funeral business," Vince said.

"What happens to the house? And us? And all this?" Frank asked.

"The purchase goes public. We change the name immediately and continue using the facilities under that name. You all may continue living here for one year, but after that, Randy and I will move in and start the remodel."

"You're changing the name?" Donnie asked.

"Just a few words of it. The Koch Brothers Funeral Home. It'll be a subsidiary of the larger Life Memorial brand."

"The town isn't going to go for the word 'cock' being on a billboard."

Vince was about to respond before Donnie interrupted: "Burgers Funeral Home has been a name in Murray for nearly a century. You're going to wipe all that out?" Donnie asked.

"This is the funeral business. Eventually, even names die off," Vince said.

"Alright, that was a little much. Calm down," Randy said. "Look, guys—Frank, this is the best deal we can make. He's right, we offered a million, but given what's happened in the last twenty-four hours, this is the best business decision for all of us."

Frank slumped down in his work chair, staring at the blank screen on the wall. "What about our dad?"

"He can stay on as long as he wants, but after a year, this house gets a face lift and becomes *our* new residence."

"It's not as if we're leaving you high and dry. We're giving you a year to square things up. We'd actually prefer if, during that year, you stayed living in the house and helped us manage the place," Randy said.

Frank lifted a blank stare to Randy who was now leaning—sitting—on his desk.

"Whoa. We didn't agree on that," Vince countered.

"You want me to work for you? To run the Cock Brothers' Funeral Home?" Frank asked.

Randy grinned. "Yeah. This way you guys can look for

something else while still having a paycheck come in—and it'll help us out—"

"Get out," Frank whispered. He lifted a finger to the door and dropped it back down on his leg. "Get out of my house."

"I assume that's a yes?" Vince asked. Neither of the Burgers brothers replied.

"We'll draw up the papers and bring them by Monday," Randy said as they exited.

Frank continued to stare off in a daze, with his head resting in his hand on the side of his chair. Randy offered an apology, and Frank maneuvered the middle finger out from under his chin. When the front door closed, Donnie took a seat on the couch across from the desk, expelling a heavy sigh and leaning his head back.

"I said get out," Frank whispered.

"You're mad at me?"

"I'm not mad at you. I just don't want to be around you right now," Frank said.

Donnie stood up. "What the hell were you thinking, man? Why would you bury those things in—"

"Wha—what are you not hearing? I.Don't.Want.To.Be. Around.You. Are you deaf? I just lost our fucking business— my business—to those pieces of shit! Which, I know *you're* incredibly thrilled about so you can go get your restaurant . . ." Frank covered his eyes with his hands and pulled them back through his hair, spewing out a guttural sigh. "Fuck!"

"Maybe it's not that bad," Donnie began softly. "They're not turning you in. You can start a new place. Build a home somewhere else."

"You just don't get it." A soft laugh came out. "And why

would you? Why would I expect you to understand any of this? When have you ever lost anything? You're always the one who has the luxury of *leaving* when things don't suit you."

"Hey, that's not—"

"It's not just that I lost this place—that sucks, yes—but it's that I lost it to *them*. Of all people. The moment that Dad stepped down, those two have had a target on my back and have done whatever they could to take this place. Shit, they just tried to go behind my back to get to you—I *definitely* didn't see that coming. They did the same thing to Dad last year. I can't count how many of our clients have come in here and said that one of them gave some embarrassing story or lie about us. So many times I've thought about selling to them—just to get them off my back. But I would rather burn this place to the ground than have those toxic taints living here. They don't care about funerals, or families; they just want the money. It's all for show: their relationships, their building, their personality. Not once have I seen them lead, let alone participate in a community event like we've done. It's not Life Memorial—it's those two! Everything they do is just . . . fake. They're fuckin' weasels!" Frank paused. "And because of something so *stupid*, they got me." He pounded his hand on the chair, then stood up and began to pace the floor. "You know, I would have been fine getting caught. I would have been fine going bankrupt because I tried like hell to keep this place running." He paused. "Who puts cameras in a graveyard!"

"What did you say earlier?"

"The cameras. Why would someone—"

"No. About them being weasels. You said *everything they do is fake*." Donnie stood with his arms folded and looking down at the floor for a moment and then: "Give me your phone,"

"What? No."

"Frank. Give me your phone, now!"

"For what?"

"I need to see your pictures," Donnie said.

"Come on, man! Really? They just showed you that video, do you really need to lecture me on more stuff? Fine, you caught me. I've been doing shit behind your back. I admit it."

"I don't—damnit! Just give me your phone! I've got an idea."

Frank's eyes narrowed. "What are you gonna do?"

"You deleted your pictures recently?"

"No . . ." Frank tossed his phone into Donnie's hand. "Password is 0073735963."

Donnie began typing it in and then looked up and smiled. "That's a blast from the past. Good game."

"The best. What are you doing?"

"Hopefully saving your ass."

43

"Don't say a word, do you hear me?" Donnie whispered.

"Yeah. Got it. What are you doing?"

Donnie opened the front door and walked down the front porch steps, shielding his eyes from the bright new day sun. "Vince, hold up." The Kochs were already in the car. "Vince!" Donnie began waving his hand, and ran to the front of the car to block them in. He motioned for him to roll down his window.

"I forgot to ask you something. Does the name Myles Hamm ring a bell?"

Vince looked at his brother and repeated the name a couple of times. "I don't think so, why?"

"He was buried in Almo Cemetery. Down 641?"

"I know where Almo is. But, no, I don't know *who* that is."

"What about Sarah Piddleton? She died in a hot air balloon accident years ago. Buried over in Frazier cemetery."

"Was she one of the ones that got vandalized?"

"She was," Donnie answered. "But you don't remember anything else about her? Or Myles?"

"Am I supposed to?" Vince replied.

"You guys did the funeral for both families. The Piddletons and the Hamms."

"Oh. Well, then that's a little more familiar. Lead with that next time. I'm running through all my mental contact—"

"Do you remember what sort of coffin the Hamm family ordered for Myles? Or Sarah?"

Vince's eyes wandered upward to meet Donnie's and his mouth opened only the tiniest bit—enough for Donnie to know he had him. The corner of his mouth twitched, as if he was about to speak, but he turned toward Randy and whispered something inaudible. "Sorry," he said. "Don't know. That's a detail that's private to the family. It's not something we log into our memory."

"Well, that's no big deal because I know what kind of coffin both families ordered. You see, I called Myles' family. He was buried in what you all referred to as the 'most elite model'—'indestructible', they told me. Made of copper. They wanted such a model because Myles was buried with a very special item. Is this ringing a bell now?"

"What do you want, Donnie?" Randy asked.

"How much do you charge for a casket made of copper?"

Vince was staring out through the windshield, choosing not to speak.

"It's cool, she told me over the phone. She paid almost nine grand for that model." Donnie held up Frank's phone, showing them a picture. He covered it with his hand to block the sun. "I just emailed you this picture and two others of Myles Hamm's open grave. The coffin was most certainly not indestructible. And, it most certainly wasn't copper. In fact, I'd be willing to bet money that the casket holding Myles Hamm was nothing more than cheap, copper-painted plastic."

Randy put his glasses on and leaned over his brother to get a look. He turned to Vince and whispered something. Vince turned to look at the photo.

"Now, why would anyone sell an elite coffin model to an old, confused, grieving woman when they actually buried him in something completely different? Could it be that someone is falsely charging astronomical prices for high-quality products, then substituting products made with anything but in order to make an astronomical profit?"

"Must have been a mix-up. Bad model. Happens all the time," Vince said.

"Really? Copper splits and breaks down like that?" Donnie asked. Vince leaned over to look at the images on the screen one more time. "Maybe you're right; maybe it was a fluke. But then how do you explain Sarah's casket? It did the exact same thing?" Neither of the Koch brothers said a word. "Do I need to send you pictures of those too?"

Vince turned now to face Donnie. "You think the police will believe these pictures? They'll ask you how you got them. Then what will you say? That you and your brother have been the ones grave robbing? See how well that goes over."

"That's exactly what I'm going to say," Donnie spoke quietly. "You see, we're not selling this place to *you*. And that's final. So, if you wanna go to the police with that tape and turn my brother in, it is at that point that we have nothing to lose. In which case, I will show these pictures, and Sarah's, and provide a list of every client you've ever buried. And we'll see how *that* goes over." Donnie waited briefly to let the threat sink in. "And in case I'm not clear, when people discover that they're being scammed by the two of you, your closing day won't be far behind. And neither will your jail sentences."

"You'd rather wipe us both out than take five hundred thousand dollars?" Vince asked.

"Nope. I'd rather stay in business. But if we go, you go. Like my brother said, we're not selling to you."

Vince tapped the steering wheel with his thumbs, nodding his head. "So, what now? What are we supposed to do?"

"Whatever you want, really. I'm just saying that if you go to the cops, we won't be far behind you. Or, a better option is that you can forget this whole conversation ever happened, and we'll do the same. We'll both go our way and continue doing our own thing."

"Will you delete those pictures?" Vince asked.

"No. But I don't expect you to delete your video."

"Good point," Vince said. He whispered something to his brother and then turned back to Donnie. "Okay. No tape. We keep quiet about your brother. And you keep those pictures to yourself. Deal?"

"Deal." The two shook hands, but before Vince pulled his hand away, Donnie gripped and pulled his arm closer. "One more thing: I want you to drop the free pickups from the hospital, and to talk to whoever you've got over there and tell them to put us back on the call list. And, I want you to leave my brother alone. Don't make any more offers to him or myself about buying this business. It's not for sale. You understand?"

"Yeah, got it."

Donnie gripped Vince's hand more tightly and leaned in closer. "And I swear to God, if I ever hear from our clients that you've called them, or communicated with them in *any way* to say something negative about me, or Frank, or this house— even if I see either of you here at our annual Christmas party, I'm gonna have Cliff hire someone to beat the ever-living *shit* out of the both of you. We good?"

Vince swallowed, and cleared his throat. He nodded slowly in agreement. "We're good."

Donnie released his grip and tapped the hood of the car. "Have a good weekend, then."

It took Donnie until he was at the steps of the house to realize that Frank wasn't beside him and was still standing speechless in the driveway. "You coming inside?"

Frank laughed. "Are you kidding me? You're going to do the casual walk-away without explaining what just happened! What was that?" He moved toward the steps and the two of them walked into the kitchen as they talked.

"I overheard you and Cliff the other day talking about Myles' grave and the coffin. I'd never heard of a coffin doing what I heard you describing, except one other time—when you were telling me about your experience with Sarah Piddleton. So, I did some digging—pun intended."

"Nice." Frank said.

Donnie continued: "I wanted to see who took care of those funerals and sure enough it was them—albeit years apart. So, I called Myles' family and asked some questions, not really sure what I was looking for until she told me how helpful the Kochs were when she said Myles had some particular requests, one of them being buried in a indestructible coffin—something made with premium material. Said they even gave her a good deal of nine grand."

"Some deal," Frank blurted out. "But how did you know

about the others? That they were scamming other people, I mean."

"I didn't. I bluffed," Donnie said. He leaned against the counter as Frank took a seat at the table. Frank was looking beyond him out the kitchen window, likely processing the situation and how close he came to his end. "I almost didn't say *anything*. Honestly, I wasn't too upset about you going down like that." Frank sensed a tone shift in Donnie's voice and he shifted his gaze to meet his older brother's eyes. "All I asked you to do was sit down and talk with me, seriously, about the future of this place. Instead of doing that One. Simple. Thing. You trespassed in a cemetery and buried human remains in an open grave. You tore up graves; you dug up *bodies*, just so you could steal a necklace, or shoes? You dismembered God knows how many corpses to collect body parts. And you did it all for what? Money? You, who gave me this whole spiel about the Kochs, and how they're fake, and how they only care about money and not about people in this town. But you do—the guy mutilating corpses. And you did it *all* behind my back. Part of me still feels like I should have let you go down."

Frank gulped. "Why didn't you?"

"Because you're my brother. And I can't stand the thought of something you love so much being taken from you by people like *that*. Believe it or not, I know how you feel." He hesitated and looked down at the floor. "Plus, I couldn't stand the thought of those two living in our house, running our business."

"When he pulled that video up," Frank began, "and I saw that cemetery, I knew I'd been caught, but, as weird as it seems, that didn't matter as much to me. All I could think about was what this would to do Dad. And Mom's business. And you. Just, this overwhelming sense of disappointment."

"Good to know you're not entirely selfish." Donnie smiled.

"I don't know what to say. That was . . ." Frank paused. "Wow. That was bad."

"Yeah. You want me to wait until later to tell you *I told you so* or go ahead and get it over with now?"

"Definitely later. Give me a heads up though so I can make sure I'm not around." Frank smiled. "What did you mean earlier when you said you know what it means to have something taken from you?"

"Yeah, about that," Donnie replied, moving toward the table. "Part of the reason I've been wanting to talk to you is because on top of wanting to figure out the future of this place—and make sure you weren't doing something stupid—I needed to get something off my chest."

A knock came at the front door, but neither Donnie nor Frank acknowledged it. "I told you I was looking to start my own place and that with all the backing I had there were plenty of options for me: Nashville, Louisville, Lexington."

"Yeah.

Dave called Frank from the foyer, but Donnie didn't hear him. "You remember how I said that my partner in New York was going to fund my next project, and that's why I was staying on board with him, even after all the stuff went down?"

"Yeah."

"Frank! Donnie!" Dave yelled again.

"Well, as it turns out, I don't have a partner anymore. And . . ."

"Frank!" Dave was now standing in the doorway to the kitchen. "Are you guys deaf?"

"Sorry," he replied, "we were chatting about something. What's up?"

"Officer Suthers is here to see you."

Frank looked at his father. "I just saw him an hour ago."

"He apparently wants to see you again. Come on," Dave said.

44

Monty extended his hand toward Frank. "Good morning, Frank."

"Long time, no see," Frank said.

"I n-n-need to speak with you about something."

"Should we be concerned officer?" Dave asked. He was standing next to Ginny by the stairs, still in his slippers and pajamas.

"D-D-Don't know. That depends on w-w-what your son has to tell me," Monty said. He gave Frank a stern look.

"Franklin, what's going on?" Ginny asked.

"Mom, I got no idea," Frank replied. "Let's talk. You mind if we all go in the kitchen and sit down? Can I get you a coffee or a water?"

"No Coffee, but I'd l-love a w-water," Monty replied.

Monty followed the Burgers family into the kitchen where Frank poured himself and Monty a glass of water. Monty scanned the room while Frank poured the drinks. He moved over to the table and pulled out a chair, turning it backwards, and took a seat. Monty took off his cap and ran a napkin across his forehead before stuffing it back in his pocket. Monty came over this morning on a hunch—and a small piece of evidence. If he could lead Frank out to the ledge, just maybe, he'd jump off. On the other hand, if he didn't take the bait . . . Monty took a breath. Thankfully the heat outside offered a cover from the nervous sweat pouring from his forehead and arm pits.

"Alright, what's up? Am I in trouble?" Frank asked. He placed a glass of water next to Monty on the table and took a mug down from the cabinet to pour himself some coffee. Monty watched as he snatched a napkin from a basket on the counter to wipe the dribble that came out of the pot.

"W-W-What were you doing in Almo the other day?"

Frank's stomach turned. "Almo? What do you mean?"

"You know w-w-what I mean, Frank."

The back door popped open, startling everyone in the room. "Yo, yo, y— Oh! Sorry." Cliff stepped inside and glanced from Monty to Frank to Donnie and then back to Monty. "Everything alright?"

"Everything is fine, Cliff. You need something?" Dave politely asked.

"Just getting my drink out of the fridge. Wanted to say 'hey.'"

Monty turned back to Frank. "Come on. W-why were you in Almo?" Monty repeated.

"Almo. Almo. The little town down 641? With all those double-wide homes?"

"That's the one. W-W-Were you visiting someone? Surely you weren't there for the shopping, and I doubt you were looking at property."

Frank took a moment before he answered: "Officer, I have no idea what you're talking about. I haven't been out to Almo in, I don't know, a while. There's nothing out there. Why do you think I was there?"

"Because I saw you. And I know y-y-you saw me," Monty replied.

"Oh. You mean the other day in the car?" Frank asked.

"Yes. The other day in the car." Monty stayed calm. He knew Frank would take this path of answering. He tapped his fingers on the table to emphasize the next words, which also helped him get through the stutter: "Why. Were. You. There?"

Frank answered back in a similar tone: "I. Wasn't. At least not in the way you're thinking. I was on my way to Paducah and got a phone call that I needed to come back. So, I turned around on the road you saw me come out of. I wasn't in Almo; I was technically just turning around.

"W-w-why were you going to Paducah?"

"All due respect, what does that matter?" Frank asked. "I'd rather not say."

"You'd r-r-rather not say." Monty snorted. "Because you don't remember or because you r-really weren't going to Paducah?" Monty smiled.

"I'd rather not say because I was picking up a birthday present for a friend of mine and I'd rather them not know where I was going—it'll give it away."

"Thanks, man," Cliff said. Frank winked and shot a finger gun toward him with a click of his tongue.

"Did you get the birthday gift?" Monty asked.

"Nope. Like I said, I had to turn around and come home."

"What was the phone call about?"

"Officer. Is there something we need to know?" Ginny asked.

Monty leaned forward and stood up to face the rest of the family. "There was a-a-another grave robbery at the Marlowe Cemetery in Almo. Your son," Monty turned back to Frank, "was in the area the morning be-b-before that robbery happened."

"What do you mean *another grave robbery*?" Ginny asked. "And why are you putting this on Franklin?"

Monty furrowed his eyebrows. "Have you not heard about the grave robberies in Murray this past week?"

Ginny slowly shook her head and looked to Dave who then explained what he knew, and Monty filled in the rest, making sure to include new information about the recent discovery in Almo. "I'm coming to your son b-b-because I have reason to believe that he has something to do with these robberies."

"You think I had something to do with a grave robbery in Almo because you saw me driving out of there the day before? Are you serious?" Frank asked.

"That's p-p-part of it, but that's not what connects you," Monty replied. Frank's heart began to beat faster. "This is." Monty pulled out a plastic bag from his shirt pocket with a napkin inside and placed it on the table with enough force and gusto to elicit a thud from his fingers. *Talk your way out of this one.*

Frank stepped closer with the others and peered at the bagged object. Monty gave them room and moved over to the counter where there was a basket of napkins sitting against the wall. *Bingo.* He picked one up and examined the stack before bringing the whole thing to the table.

"I don't understand," Ginny said. The evidence in the bag was the same style napkin as the ones sitting in the basket. On the napkin, in large black, block letters was the word DONUTS. The D was crossed out and replaced with what was designed to look like a handwritten G in red permanent parker. Beneath it read @ VIRGINIA JAN'S.

Monty dropped the basket next to the plastic bag. "I f-f-found that napkin in the dirt at Frazier's the other day and didn't think much of it. Everyone goes to that place. It didn't occur to me until this m-m-morning that those napkins are an old design. Virginia Jan's doesn't use these anymore," Monty said, picking up the evidence bag. "They use these." Monty pulled another napkin out of his front pocket and laid if flat on the table. It was like the other except it did not have the red marker design going through the D in DONUTS. Monty continued: "When I bumped into you this m-morning, you handed me *your* napkin to wipe the spilt coffee off my arm. It w-was the same d-design as the o-one I f-f-found at F-Fraziers. And then it hit me: who else b-but the owner and her f-f-family would still have napkins with this design?" Monty looked at Ginny. "Am I right, Mrs. B-B-Burgers? W-Would anyone else b-b-besides your son still have access to these?"

Ginny looked at Dave who looked just as clueless about what to say as Frank did. "I'm sure . . . there's got to be . . . I'd have to ask and see. It's possible—Frank what's going on? Did you have something to do with all this?"

"Mom, I got no clue what this is about," Frank replied. He looked at Monty. "You can't pin this on me because of a napkin."

"I c-can't. You're right. But it's enough to justify getting a w-w-war-warrant to search your house for something that would pin you to it." Monty wasn't sure what he expected to get out of this conversation. He knew Frank wouldn't confess, but at the mention of the word *warrant*, Frank crossed his arms and looked to Cliff. And Monty could see his breathing was beginning to pick up.

Despite his increased confidence, his anxiety over the situation kept breaking his stride in smoother communication. He couldn't calm his brain down enough to communicate the words without forcing them. His mind was building barriers for speaking words he normally had no problem saying. He turned to Donnie and took a breath. "W-What about you? You know anything about this?"

"Don't look at me. If my brother has been out there digging up graves, I can tell you that I'm not a part of it."

"I find that hard to believe. From how it looks to me, y-you-you're just as likely as he is to be out there."

"Excuse me?" Donnie asked.

"Is it r-r-really a c-c-co-coincidence that all this started happening w-what? Two, th-three w-w-weeks after you got let go?" Monty asked.

"Hey, hang on a second—" Donnie tried to take hold of the conversation, but Frank cut him off.

"What are you talking about? He wasn't let go. He came back here to open a restaurant and help out with business."

Does he not know? "Is that w-w-what he t-t-told you?" *Calm down. Breathe*. He didn't plan on attacking Donnie, nor did he count on Frank not knowing what happened to his brother. "Seems like a risky way to g-g-get b-b-ack on your f-feet."

Frank looked at Donnie and then back at Monty. Dave spoke up. "Alright officer. I'm going to have to ask you to leave until we can get a lawyer."

"No, no. We don't need a lawyer because Frank didn't do anything, and neither did I," Donnie said.

"Yeah, how dare you come in here and accu—" Frank began, but Donnie cut him off. Frank said *okay* and closed his mouth.

"You've got nothing on him, and you know that. Yes, by the way, it is a coincidence that this whole thing started to happen when I got back, but that's not evidence of my—or his—involvement. Let me ask you something, how long did it take you to put this story together in your mind? You realize you've built your entire case on a napkin? Not car keys, footprints, name tags, or even a single eyewitness; your whole case rests on *this*?" Donnie picked up the bag with the napkin in it. "Is that why you've been sleazing around our house, and around Cliff's gym? So you could concoct a series of events that would allow you to pin this on someone, and make up for the fact that you aren't a good enough cop to find the actual criminal?"

"W-w-watch it, son." Monty pointed his finger at Donnie.

"Did it ever occur to you that my brother, who tends to wrap his coffee mug up in these napkins, was probably walking around in Frazier's Cemetery and dropped the napkin at some point—maybe days before? He takes walks there all the time—ask Willie."

Frank interjected: "Wait, I told you all this. A week ago when you came by the first time. I told you that I take walks in that cemetery every morning. And yeah, I take a coffee mug wrapped up with a napkin. I could have just dropped one at some point and the napkin got mixed in with the dirt while someone was digging."

"Or while you were digging," Monty offered.

"Did you really come over here to arrest me based on *this*?"

Monty went quiet.

"You should have stuck with teaching high school." Donnie walked over to the back door and opened it. "I'd like you to leave. And the next time you get a theory going in that head of yours, I suggest you run it by someone with some logic like your girlfriend at the diner."

Monty turned around as if a gunshot rang out. "W-W-What did you say?" Monty asked.

"Oh, is that supposed to be a secret?"

Monty was frozen.

Donnie continued: "Didn't Sophia tell you that she and I were close? She's told me everything about you. Were you trying to keep it a secret that you were making moves on a girl who is almost half your age and married?"

Monty was dumbfounded. He should not have involved the other brother. He was disappointed that he had come to their house with so little evidence, and now he had become unexpectedly ashamed. His teeth were clinched, and he was breathing heavily through his nose. He knew if he tried to talk, he would only stutter through his thoughts. He needed to get out of here. More importantly, he couldn't let them know this interrogation was a bluff. He circulated thoughts and sentences through his mind to try and salvage his pride, constructing them with words that would take as few stutters as possible. He also needed to save face regarding Sophia. "There's n-n-nothing g-g-going on with h-her," Monty said.

"That's not what she said. If I were you, I'd be careful with that. Her husband, Nick, has a bit of a temper."

For a moment, Monty's brain lapsed back to the previous night and their encounter in the parking lot. Donnie motioned with his finger for Monty to leave.

"If you're hiding something, y-y-you'd be b-b-better off t-telling me now," Monty said.

"Get out of our house," Donnie said.

Monty reached for the plastic bag on the table, put it back in his pocket, and locked eyes with Frank as he buttoned it back. "I know it's you. I d-d-don't know how, but I'm gonna f-f-f—" he paused and breathed. "If I need to get a w-w-war-warrant to search this place—or your place," he eyed Ginny, "I will." He moved away from Donnie at the back door and walked through the family toward the front.

45

Dave and Ginny stood by the doorway talking with each other, then turned to Frank. Frank attempted to explain that everything was a misunderstanding, but Dave cut him off.

"Misunderstanding or not, that is our name—my name—on that sign and the last thing we need . . ." Dave paused. "The last thing you boys need is bad press."

Ginny said to Donnie, "And you! I don't care what that girl told you about him, what you said was very disrespectful. I want you to apologize to him."

Donnie let out an astonished laugh. "Apologize? For what?" Donnie asked. "The guy came in here accusing us of something absurd that we didn't do, based on some shoddy evidence."

"Donald. He is a respected public figure in this town, and a very sweet man who's given my business a lot of support."

Frank snickered. Both Ginny and Donnie looked at him. "What? Was that not a cop and donut joke?" He cleared his throat. "Sorry."

Ginny sighed. "I want you to apologize to him for saying those things. They were rude and insensitive. You don't know anything about his feelings and you used it to embarrass him."

"Mom, tha—"

"That's enough." Ginny cut the conversation to a halt.

"Sorry, Mom," Frank said.

"Sorry," Donnie echoed.

"Until the police resolve this whole thing, I think it's a good idea for *you*," looking at Frank, "to stay out of the cemeteries."

"I have to go to cemeteries," Frank said.

"You know what I mean. You probably need to stop going for walks so late at night in them. If you're walking around in one that happens to be vandalized, he's going to come back here."

"We'll be fine. Don't worry," Frank said.

"Franklin, now stop it! You're a grown man and more than capable of living your own life, but I expect and trust you'll do what's best for this house. I don't want it getting around that the owner of my family's business is a grave robber. Are we clear?" Ginny asked. "It's not only this home you're affecting—I've got my restaurant."

"Yes, ma'am. I'm sorry."

"I'm going to go to go work in the garden."

"Bye, Mrs. B," Cliff offered.

"Goodbye, Clifford," Ginny offered.

Donnie, Frank, and Cliff all stood in the foyer entrance in silence until Ginny and Dave were out of ear shot.

"Is it rude to tell her that Cliff isn't short for Clifford?" Cliff asked.

Donnie laughed. "Frank and Donnie aren't short for Franklin and Donald. My birth certificate literally says Donnie. That's just her thing." He looked to Frank for affirmation and saw him walking into the kitchen. He heard the back door slam.

"What's up with him?" Cliff asked.

"I think I know. I never told him about New York," Donnie replied.

"Ouch. Hearing it from a cop probably wasn't what you had in mind, huh? I told you to tell him," Cliff said.

"Yeah, thanks."

Frank was sitting on the porch swing. Donnie closed the screen door and walked over to the basketball hoop. He attempted a shot and missed, making a joke at his own expense. Frank didn't say a word or even stifle a laugh.

Donnie put the ball on the ground and walked over to the swing. "So, I guess I should probably tell you why—"

"Why didn't you tell me?" Frank asked.

Donnie took a seat and let out a long breath. "Because . . . it's embarrassing."

"How could you be embarrassed around me? We've seen each other at our most embarrassing points already. Remember, I shaved your junk before senior prom?"

"That was definitely not me," Donnie replied. "And I'm a little concerned that you probably tell people that."

"Maybe it wasn't, but we did used to play strip poker with our stuffed animals back when we were kids," Frank said.

Donnie nodded his head. "You got me there. Playing strip poker with my brother and stuffed animals is definitely a low point of my life."

"You thought high school was a low point? I thought it was pretty awesome," Frank said.

Donnie let a laugh escape through his nose, "Shut up." They sat quietly for a moment before Donnie spoke again. "I don't really have a good reason for not telling you. I guess I was just waiting until I had something else, or until I had my investors back."

"So, what happened?"

"Exactly what I said. I was let go."

"What'd you do?"

"Nothing. I got screwed over. Calvin opened that place last year with me on board as the executive chef. His son moved up there in April and started working as the sous chef. Calvin was also planning to be one of the major backers for my own restaurant. About six weeks ago a customer's order went wrong—though I'm pretty sure now it was staged—and Calvin used it as an excuse to fire me and bump up his son."

"Must have been a pretty big mistake," Frank said.

"They were celebrities."

"Would I know them?" Frank asked.

"Yeah. My name got dropped in several blog posts about the restaurant. Surprised you didn't read about it."

"I rarely get on social media other than to check client backgrounds. Who was it?"

"Doesn't matter. It was a setup. Two of the customers were allergic to shellfish. They said I recommended the tasting menu because it would be free of it. I never said that—never even recommended the tasting menu. When I heard who it was, I came out and introduced myself, made some suggestions; asked if anyone had any allergies—they didn't. Thirty minutes later, someone's yelling for a doctor."

"You really think Calvin set that up?"

"Definitely. It's nothing to deescalate a situation like that, but he completely rolled over on me—and my reputation. Dude's got pull with some pretty high up people too. Completely screwed me. He wanted his kid in there and needed a clean way to get me out, and put me in a position where I couldn't compete with him. I asked him about our agreement to open another spot next year; he told me he never agreed to that—didn't even know what I was talking about."

"Damn."

"Yeah. Like Dad always says, get everything in writing. So, here I am."

"Mom and Dad know?"

"Yeah they were the first ones I called."

"Are you serious? We talked every week!"

"I know. *I know*. I would call you and think I'd tell you and then you'd start talking about something going on here, or some problem the home was having and . . . I don't know. Just didn't want to add one more thing. Dad said I should just take a break, cool off, and work at home for a bit. Mom has been trying to help me get another place started. They kept pushing me to tell you but, I never found the right time. It's probably why I was such a dick these last couple of weeks. I was worried that if this place got shut down or if you did something to screw up our business, then I'd really have nothing. It would take *forever* to get backers to trust me at that point." Donnie patted his pockets checking for his phone, and asked Frank if he'd seen it. Frank shook his head and followed Donnie into the foyer.

"So, what are you gonna do?" Frank asked. "Are you looking at opening a restaurant in Nashville? Or was that just made up too?"

"No, that's real. I'm looking in Nashville, Paducah, St. Louis, Louisville." Donnie stepped into his office and immediately noticed his phone on the desk. "Got it. Yeah, the only thing I wasn't truthful about was that I got fired. I've been honest about everything else."

Frank entered the room and leaned against the door frame.

"Well, elephant in the room; are you looking at getting out of here as quickly as you can or . . . you plan on sticking around for a while?"

"That depends," Donnie replied. He raised his eyebrows and tipped his head forward to Frank.

"On me?"

"Yup. You nearly screwed this whole thing up."

"Yeah, I know—"

"Stop. I'm being serious, Frank. This was really close. I can't stay on here if I'm going to be constantly at risk of going to jail. But, on the other hand, I don't want it to close down—and I could use a break from culinary politics just doing some light fare and experimental dishes for the funerals."

"So, you're staying?"

"Here's what I'll do. We got the Kochs off our back—at least for now—which should give us some breathing room to focus on publicity and doing some maintenance. How much money have you made with all this?"

"Probably like forty or fifty," Frank replied, hesitantly.

"Forty or fifty!"

"Yeah, there've been a few—"

"Doesn't matter. At this point, we can't give it back, so, if you'll agree to work with me on spending and include me on decisions you make—not for approval, but just to communicate—then I will give you . . . my full service. I'll help with the planning; I'll help run the services. I'll even create a menu for people that rivals any restaurant in town. I've realized these past couple weeks that you're pretty freakin' good at dealing with our clients. Your methods for community engagement are weird but you're getting our name out there and you make people feel good—I think people need this option. But not at the cost of my reputation and our family's future. Funeral Homes don't rob graves. And we definitely don't mutilate corpses. So, if you can promise me that you'll not do any more illegal activities, then I'll stay on until early next year."

"Jeez, that long?"

"Here's the deal though," Donnie said, running his fingers around his mouth. "In January, if, with all the work, and the advertising, and the bangin' food, we are still no further along that we are right now—only doing one or no funerals each week—I want you to promise me that we can seriously talk about selling the place. Not to the Kochs, but at that time, we'd have done all we could. And, I want you to be open to *being honest with yourself* that maybe the season of this place has come to an end."

"That's only like six months away," Frank said.

"Yup. But plenty of time for us to know if we can bring this thing back to life," Donnie said.

"Pun intended," they both said dryly.

"I'm gonna give it everything I've got, but if by next year I feel like we can't make it—and you'll have to trust that I genuinely want it to stay open—then I *will* sell my half of the business. And I would hope that you can, by that point, do the same." Donnie looked at his brother. "Does that work?"

Frank's head began to nod. "I guess I could always open a new place," he said.

"Or go manage another funeral home. You don't have to do your own—take over someone else's."

"Yeah. That could work. What about you? I take it that selling your half would give you a good start toward the restaurant?"

"The money would be great, definitely, but I don't need it. I've still got two guys willing to put up money for the idea I have if I do open it in Nashville, and I think by the end of the year I'll have two other investors, which should give me enough to get started. But I've got someone else who's willing to fund almost an entire project if I do it in Paducah—he was my boss when I was in West Virginia. The more I think about it, keeping this place going works in my favor on a business standpoint. So, if you can back off on the illegal crap, I'm here."

Frank turned and looked at Donnie. "I want you here."

"Okay. Let's do it," Donnie reached out his hand to shake Frank's but his brother snatched him up in an embrace. "Man, you smell good."

"Victoria's Secret lotion mixed with Abercrombie Woods. Women love it," Frank replied. He set Donnie down.

"I don't say it enough, but you know I love you, right?"

"Damn right, you do." Frank smiled.

"I mean, don't get me wrong, I definitely hate you," he put his hand on Frank's shoulder, "but I love you." The two of them laughed. Heartily. Donnie stepped back and put his hand behind him to lean on the desk but accidently knocked the box of chess pieces off and onto the floor. "Oh!" Several wrapped pieces tumbled onto the carpet.

Frank knelt down to put them back into the box, but Donnie assured him he would take care of it. "I got it. I'll unwrap them so I can put the entire board on the desk."

"Aright. I'm gonna go eat, then."

"You didn't eat yet?"

"When have I had a chance this morning?"

"Good point." Frank turned to leave the room as Donnie knelt onto the floor and began organizing the pieces by color, then he fell into a cross-legged position to unwrap them. He pulled out the game board from the box and examined it to make sure it hadn't cracked when it hit the floor. He saw the envelope taped to the bottom when he turned it over. "What's this?" The word 'thanks' was written across the envelope's flap.

"Frank!"

"Yeah!"

"Come in here, will ya?"

Frank walked into Donnie's office holding a bowl of cereal. "What's up? Why are you on the floor?" He walked over to his brother on the floor and paused, sniffing the air. "Did you fart in here?"

"No. I found—you're eating a donut and cereal for breakfast?" Donnie asked.

Frank spooned puffs into his mouth and made an audible *mm-hmm*.

Donnie raised his arm, holding the envelope. "I think that's yours."

"What is it?"

"I don't know. I pulled the board out and that was taped on there. Didn't want to be *you* and go through someone else's mail," Donnie said.

Frank set the bowl down and took the note. It was typed on blank letterhead. Frank read it aloud:

Hello friend,

The contents of this box are the result of several weeks of work. Your help on this project has been enormously appreciated. Inside, you will find a full chess set carved from two sources: one is animal, the other is human— from the bones you retrieved for us. I have a list of individuals willing to pay for luxury sets like this one upwards of twenty thousand dollars. Please accept this gift as a token of our appreciation for your work, and we ask that you also consider a partnership. We are willing to offer a fifteen percent cut on each set sold and one thousand dollars for each part rendered by your service: currently there are fourteen requests pending. If and when you are willing to help, please connect with our contact on the forum as we have done in the past and title your initial post as 'Kings and Queens.' We will make contact from there. Should you be unwilling to accept this offer, please keep the set as a gift. We look forward to hearing from you soon.

Blessings.

"Whoa," Frank whispered.

"Ew. These are human bones?" Donnie asked.

"Do you know what this means? Fifteen percent of twenty grand is what? Three thousand? Plus an extra thousand for each part? This is what we're looking for!"

"No. Absolutely not," Donnie said. "We're done with the illegal stuff."

"The guy's got fourteen requests! What's fourteen times three? Forty . . . two? Forty-two thousand? That's not counting the parts. That's an extra fifty grand for us and all we have to do is replace a few bones with plastic mannequin do—"

"Frank! Did you forget what happened here an hour ago? You almost got caught. We're not taking this deal. I'm not going to jail for a chess set!"

"But we wouldn't go to jail because we're not going to get caught. No one ever inspects the bodies that closely, and I know a place where we can get silicone body parts for dirt cheap. They look just like the real thing."

"You take this deal, and I'm out," Donnie said, calmly.

Frank's whole body sagged with disappointment. Donnie could practically hear his brain deflate. "What if we try it out first—"

"No," Donnie cut in. "Not if you want me working here with you. That cop's already on to you. You screw up again, and it's over."

"Gahh! It's fifty grand, though!"

"And we'll make the fifty grand, just not that way."

Frank took the letter and read through it again as he walked toward the office door.

"I'm serious, man," Donnie said, getting up off the floor.

"Yeah, yeah," Frank called back.

"Don't make me start inspecting all the corpses before the viewings; you know I'll do it."

"Okay. I won't take the deal."

"Shred that note," Donnie called. Frank had walked into his own office across the hall.

"Shredding it now," Frank called back.

Donnie stared at the beautifully carved skeleton bones on his desk and let out a sigh. He heard the high-pitched whirring of the shredder's motor from the other room. He knew his brother too well to believe that Frank could say *no* to fifty grand that easily.

He would indeed have to start checking the corpses.

There wasn't a doubt in his mind Frank never shredded that letter.

EPILOGUE

The package arrived shortly after Monty Suthers left the Burgers home. It laid unnoticed against the wall a few feet to the right of the front door through the morning and much of the afternoon. It wasn't until Frank finished fixing the doorknob that he looked over and saw it sitting there.

It was addressed to Frank Burgers: no stamps, no return address, no recipient address. "Hmm," he mumbled, looking around the front porch and yard. "Weird."

"Knob's fixed," Frank called out, closing the front door and walking inside.

Donnie yelled from his office: "It's about time. Hey!"

"Yeah," Frank poked his head in, leaving his body and the package out of view.

"I think I'm going to drive up to Nashville for dinner. You wanna go?" Donnie asked.

"Right now?"

"Yeah," Donnie replied. "In half an hour, maybe?"

Frank narrowed his eyes. "You're going to see that girl, aren't you?"

"I may stop by there," he smiled.

"Uh huh." Frank grinned. "I'm not trying to be a third wheel."

"If you go, it'll make it less weird. I can play it off as you and me hanging out."

"I would normally go with you but I'm still pretty wiped. Rain check for your second date, alright?"

"It's not like that," Donnie said.

"Have fun." Frank patted the door frame and moved into his office. He set the package on his desk and used his pocket-knife to cut a slit into the tape across the top flaps. The pink material inside appeared, at first, to be some sort of gift wrapping, but at pulling both flaps fully open, Frank quickly released the box and jumped back, cursing to himself in a whisper.

He didn't need the picture of Sarah Piddleton lying on top to recognize what he was looking at—the buttons gave it away: several of them pinned to a dirty and tattered pink cardigan sweater. Tucked underneath was a black-and-white picture of *him*, clearly visible, standing beside Cliff in front of the open grave, holding the plastic bag of Sarah's bones.

The photo of Sarah resting on top had to be taken from an old yearbook. It showed Sarah smiling in her classroom, sitting at her desk in front of the chalkboard, and wearing the very same sweater she was buried in.

The same sweater Frank had thrown back into her grave a week ago.

The same sweater he was now staring at inside the box.

Below the picture of Sarah was a message in red ink:

There is a working payphone at the RacerFan Gas Station across from the Arena. I will call it at 11p.m. tonight. Answer it.

"Well, shit," Frank whispered.

To be continued in Part II

Author Note

People have asked why I chose to set the story in a real town instead of making one up, and the best answer I can offer is that it wasn't my intention; Murray sort of wrote itself in. As the story was coming together I realized I was writing what I knew: the streets, buildings, lifestyle, cemeteries, weather—it was all Murray! In the end, this Western Kentucky town became the home of the Burgers Family and I couldn't be happier. I have so much family history in this town and am grateful that it was home to me for a short while. One of the most unique parts of this area is Land Between the Lakes. This peninsula is rich with stories, history, and will continue to show up in future novels—especially part II.

Part I of this story came together with the help of several individuals. The most important is my wife, Gina, who has put up with this story and these characters for nearly two years, and who made sure this project got done. In complete random order, I also wish to thank Bob Pfannerstill, Chris Rhatigan, Jaye Manus, Ginny Willman, Maura Cravey, Tara Hofsiss, Sandy Abate, Rachel Kuldell, Katrine Long, and Kim Hofsiss; you all know what you did. Thank you!

Hannah, I could not be happier that you decided to work with me. Your ideas and work gave this novel a Mario Mushroom and I am still smiling over what you've done.

And finally, Matt Markgraf. None of this would have happened without you.

—C, November 2019

Clayton Tune has spent the majority of his life living in Northern VA, but was born and attended college in Western Kentucky. He has degrees in Theater, Biblical Studies, and is a Licensed Massage Therapist.

When he is not writing, he enjoys watching most any sport on TV. He is a loyal fan to the Tennessee Titans, Washington Wizards, and the Washington Nationals. Clayton is married with two children and is an avid collector of anything from the '90s.

The Burgers Brothers' Family Funeral Home is his first novel.

Made in the USA
Middletown, DE
30 August 2021